Steady rain drumming on the tarp of the wagon masked the approach of two strangers on horseback who quickly flanked the wagon team. One rode a Morgan and wore a torn hat like the man Mark caught watching him in town. The other character rode a pinto and hid his face with a hat pulled low. He matched the other person in the pair from town that watched him come out of the bank. Uneasy, Mark brought the wagon to a halt, hoping the boys had ridden far enough ahead that the two strangers didn't know they were there.

"What can I do for you gentlemen?" Mark said loud enough that Sarah might hear him, and she and Lydia would be quiet and stay out of sight.

"We're heading north to Nebraska for a spell and that rifle you won in town sure would come in handy. We were wondering just how good a shot you really are," said the older man.

"I shot against you," the younger man continued. "And the way I see it, you should hand over that rifle if you want to live. With that gun, I could win every competition."

In unison, both men drew their pistols, cocked the hammers, and pointed them at Mark.

Previous Books in this Series:

SETTLER'S LIFE — Book One of the A Plains Life series, released September 2018 and is now available on Amazon, iTunes, and Audible.com in paperback, e-book, and audio book formats. Published by The Wild Rose Press, Inc., Cactus Rose Division.

Second Chance Life

by

Judy Sharer

A Plains Life, Book Two

Second Chance Life

COPYRIGHT © 2019 by Judy M. Sharer

Cover Art by *Diana Carlile*

The Wild Rose Press, Inc.
PO Box 708
Adams Basin, NY 14410-0708
Visit us at www.thewildrosepress.com

Publishing History
First Cactus Rose Edition, 2019
Print ISBN 978-1-5092-2807-2
Digital ISBN 978-1-5092-2808-9

A Plains Life, Book Two
Published in the United States of America

Dedication

This book is dedicated to my mother,
Roberta Sorenson,
my family, my beta readers, and dear friends,
for their constant encouragement
and overwhelming support.

Chapter One

Early March 1859

Sarah Clark Hewitt wrapped her shawl tighter as the door closed behind her. She couldn't believe fourteen years ago she and Samuel Clark wed. So much happened since that day. Samuel died last year while hunting with Mark, leaving Sarah and their two children, Jack and Lydia, alone. Samuel's death brought Mark and Sarah together and their love grew. Sarah couldn't think of a more appropriate time to recall old memories and dream of her new life with her husband Mark. Climbing the knoll to the old elm tree, she stood silently in front of her first husband's grave.

She so longed to hear Samuel's voice once more, picture his smile, and sense his warm embrace. She summoned to mind words she heard him say hundreds of times, but the vibrant tone, subtle hints of sarcasm, and caring certainty were gone. All she heard now were the words.

Samuel's touch was always gentle, his words encouraging, and his promise the same. They owned their land free and clear and could nurture the site into a flourishing farm. This was the couple's dream when they traveled west from Pennsylvania to Kansas five years ago. A successful farm was still her dream, and now that she and Mark were married, they set new goals for the farm…new dreams. They would turn the farm into a ranch and raise cattle and horses. This year, the family wanted to clear more land for additional crops, fence in a pasture, and strengthen the herd. The changes would take place, as soon as the weather cooperated.

Sarah sat on the ground beside her late husband's makeshift marker. She ran her hands over the slight round of her belly in anticipation of the new life within. "God works in ways we may never understand, sweetheart," she said as she found peace in her heart.

A breeze lifted the hair off the back of her neck. A gentle kiss from Samuel maybe? Her eyes turned to the eastern sky and warmth enveloped her. God sent a sign; Samuel was close by.

****

As his wife walked up the knoll, Mark looked on from the barn and understood her wanting time alone. He remembered that Sarah and Samuel's anniversary was today and didn't want to intrude. Samuel and Mark grew up together as best friends. After Samuel's death, Mark stayed on to help the family and, in time, he and Sarah fell in love. She would always love her first husband, but she was his wife now. Mark loved her two children, Jack and Lydia, as his own. The promise of a baby brightened his outlook on life although his concern for Sarah carrying their child full term after she lost her last child at birth was a blanket of worry.

A brilliant flash illuminated the western sky over the vast prairie. In the distance, gray ominous clouds formed in the west, heading their way. *If the storm stays on course, it's heading right toward us.* Mark never experienced a violent storm of this magnitude. The wind carried the rain-laden ominous clouds closer. He ran toward Sarah, yelling to the children, "There's a storm coming! Quick, latch the shutters and get to the root cellar."

"Sarah! Sarah, look to the west. A storm is coming. You need to get to the root cellar." He rushed to help her down the hill and then ran to secure the chicken coop and herd the horses from the barn. He glanced again to the west. Black clouds churned overhead, filtering out the light of day. The wind swirled and spears of lightning split the sky. *I pray this storm passes quickly. If gusty winds kick up, there could be a twister.*

Deafening claps of thunder accompanied the slashes of lightning. The ground rumbled. Mark counted the seconds between the flashes and the boom of the thunder to judge the distance. The storm would be upon them momentarily. Checking to make sure everyone was inside, he secured the root cellar door. Rain started to pelt the ground above and hit the door with such force the clatter sounded like nails hitting a roof.

"Do you think we'll be safe here?" Sarah asked, as a crack of lightning radiated the sky and immediately a deafening boom rumbled and shook the earth. Everyone recoiled.

"The storm is close. That strike hit nearby." Mark opened the door a crack. "Smoke. I smell smoke." He glanced at the house, then the barn. "It's the barn!" he yelled. "The barn's on fire!"

Smoke streamed from the barn roof.

Mark shouted, "Jack, release the chickens from the coop, then fill some buckets." He grabbed the back of

Lydia's dress as she got up to run after Jack. "No, sweetheart, you need to stay with your mother."

"But what about Momma Kitty and Muzzy? They're in the barn. I'm afraid they'll die."

"They'll get out. You stay here."

Mark flung open the front doors of the barn. Flames licked their way along the roofline. Smoke billowed as he struggled to cut Daisy the milk cow's lead and shoo her out to safety. Next, he piled lanterns in the spring wagon, heaving in the plow and bags of seed that he covered with a canvas, then dragged the wagon out to the yard. Returning, he threw saddles, harnesses, ropes, buckets and Sarah's garden tools into the covered wagon.

Jack helped him maneuver the wagon free of the fire. Wind drifted onto the canvas roof and live embers burned brightly.

Mark yelled above the noise of the howling storm, "Save the canvas, Jack. Then get Daisy to the corral."

Racing for water, Jack doused the canvas first, then searched for the milk cow.

Unbearable heat, flames, and dark smoke met Mark as he dashed back into the barn. He needed to save the tools and other necessities before abandoning the barn to the all-consuming furnace within. He grabbed what he could carry, then Lydia's cats skittering along the wall toward the door caught his eye. The smoke thickened and new flames blossomed. With every breath, the intense heat seared his lungs.

When in the yard, he dropped the tools and doused himself with a bucket of water.

He yelled over the storm to Jack, "Get back to the root cellar. Nothing will keep the barn from burning to the ground."

Jack returned and explained the situation to his mother.

"Jack, you stay with Lydia, and don't come out again," she said, and ran to find Mark coming out of the barn. She handed him a wet towel she had grabbed from the clothesline. "Mark, you've saved so much. Please don't go back in! I couldn't bear the grief if something happened to you."

"Just once more." He tied the wet towel over his nose and mouth, and plunged back into the inferno. His eyes streamed with tears from the smoke. *I need to get Samuel's woodworking tool chest.* He crawled along the floor beneath the smoke to where the chest sat.

A loud crack resounded. A rafter gave way. A flurry of sparks exploded to release smoldering hay from the loft and send flaming pieces of wood to the barn floor. Samuel's tool chest in his arms, Mark sprinted toward the barely discernible opening as the firestorm exploded behind him.

Five strides and he cleared the barn door. Ten more and he dropped the tool chest. Bending over and breathing deeply, he rubbed his eyes. The rain blessedly cooled him. He coughed to clear his lungs, wiped soot from his blackened face.

A quick glance at the farmhouse roof showed no burning embers or flames. Drawing in deep breaths of relief, he wiped his mouth and forehead with his sleeve and murmured a quick prayer of thanks.

Sarah helped Mark back to the root cellar to wait out the storm.

When Lydia saw Mark, she called out, "Did you save Muzzy and Momma Kitty?"

"I got a glimpse of them heading toward the door, sweetheart. I'm sure they got out. They're scared and probably hiding somewhere. They'll come out when they're ready, after the storm passes."

Tears ran down Lydia's cheeks. "I prayed you would get out safely." She embraced Mark with a hug.

"God must have heard you, sweetheart."

"But Father, you're hurt."

"Only a few minor burns and a scrape is all. Nothing your ma can't fix." Mark raked his fingers through his hair plastered to his head, and then they enveloped each other in a hug and waited.

As quickly as the storm blew in, the lightning and wind raced on. The rain eased to a steady drizzle, and the sky brightened toward the west. The family ventured from the root cellar to find the barn still in flames as smoke wafted toward the sky. Five full buckets remained, but the structure was a total loss. No sense in wasting the water.

The family looked on in disbelief as the barn Samuel and Mark built together was reduced to charred timbers.

Seeing defeat on Sarah's face and in the slump of her body, Mark kissed her on the forehead. "Sarah, why don't you take the children inside to get dry?" He coughed; his voice hoarse from the smoke he inhaled. "Then, when the rain stops, we'll all look for the cats. I'm sure they got out in time," he reassured Lydia.

The storm that caused the devastation lingered long enough to put out most of the flames, leaving smoking piles of charred timber behind.

Damage appeared limited to the barn and chicken coop. The barn and coop could be rebuilt, but Sarah and their unborn child were his immediate concern. He couldn't let her down now. No, he wouldn't give up. The child about to enter their lives was a blessing of love. A barn fire wouldn't take away their happiness.

To make sure the remaining flames didn't spread, Mark doused the hot spots and then corralled the horses while Sarah and Lydia fixed supper. His stomach told him they'd worked straight through the midday meal.

After Sarah tended to his wounds, she set supper on the table.

"Jack, you were brave today. We could have lost the chickens and the wagon's canvas if you hadn't taken action." Mark looked at the children.

Jack's face brightened.

"The barn is a loss, but we must give thanks for what we have. We're all safe, the animals are safe, and the house isn't damaged. We can rebuild the barn. I'm sure Seth Frazer and Joe Spencer would help."

Mark looked at Sarah, who let out a long sigh and said, "But we can't afford to rebuild the barn."

"We'll talk about this later, sweetheart," Mark said, seeing the uneasiness on the children's faces. "But rest assured, we will rebuild."

After supper, Mark checked the barn, dousing smoldering fires so they wouldn't spread, while the children did their chores and looked for the cats without success.

****

Later, while the children played a game of checkers to take the edge off, Lydia stopped for a moment and said, "I think I hear a faint meow. There, I heard the meow again. Did you?"

"Yes, I think so," Jack said, as he and Lydia ran

outside.

Lydia called out, "Momma Kitty, please meow again." From a patch of grass by the well, a soft noise rose. "I heard her, but I can't see her."

Mark stepped closer. The lamp he carried gave off enough light for Lydia to spy the cats. Muzzy lay in a tight ball, hair visibly scorched and a patch of charred skin exposed. Momma Kitty sat beside her, an open wound on her back and her front paws singed and bloody.

"Ma, we have to help them," Lydia pleaded.

"Yes, let's get them inside, and I'll dress their wounds." Sarah ran back to the house to assemble salve and bandages.

"Lydia," Mark said. "Why don't you fetch some food and a plate of milk? I'm sure the cats will want to eat when your ma finishes. I'll hold Muzzy for you."

Lydia dipped into Sarah's stew crock, picked out a big piece of beef, and tore the meat into bite-size pieces before pouring a generous amount of cream onto the plate.

Sarah attended both cats' wounds. Once she finished, Lydia and Jack fed the recovering pets the much-appreciated meal.

"They can stay inside tonight," Mark said, then looked at Sarah for reassurance.

"Yes, they should stay inside so we can keep an eye on them," Sarah agreed.

"Can I sleep downstairs in case they need me?" Lydia begged.

"Of course, dear." Sarah gathered the bedding.

Once the cats cuddled into their soft nest, the excitement of the day drew to a close. Lydia settled under the quilts, and Jack climbed to the loft.

****

While Jack and Lydia slept, exhausted from the day's events, Sarah poured Mark coffee and made herself a cup of tea. Sitting at the table, sipping from his steaming mug, Mark said, "At least the barn caught fire and not the house. We can rebuild. If we fix up the lean-to and enclose one end, Daisy will have a new home behind the grain shed for now. Most of the seed was saved, but I'll get more before planting is over.

"It won't be easy, Sarah, but we'll make it. Keep remembering God doesn't give us more than we can handle."

"I wish I had your optimism. Yes, we have the house, but without a barn, what will we do?"

"Don't worry dear, we'll rebuild. Our new dreams will just take us a little longer to achieve."

****

The next morning, Mark walked into the house after dousing a few small fire flare-ups that occurred in the rubble overnight.

"First things first," Mark said as he sat talking with Sarah. "Jack and I need to build a makeshift coop and gather the chickens. Then we'll get Daisy settled into her new home, and when it's safe, we'll comb through the ashes for anything salvageable.

"I'll make a list of materials we'll need to rebuild the lean-to and the chicken coop, then pick up lumber and more seed on the next trip to town."

Chapter Two

While making the materials list, Mark said, "This year I think we should focus on clearing the barn rubble and not scrub any additional land. We'll plant what's already cleared and pray for good crops. Jack and I can start plowing tomorrow. The timing is a little early, but the frost is out of the ground. After the rain, the soil will turn over easier and take less time to plow."

"You're right, Mark." Sarah stood, walked to the stove, and warmed her tea. "The crops are most important. Maybe if this year's harvest is sufficient we can sell the extra grain and think about rebuilding next year. Our dream will be delayed but not forgotten. We just don't have the money right now."

****

After several days, the small fires burned out and made combing through the ashes possible. Mark found only a few tools and a couple of glass jugs and crocks worth saving.

The smell of burnt wood hung in the air. Mark and Jack took a couple of days off from the fields to cut salvageable rafters and board ends that could be incorporated in the repairs. Afterward, they raked everything into a pile in the center of the old structure and set the wood ablaze. Clean-up would take time. "The sooner the site is prepared," Mark insisted, "the sooner we can start rebuilding. However, planting must come first."

Mark and Jack plowed the soil, took turns at the reins, and swapped horses when needed. Each day they hauled a load of wood ash from the barn out to the fields and spread the ash to enrich the soil.

The duo tilled seven of the farm's fifteen cleared acres. Four still needed tilled, and the other four acres were pasture, which reseeded itself. Seeking relief from the backbreaking work of plowing, Mark announced he would leave early the next morning for a trip to town to pick up more seed and stop at the mill to get lumber for the chicken coop and small projects he wanted to complete.

****

Anticipating Mark would be able to mail letters, Sarah penned her mother in Pennsylvania a letter to catch her up on news:

April 16, 1859
Northwest Border,
Riley County, Kansas
Dearest Mother,

So much has happened I am not sure where to start.

First, I am excited to tell you I am three months with child and all is well. Mark and the children are so excited and help as much as they can. I pray my pregnancy goes well, for I could not bear to lose this child too. Please share our good news with the family and ask everyone to keep us in their prayers.

I hope you and the family had a joyous Christmas. Ours was especially nice. Mark surprised us all with gifts and the children were pleased with the items they made for each other. I worried about the holiday being the first without Samuel, but we remembered him each in our own way.

A lightning storm a few weeks ago caused a fire and destroyed the barn and chicken coop Samuel and Mark built. Mark saved the animals, most of the seed, the wagons, and the tools. We are grateful God spared the house. Lydia's cats suffered burns, but they're fine now. She was so attentive and compassionate with them, I am sure she will make a fine mother someday.

Mark insists on rebuilding the barn. Maybe next year we can afford the added expense if we have extra crops to sell.

I pray all is well back home. I so wish we lived closer. Let us know if Matthew and Emma still want to come to Kansas. They are more than welcome to live here. The children would love having them with us.

Take care, Mother, and tell Father and everyone we send our love.

Your loving daughter,

Sarah

Then she took out another piece of paper and wrote to Mark's mother, sharing some of the same news and leaving a space at the end for Mark to write a few words.

Sarah knew Mark's mother, Ruth, only slightly from what Mark shared. She vowed to write to get better acquainted. She also would encourage her mother to seek her out, since they both lived in Tidioute. They knew each other, but how well she wasn't sure. Maybe Mother could have Ruth come for supper one night. She'd suggest the meal in her next letter.

Chapter Three

Upon arrival in Dead Flats, Mark headed to the Postal Office. He greeted the clerk, paid the postage, and sent Sarah's letters on their way. In a hurry to get to the hardware, he never thought to ask for any mail.

Crossing the street to the bank, he withdrew enough money to buy supplies. The account held the reward received from the attempted stagecoach robbery when Samuel killed two outlaws and got shot in the process. Before Samuel died, he made Mark promise to impersonate Samuel in order to collect the money for the family. Sarah believed the money came from a different source, Mark's share of a gold mine in California.

Fortunately, there was sufficient seed in the bins at the hardware store to replace the loss from the fire. Mark explained about the fire destroying the barn and, while gathering supplies to rebuild the coop, overheard the clerk and another customer talking.

"This week's local newspaper forecasts a dismal year for crops." The clerk flipped the page to the article to show the man. "They even printed a planting chart for farmers to reference for this year's planting."

"It sure doesn't look good," said the customer.

"And I doubt next year will be any better. The chance of a severe drought has people already concerned about whether to stay or leave the area." The clerk turned to Mark.

"We're staying," Mark spoke up. "We've started to plow our fields already, and since the frost is out of the ground, we'll risk planting right away. This way we'll get a jump on the growing season and hopefully, with a little luck, harvest full crops. Probably only one cutting, but maybe we'll have time to clear more land and plant a late crop."

"Well, that might work. I wish you the best." The clerk helped load the wagon.

Mark drove the wagon to the dry goods store. *Sarah didn't ask for provisions, but if this drought does hit, prices will go up.* He stocked up on a few essentials like sugar, cornmeal, salt, molasses, flour, and dried beans, and splurged on coffee and a jar of maple syrup he discovered tucked behind some canned peaches.

Then, thinking of the smile on Jack and Lydia's faces the last time he brought home candy, he said, "Please add two three-cent sacks of candy and a newspaper to the order. That should hold us." No telling what would happen if a drought hit, but he'd be as prepared as possible.

Passing the church and crossing the creek on the way out of town, he speculated, *The newspaper's been wrong before. Maybe the prediction will be wrong this year. I'll wait and see what happens. In Sarah's condition, she doesn't need more to worry about. She worries enough.*

****

Arriving at the sawmill, Mark explained to the owner, "Our barn caught fire a few weeks back. The family and all the animals are safe, but the barn is a total loss."

"Sorry about the barn, but glad your family's all right," the mill owner replied. "We didn't get a drop of rain here and we sure could use some. I hear tell a drought is predicted for this year."

"Yes, I heard that too. I sure hope not. We lost a quarter of our hay and some of our seed. We'll need a good year to recoup our losses."

"Well, you're in luck. We cut logs hauled in last week. I can sell them for a good price, especially if you're willing to load 'em yourself. Over there," he pointed to a good-sized pile, "that's them."

"I'll take as much as I can haul today and come back four or five more times with a helper to load the rest. Now, what kind of money are we talking?"

"I don't take credit."

"I have money."

The men haggled on the price and finally settled on a reasonable amount. Next trip, he'd have to withdraw money to pay for the rest. Mark paid what he could, drove the wagon around to the pile of lumber, and began loading. The sun was high in the sky by the time the wagon was stacked full. Sweating and tired, arms and back sore, he headed toward home. After traveling four hours, his belly started growling. He stopped for the night. He'd get an early start in the morning so he could rest the horses along the way. The food Sarah packed for supper would taste mighty good with a hot cup of coffee.

****

Stiff and sore the next morning, Mark found himself getting a later start than expected. Stopping more often than usual to stretch and water the horses, Mark didn't arrive home until after supper.

Jack ran out to greet him and started unhitching the horses. "Mother said for you to come in and eat before we unload. You must be tired, Mark. Let me unhitch the horses. I'll feed and rub them down."

"Thanks, Jack. Tomorrow we'll unload at the east end of the old barn, and you and Lydia can help. But right now, supper sure would taste good."

Entering the house, he rubbed a few cramped muscles in his arms and sat down to eat. Mark relished his food. "This beef stew is your best ever, Sarah."

"You must be hungry, Mark. This is the same beef stew I make every time." Filling his cup, she boasted, "Here, enjoy a cup of my best ever coffee with your meal, too."

Almost finished with his meal, he commented, "I'll need help unloading the lumber tomorrow, but all I want to do now is crawl into bed."

****

The next morning, Mark awakened to Sarah's voice calling him to the table. The smell of flapjacks filled the house. Sitting down to eat, he said, "I see you found the maple syrup."

"Jack brought in the supplies last night, and that's when I discovered the jar."

"Thanks for the help, Jack." Mark sat down. "You didn't ask for anything, Sarah, but since I was in town I figured a few extra provisions couldn't hurt. We'll work on getting the crops in and give the lumber time to dry." Mark added, "I also need to make a few more trips for lumber."

Sarah didn't question his comments. He knew he'd have to mention rebuilding the barn this year again, but for now he'd let the conversation rest. Instead he asked,

"The creek and the well have never run dry, have they?"

"Not since we've lived here, they haven't. Do you ask because of the possible drought projected for this year?"

"You read the newspaper last night, didn't you?"

"Yes, I stayed up and read. News from town is always welcomed."

"Don't be too concerned."

"Is that why we're planting earlier than usual?"

"Yes, let's hope we don't get a late frost."

Mark put his arm around Sarah's waist and brought her close. "Let me worry about the crops, sweetheart," he whispered in her ear. Placing his hand on her belly he said, "This little one needn't worry. We'll be fine, because we have each other. There isn't anything his parents can't do together."

"Or *her* parents," Sarah said playfully. "Did you remember to mail the letters while in town?"

"I sent them."

"No mail from back east?"

"I'm sorry, sweetheart; I never asked, and the postmaster didn't mention any letters. Don't be too upset with me. I'll be going back for more lumber soon. I can check then."

"I'll forgive you this time." Sarah kissed his cheek, patted his shoulder, and sent him on his way.

****

Mark laid out the first two layers of boards to show Jack and Lydia the process. "So when we finish a layer, Lydia, you lay a stick at both ends to create a gap between the layers to allow air flow, which will help the lumber dry."

It took less than an hour to unload and stack the wood. Afterward, Jack helped shovel a load of wood ash into the wagon to spread on the field.

Two weeks later, Lydia helped with the planting. She dropped a few kernels in each hole she made with the end of an old pitchfork handle, and Jack kicked dirt to cover them. They took turns to make the tasks less boring. Yes, planting this early was risky, but the days were warmer than usual, and the family was willing to take the chance.

Although they started planting early and the cornfields were completed, late May arrived before they finished all but four acres. Mark saved the most weather-susceptible crops to plant last and already plowed the garden plot for Sarah, figuring she and Lydia could plant the seeds while he made a run to town for another load of lumber. *Should I tell Sarah my plans to rebuild the barn this summer? No, she'll worry if she knows I'm spending money on building supplies right now.*

Mark announced, "I'll leave in the morning. Anything you need from town? We're going to need more nails and lumber, so make a list of provisions."

"Another trip for lumber? Those chickens will have a nicer house than ours," Sarah joked.

"Can I go along, Mark?" Jack asked.

"Not this trip, Jack. I won't be long. I'll leave early and get back late the following night. Besides, your mother will need help planting the garden. You and Lydia can both help this year."

"Sure, I'll help plant the garden. I can carry the water buckets for you, Ma."

Mark winked.

Jack winked back.

****

Come evening, Sarah wrote her mother, and keeping true to her vow, wrote Mark's mother a short letter, too.

May 15, 1859
Riley County, Kansas
Dear Mother Hewitt,

We have been busy. The crops are almost planted so we will start on the garden next. Lydia and Jack will help me plant while Mark heads to town for lumber and supplies to rebuild the chicken coop and the lean-to for our milk cow, Daisy. Since the fire we've made adjustments.

Mark is wonderful with the children. He is patient and understanding while teaching Jack, and he compliments Lydia on her cooking, sewing, and completion of chores. He makes life on our farm fun and challenging instead of hard work.

After signing our last letter, I realized I do not know much about you other than what Mark tells me. I would be interested in hearing some of your memories about life when Mark was young and still living at home, and I will share events happening here each time I write.

Mark talks about you often, Mother Hewitt. I know he misses you. I pray this finds you in good health and good spirits. Please write when you can.

Your loving daughter-in-law,
Sarah

As she always did, Sarah left the pen out and room at the bottom of the letter for Mark to write a few words to his mother. Maybe in the next letter she'd have the children add a few lines. After all, Mark's mother faced the same possibility as her parents. Ruth might never see her son again. She put herself in her mother-in-law's position and realized when Jack and Lydia married, she too would feel the hardship.

****

Mark wrote a few lines to his mother, and then Sarah dripped wax and sealed the letters. Sitting at the kitchen table across from Sarah, Mark said, "This load of lumber isn't for the chicken coop, Sarah. You're right; we have enough to build the coop already. The owner of the sawmill gave me a deal on enough lumber to rebuild the barn. I figured as long as we have the money, we may as well take advantage of the good price and rebuild this year."

"Have the money? What do you mean?"

Mark knew the reward money hidden away in the bank would cover the cost of the barn with money to spare. The only problem was the promise he made to his best friend Samuel as he lay dying after the attempted stagecoach robbery. He couldn't tell Sarah about the money. She wasn't aware they didn't have to pinch every penny as she believed. How could he possibly explain? Once again, he debated, *Must I lie to keep my promise to Samuel? Must I keep lying, or has the time come to tell Sarah the truth? But I promised myself I'd take Samuel's secret to my grave.*

"No, Sarah, we can rebuild both the barn and the chicken coop."

"Mark, we must be realistic. We don't have any debt right now, but I don't think they'll give us that much credit. To take out a loan would be folly. We could never pay the debt."

Before he knew it, he deftly spun the story of the stagecoach robbery where he, not Samuel emerged the hero. To keep his promise, he said he was the one who rescued the cash box, killed two outlaws in self-defense, and claimed the reward money for his bold actions. He said all this took place last spring before he met up with Samuel and the accident that claimed Samuel's life. He couldn't force himself to break Samuel's trust and so, once again, he lied. *All a man has is his word. If Sarah ever discovers the truth, she might never forgive me.*

"I collected the reward money after I brought Samuel's body home to you and stayed on to help you and the children. I lied to you about where the money came from. You had already been through a devastating winter and just lost Samuel. I didn't want you to worry.

"I told Samuel about the robbery and killing the two bandits. He said you wouldn't approve, so I lied about the source and the amount of the money. Now the reward money will pay for the supplies we need to rebuild the barn. Our future dreams can still come true."

Mark let out a long breath. "Please forgive me, Sarah."

Sarah stared at Mark for a moment, then gasped. "Forgive you?" She turned away from him in her chair. A sob escaped as she rose. "How could you lie to me? I'm your wife. Have you no loyalty?" Unable to contain herself, she rushed to their bedroom.

What have I done? Every part of him ached to go after her, take her in his arms, and promise her everything would be all right. They could rebuild the barn.

Instead of consoling her, he blew out the oil lamp

and walked outside. Gazing at the night sky, he reassured himself, *With Sarah's steadfast belief in Thou shall not kill, if Sarah knew the truth the situation would be worse. The real truth that Samuel intervened in the stage hold-up and killed the two robbers still haunted him. I've only lied to honor my promise to Samuel as he lay dying and pleading with me never to let Sarah know what really happened that day. Could Sarah ever forgive me?*

Loyalty, she said. I was loyal to my friend yet told Sarah about the money and in doing so told another lie. My web of deceit has grown more entangled.

Guts churning, he feared what Sarah would say or do in the morning. Would she think less of him? As he propped himself up against the well, he looked in the direction where the barn once stood. Doubts drifted in and out of his mind, and he soon dozed off.

He awoke in the middle of the night and thought about returning to the house, but instead fetched a horse blanket from the barn. This time his mind wouldn't settle and instead filled with possible scenarios. The one that scared him the most was, *What if Sarah is so upset she asks me to leave?*

Chapter Four

Sarah tossed and turned, sleep evasive as her mind raced with questions. *Mark lied to me. Will I ever be able to trust him again? Did he lie because he killed two men and was afraid telling me would make me hate him? Why didn't he share this with me sooner? What else has he not told me?*

Mark said the money that paid for seed and supplies last year was sent by his partner who had a successful gold mine claim. He lied. Can I forgive him? Samuel never lied. Truthfulness is an unspoken bond between husband and wife. I realize to compare the two men is unfair. But why did he feel he couldn't trust me?

Sarah buried sobs of frustration and confusion in her pillow.

She and Mark never talked about trust, truth, loyalty, and the destruction a lie could generate in a marriage. Until now there was no reason to believe anything but honesty existed between them. Sarah believed in trust and honesty. *Why did Mark lie?* She reached for her Bible and the pages fell open to Matthew. Her eyes focused on Chapter Seven, then verses one to twenty. She read, "Judge not, that you be not judged. For with what judgment you judge, you will be judged; and with the measurement you use, it will be measured back to you."

By the end of the passage, Sarah knew she had

been harsh with Mark and understood what she must do tomorrow before he left for town. Exhausted, she fell into a fitful sleep and awoke unrefreshed after a few hours. She expected Mark in bed beside her, but he wasn't.

She did love him. He was a good man with good intentions, but the fact remained his lie cut deep. She needed to know the answer to the question that kept her in turmoil all night. Why did he feel he couldn't tell her the truth? But where was he? Did he leave for town already?

He wasn't inside. She grabbed the bucket off the table to fetch water and see if the wagon was still there. She found him sitting on the ground propped up against the well, looking at the dismal remains of the barn. As she approached, he never spoke until she greeted him, "Good morning, husband."

"Good morning, wife." He scrambled to his feet.

"Were you out here all night?"

"Yes, you needed time alone." He dusted off his pants.

"Mark, we need to talk. I must know if you've told other lies." Sarah placed the bucket on the ground.

"Well, there are a few details I didn't tell you. Let me explain. Don't take my family away from me. I've hurt you, Sarah, but please don't ask me to leave. I love you and our children. Think about the baby. I can't live without you."

Sarah was shocked. She'd need time to regain trust, but she never considered asking him to leave as an option. *I'll give him a chance and keep an open mind, but he better not lie again. If I can't trust him, I don't know what I'll do.* The scripture she read last night about judgment came to mind.

"Come inside. I'll put coffee on and start breakfast."

"Let me draw the water for you. I'm afraid you're overdoing. You're upset with me, and your eyes tell me you didn't sleep much last night. You should rest easy for the baby's sake." He placed the brimming bucket inside the door and added, "I'll go wash at the creek. I'm sure I smell of smoke from sitting out all night."

"Let me fetch you soap and clean clothes." Sarah looked at Mark with new understanding.

****

Jack bounded down the ladder from the loft. "Mark, why haven't you left yet?"

Mark, sitting at the table with his coffee, explained, "I've decided to wait one more day before going. We'll work the fields today, and I'll leave tomorrow."

After the children left to do their morning chores, Mark entreated, "Please, Sarah, Samuel was very clear. He insisted I never mention the attempted stagecoach hold-up and the reward money. He said to take this story to my grave and never tell you. Said you'd call the reward blood money for killing two men. Even though the driver and a boy about Jack's age were saved, Samuel thought you'd think of me as a killer. The outlaws killed the boy's father during the shootout, leaving him an orphan."

"The poor child." Sarah held her hands over her heart.

"The driver took a bullet in the arm, but when I collected the reward money, the sheriff told me he was fine. He also shared he found someone to care for the boy.

"I never noticed the cash box until the driver pointed under the seat. The box was padlocked. The whole mess began when I stopped to help put a wheel back on the coach. We got the wheel on, and then, out of nowhere, two riders charged us, shooting to kill. And, well, you know the rest."

"You were lucky you weren't shot, Mark." Sarah clasped his hands in hers.

"Samuel said not to tell you the details, but I have to, Sarah. I can't lie any longer. The money is ours and belongs to both of us. You see, we can rebuild the barn and continue our dream for the ranch. If Samuel were here, that's what he'd do. He'd rebuild and use the money to take care of you and the children. And that's what I've done. Please forgive me, Sarah. I should have told you before we were married, but Samuel insisted, so I didn't."

Sarah looked into Mark's eyes and knew everything he told her was also what Samuel would have said. Samuel knew she could never approve of such actions. Her beliefs didn't approve of killing. But something Mark mentioned struck her as odd. Something didn't sit right, but she couldn't quite put her finger on the words.

She nestled into Mark's welcoming embrace. Then, gazing directly into his eyes said, "Samuel was right, I don't approve, but in my heart I do understand you would never intentionally kill anyone unless they threatened you first."

"Thank you, Sarah. Now we can put this behind us and look to our future."

"Yes, if you're sure there's nothing else you want to tell me about your past."

"Nothing I can think of." Mark smiled and Sarah returned the smile in full measure. He continued, "On our next trip to town, I want to combine bank accounts and tell the bank president my wishes in case anything happens to me."

"Are you sure, Mark?"

"I'm sure."

Chapter Five

At midafternoon Mark arrived at Dead Flats and headed straight to the bank. A sign with faded red lettering dangled from a rusty chain, proclaiming the false-fronted building across from the bank as the Windy Plains Saloon. In the road near the sagging boardwalk sat a small Conestoga wagon with a crude rendering of a native medicine man decked out in full garb printed on the side. Above the image Mark read: "Doctor Hollingsworth's Magic Elixir."

A tall, red-haired man dressed in a ragged, once-elegant suit, stood on a makeshift platform at the back of the wagon. He orated in a loud voice, "Brought to you from Chicago and parts east, the one, the only, Hollingsworth's Magic Indian Elixir! Only one dollar a bottle! Are you rundown, tired of feelin' poorly due to hard work or lack of sleep? A small measure daily will increase manly vigor, aid in sleeping, and banish aches due to arthritis and rheumatism. Friends, I tell you, this elixir will cure female complaints as well as colic and fevers in infants!"

A small group of townsfolk gathered around.

THE BEST IN THE WORLD announced the sign on the wagon. "I just got in from Chicago, where I sold out, the demand was so great. This new supply arrived today, and I am giving you fine ladies and gentlemen the first opportunity to buy.

"It's made from secret ingredients Dr. Hollingsworth himself learned from a Cherokee medicine man on his deathbed." The Irish peddler's voice raised. "Only one dollar!"

"I'll take one," a voice in the back rang out.

"Give that wise woman a bottle," the peddler told the lad standing nearby, his arms cradling many bottles.

The tow-headed youth, clad in a worn shirt and pants looking two sizes too big, passed out bottles and collected the money. He turned toward Mark as he gave the buyer her purchase. His shirt open at the collar revealed a dark red mark in a crescent shape on his neck. This caught Mark's attention. The lad stopped, hitched up his oversized britches, and Mark remembered the shape was the same as Samuel described on the orphaned boy from the stagecoach robbery.

"Are you next, sir?" the boy asked Mark in a clear, proper voice. Mark shook his head. He couldn't be sure this boy was the same lad, and he wasn't convinced he wanted to know. The boy's hands and wrists appeared chafed, and then he looked him fully in the face.

Mark's mind flashed back to the day of the robbery and the loss of his best friend. He refocused quickly and walked to the hardware store to pick up the supplies he needed. After loading, he left the horses and wagon at the livery so the horses could eat and headed toward the Wild Rose Hotel dining room.

The peddler's wagon was parked down the alley. The boy stood at the back door of the hotel, obviously hoping for a handout. He wasn't receiving proper care, and that didn't sit right with Mark.

Many times on the frontier local magistrates placed

unwanted, orphaned children with any family that would take or buy them. Often these children were used like slaves, given the dirtiest jobs to complete around the house or workplace, and, in some cases beaten and starved.

Mark already spent more time in town than he planned. *If I leave now I'll be spending the night outside of town to get an early start. I might as well get a hot meal while I'm here.*

Later, after a dinner special he finished down to the last crumbs of apple pie and last swig of coffee, he was full, unable to eat another bite. Unlike the boy he recalled begging at the back door.

As he walked toward the stables, Mark again spotted the Conestoga wagon. The peddler and the boy were nowhere around. Mark wanted to walk by, forget about the past, yet he needed to find out for sure. Was he the orphaned boy named Billy, from the stagecoach robbery? Surely he'd respond to his name. From the interview with the sheriff when he collected the reward, Mark knew the boy's name was Billy Henry, he lived in Kansas City, and his father was a lawyer.

"Billy Henry!" Mark called out as he approached the wagon. A tousled head emerged from under the tarp at the rear.

"Billy, is that you?" *He wouldn't have reacted if it weren't. Now what?*

The peddler stepped down from the front of the wagon. "You want something, mister?"

Ignoring him, Mark walked up to Billy and asked, "Where's your father, Billy?"

"How do you know my father?" Billy demanded.

"Your father's a lawyer. His office is in Kansas

City. He did work for me on a land purchase, and I met you and your mother when you walked in during the meeting. I can't believe she would let you come this far from home alone. Come out from the wagon so we can talk." Mark motioned to the boy, but the boy looked at the peddler and back at Mark and didn't budge. Mark stepped closer and discovered the boy was trussed to the side rail with his hands behind his back.

"Cut him loose!" Mark demanded, incensed to see the boy cowering in fear.

The peddler released the boy, explaining, "I was gettin' ready to play cards at the saloon. I tied him so he wouldn't try to run away when I'm gone. He tried when I first got him, so I tie him up when I leave now. It don't matter how good I treat him, I can't ever beat any sense into the lad."

The peddler stood beside the freed boy, hand on his shoulder. "The boy is in my custody now. Tell him, Billy. Tell him what happened to your family."

The boy, cowering under the peddler's heavy grasp muttered, "My father is dead and so is my mother. The sheriff in Marysville told me I had to go with Rusty and work."

Rusty's whiskey-roughened voice broke into conversation. "Can I talk to you privately? Shall we be on a first name basis, then? You can call me Rusty, on account of why ya can see," he said, lifting his hat, pointing to his head, where a red fringe of hair surrounded a pink scalp. "My name's O'Bryan, from the Old Sod, I am."

Mark gave Billy a look that pleaded with him to play along, then addressed his next remarks to Rusty. "My name is Mark Hewitt. This boy's father was a business associate."

"But I paid the sheriff in Marysville two gold eagles for the boy. He belongs to me now. You heard him. His parents are dead and I'm all he has."

Gritting his teeth, Mark grabbed the front of the old man's shirt, drew him close, and shook him hard. "Understand me. What you say isn't true. I know for a fact the boy's father has a brother and I plan to return the boy to his family. If you are wanting your two gold eagles back"—Mark dug into his pocket—"here, take these. The boy is coming with me."

Rusty pocketed the money. "You go with this here fella, Billy. He wants ya now. Git." Then the old man turned and headed to the saloon.

"Billy, gather your things and let's get out of here," Mark told him. "Anything that's yours, bring with you. You're not coming back."

"I don't have much, mister," the boy said as he stuffed a few items in a sack.

Mark took the sack and gave Billy a hand out of the wagon onto the street. As soon as his feet touched the ground, the boy snatched at his belongings.

"Whoa, there. I won't hurt you."

"Give me my things. I'm not yours! I don't have to mind nobody!" The boy kicked and landed two hard strikes to Mark's shin.

Mark grabbed the boy's collar and Billy flailed about, trying to get free. Finally exhausted, he quieted.

"I won't hurt you, son. I'm here to help you. Are you hungry? I think the hotel dining room is still open. I could go for a big slice of warm apple pie with ice cream and a cup of coffee. If you're not hungry, you can come watch me eat."

The boy settled and Mark leaned back. "My name is Mark Hewitt. Let me start over. Here's your sack. You don't know me, but I know about you. I'd like you to come home with me and meet my family. Two siblings about your age live at the farm. I think you'd like both of them. The boy's name is Jack and he just had a birthday. He's thirteen. Lydia, his sister, is eleven. You'll like living on a farm, and you'll take care of your own horse."

"But I don't have a horse." The boy scuffed his foot in the dust.

"Can you ride?"

"Yeah, I've ridden some."

"If you come with me, I'll teach you how to ride and you'll have your own horse someday."

Mark guided the boy toward the yellow lanterns lighting the door of the hotel, where they found a seat in the dining room. "I ate here earlier. The specials are beef stew and meatloaf. Both come with mashed potatoes and green beans. Either sound good to you, Billy?"

"They both sound good."

"Tell her what you'd like." Mark motioned toward the waitress.

"I'd like meatloaf with lots of mashed potatoes and gravy, and beans...please."

Mark said, "I've already eaten, but I'll have coffee and please fetch a tall glass of milk for the boy. Then we'll each have a slice of apple pie with ice cream." Mark looked at Billy and asked, "You do like apple pie, don't you?"

Billy's head nodded like a wooden bobber with a fish on the end of the line. He polished off the heaping plate, sopping up the last of the gravy with a roll, then attacked the pie and another glass of milk. As Billy ate, Mark imagined the hardships the boy suffered. Finally finished, Billy's eyelids drooped as he yawned.

"Well, Billy, my horses and wagon are at the stables. I am headed there to spend the night where we'll be warm and out of the weather. Tomorrow will be a long day. We can talk more in the morning. I truly hope you won't try to run off. I promise I won't hurt you."

"I won't run off, mister, but tomorrow you'll have to tell me how you knew my folks."

"Fair enough," Mark agreed.

At the stables, Mark fashioned a bed for them, out of straw, in the back of the wagon. "You warm enough, Billy?" Mark asked as he covered them with his horse blanket and settled in for the night.

"Yes, mister."

"You can call me Mark. You don't have to call me mister."

"Thanks Mark, for buying me supper. I haven't eaten pie in I can't remember how long."

"You're welcome, Billy. I'm glad you enjoyed the food. Wait until we get to the farm. Lydia makes real good pies."

Within minutes, the exhausted boy was fast asleep.

Mark understood the boy was confused and probably afraid. Tomorrow he'd prove there was no reason for worry. Billy needed time to heal his emotional scars and pent-up anger. Mark's actions would show Billy there was nothing to fear.

****

After a breakfast of flapjacks with maple syrup and

sausage, Mark ordered a dozen buttermilk biscuits to be wrapped so he could take them with him. He stuck the package inside his coat for later. The bill paid, they walked across the street to the dry goods store.

"We need to pick up new clothes and shoes for you before we leave town."

"Where's your farm?" Billy asked.

"It's on the border of Clay and Riley Counties, a good day and a half's ride from here," Mark answered.

"How many others work this farm? Any slaves?" asked Billy.

Mark lowered his voice. "No slaves. Only my family. You'll meet them all tomorrow. My family doesn't believe in slavery."

"My parents didn't either," Billy whispered, picking up on Mark's hushed tone.

"Come on, Billy, let's get what you need." Looking at the boy, Mark could see every stitch on him, from tattered hat to outsized shoes tied on with rawhide, was falling apart.

"Come to think of it, I could use new trousers myself." Mark picked up a pair and added a blanket and staples for Sarah to the growing pile. He chose a bolt of pink and one of blue calico fabric with buttons to match the tiny design on the material for Sarah and Lydia. He asked the clerk, "Could you wrap them with pink and blue ribbons for me? My daughter will use them to tie up her hair."

Mark barely recognized Billy, outfitted head to toe with new clothes. Mark added a pair of trousers and socks to his pile for the growing Jack.

Mark motioned to the counter. "Billy, pick out three half-dime's worth bags of candy, one for yourself and the others to share with Jack and Lydia." Billy's eyes grew wide, peering through the glass at all the sweet choices.

The next stop was the postal office, where he mailed Sarah's letters and picked up three for the Hewitt family, and then on to the stables to retrieve the wagon so they could get to the sawmill and load lumber before heading home to start Billy's new life.

Chapter Six

Billy glanced back at the town as the wagon crossed the bridge. Was he really free from Rusty? He was wearing new clothes and shoes for the first time in a year, that this stranger bought him. He could start a new life. Could this all be true? But why?

"Thanks for the clothes and shoes, mister."

"Sure, Billy. We'll be back to town next month, so if you think of other things you'll need, we'll pick them up then. Remember, you can call me Mark if you want."

Billy was quiet for a while, then asked, "Mark, how well did you know my parents?"

"Honestly, I didn't know your father personally, and I never met you or your mother like I told Rusty. I wanted him to believe me, so I sort of stretched the truth."

"You lied?" Billy's eye's widened. What had he gotten himself into?

"Well, not exactly. I learned about you from the Marysville sheriff. I knew how you lost your father and that he was a lawyer. I wasn't in town when you arrived on the stagecoach, but word travels. It's a coincidence that we ran into each other.

"I took a chance when I called out your name. I'm glad you're free from Rusty, and I'm pleased you're coming to the farm to meet my family. You'll like

37

them. I hope you'll want to stay."

****

Soon Mark and Billy arrived at the sawmill.

"Now comes the hard work. See the pile of lumber over there?" Mark pointed to a stack next to an old plow. "We need to load those boards to take home. The lumber is why I traveled to town in the first place. Are you sure you're up for helping?"

"Yeah, I'll help. Why do you need so many boards?"

"Our barn burned down this spring during a thunderstorm, and we must rebuild."

As they loaded boards, Mark taught Billy the difference between hard and soft woods and what they were used for. After paying his bill, Mark said, "We'll be back in two weeks for another load." He and Billy climbed back onto the wagon.

On the road again, Billy's eyes closed and his head bobbed, and Mark said, "Crawl in the back and take a nap. You won't miss anything, and I'll wake you in time to eat."

Without hesitation, Billy jumped over the seat to dig out the blanket they bought in town. Soon he was sound asleep.

The next thing he heard, Mark called him to "Wake up."

"What's happening?" Billy asked as he climbed over the wagon seat.

"It's time to make camp. You hungry?" Mark asked, as he headed the horses off the road and eased them to a stop.

"Sure am."

With a fire started, Mark handed Billy a couple of

biscuits and jerky and set out the sack of dried apples Sarah packed. "Dig in. You're nothing but skin and bones. Don't worry. Sarah, my wife, will fatten you up. She's a good cook."

****

On the road again the next morning, Mark said, "Tell me more about your folks."

"Well, my momma died having a baby, and the baby died too." Billy shrugged his shoulders and sighed, "Poppa said he couldn't live in Kansas City without her because of the memories, so we headed to Colorado. And you know how Poppa died in the stage hold-up."

"I only know what I heard. If it's not too painful, could you tell me the story?" Mark asked. "Sometimes talking to someone about the pain you carry around helps relieve that pain a little. You can talk to me if you want. I'm a good listener."

"Well, you're the first person who's cared enough to want to listen. I'll tell you what happened. It's been almost a year since I lost my father in an attempted stagecoach robbery. I think of that day often. My whole life changed and there was nothing I could do.

"If only I did what father told me: get in the stage, lie on the floor, and don't get up until told. If only I hadn't looked out the window. Poppa got hit with the first shot. He fell to his knees, then to the ground. If the farmer hadn't stopped to help put the wheel back on the stagecoach, we might all have died.

"The farmer decided to charge the robbers head on. Said we were sitting ducks if we didn't. Within minutes both the outlaws were dead. He killed them both. I was bandaging the driver's arm when the farmer rode off. I never thanked him for saving my life. I can't even tell you his name, but I could identify his face."

Billy hung his head. "When the stage finally arrived in Marysville, the driver turned me over to the sheriff. The only things I had were my father's coin pouch with a little money, his watch, and our two suitcases.

"They buried my father in the town cemetery. Without enough money to take the stage back to Kansas City, I was at the mercy of the sheriff, who gladly turned me over to Rusty. 'Do what he tells you, boy,' I remember the sheriff saying as Rusty took me out of the office.

****

"At first Rusty treated me all right. I drove the wagon, took care of the mules, cooked, and helped him with his shows, as he liked to call them. His wares were bottles of elixir, pots and pans, and silverware he'd pick up from time to time to resell, if he could buy them cheap enough. He was a stout, tall man. But he could sweet talk the ladies into buying his wares and could convince the men the elixir worked on their ailments too.

"Then, one night, Rusty got drunk. When he returned from the saloon he asked why I let the fire go out. Couldn't I do anything right? Said, 'You're just a dumb lad.' He slapped me around and shoved me backward. I almost fell into the hot coals of the fire. Before I knew what happened, he tied my hands to the seat of the wagon. He left me there all night while he passed out, wrapped in a blanket.

"The next day when he untied me, I vowed to get away, as far away as possible. My tolerance turned into hatred. I knew where he kept the locked cashbox, and that a few blows with a cast iron pan would break the lock, but waiting for the right time took patience. He tied my hands every night so I wouldn't try anything while he slept. I wanted to kill him more than once, but I couldn't kill him in cold blood. People would figure I killed him, and I didn't want to go to prison. The cussing and slapping me around became threats and beatings.

"Biding my time, I waited for the right moment to make my move. I overheard a conversation between him and an elderly woman who lived in town. The lady owned sterling silverware and other items she wanted to sell. He would be gone a few hours. Here was my chance. I'd bite my ropes off if necessary, break the lock on the cashbox, buy a ticket for the stage, and get away. I didn't care where the stage was headed as long as I could get away.

"After the morning meal, I anxiously washed the pans and dishes and put them away as usual. Then I prepared for the morning show. We usually did two shows a day, one late morning, then late afternoon. As I started the preparations, Rusty said, 'No show this morning, boy. Get in the wagon and mix more elixir.' I memorized the recipe; I made elixir so many times. A cup and a half of water, a fifth of rye whiskey, three tablespoons sugar, and six tablespoons beet juice. I'd mix everything in a crock and ladle the mixture into the bottles."

Mark said, "So that's what elixir is made of. That stuff wouldn't cure any ailment I ever had."

"I know, but Rusty's performance always sounded so good we sold out in every town. That day I took my

41

time, knowing he always liked the elixir bottled the same day. We were running low. If he hadn't cancelled the morning show, we'd have sold out and needed another batch made for the afternoon show anyway. I could make it, bottle and cork it, and put on the label in an hour, but I always took my time. Rusty knew if I made the elixir, the amounts were consistent, and consistency sold the product, he always told me. The color always had to be the same in each bottle.

"I heard the town clock chime half past. My timing was perfect. I had mixed the batch but hadn't bottled any yet. Rusty opened the back flaps of the wagon to check on my progress and said, 'You haven't even started bottling yet. This needs bottled, and I have to leave soon.' He paced back and forth restlessly.

"I said, 'I know what I'm doing. I've done this a thousand times. I'll finish this and then go get us leftover food from the hotel's back alley. The owner has seen me and hasn't reported me once to the sheriff.' Other than selling his elixir, the things Rusty liked best were eating and gambling.

"Rusty wasn't happy but finally agreed. 'Oh, all right. Just this once. But when I get back, there'll be hell to pay if everything's not done.' Rusty looked at his watch and headed for town.

"I hurried and bottled the elixir, slapped the labels on, and cleaned up everything. The cashbox would be in the trunk where it always was…locked. Rusty took money with him to purchase the widow's wares, but when I broke the old lock on the trunk with a cast iron skillet with one blow, the cashbox was there. I shook the box and coins rattled. He hadn't taken it all. I only needed enough to buy a ticket so I'd never have to deal with him again.

"I grabbed the cashbox and the skillet. This was my chance. After six whacks the lock hung open. There were three double-eagle twenty-dollar gold coins and a few silver coins. I grabbed all the money and headed for the ticket office to catch the morning stage.

"Well, you can see I didn't make it. Rusty threatened to turn me over to the sheriff for stealing if I tried it again, and he whipped me good. He said, 'I don't care if you rot in prison, and that's where you're going if you try this again.' I figured he meant every word."

"Why, that's quite a story." Mark shifted his weight on the wagon seat.

Billy turned and stared right into Mark's eyes. "Don't you believe me?"

"Yes, I believe you, every word. I'm sorry you had to put up with Rusty as long as you did. "Did he gamble a lot?" Mark asked.

"Lately, every town we stopped at he gambled. Most nights he'd come back and fall asleep, but sometimes he came back angry or hungry and wanted me to cook him some food."

"Don't you have any relatives like grandparents or an aunt, or uncle? Is there anyone related to your ma or pa you can remember?"

"Not that I know of. You mentioned something about an uncle, but my folks never talked about anyone and nobody ever visited. I only remember my momma, poppa, and me. The sheriff in Marysville asked me the same question before he gave me to Rusty."

"Billy, I lied about you having an uncle, to get you away from Rusty."

"I thought so. I did have a photograph of my parents, but Rusty got mad at me once and threw it in a creek. He wouldn't let me go after it, and soon the current carried the tintype and frame downstream."

"I'm sorry about the photo, and I'm sorry about the way Rusty treated you, Billy." They rode in silence for a while, and then Mark asked, "Have you been around livestock or on a farm much?"

"No. Just Rusty's old mules."

"Well, you'll have chores to help with, and we have fields to plant. Plus we have to rebuild the barn and the chicken coop. Jack can teach you to ride a horse. You'll catch on."

Talking made the time pass quickly, and late in the afternoon they crossed the creek to the Hewitt property. Billy leaned forward as the fields and then the house appeared in the distance. Excited, but nervous at the same time to meet Mark's family, he asked. "What are the boy and girl's names again? Jack and Lydia?"

"Yes, Jack and Lydia."

"What if they don't like me? What if they don't want me to stay?"

"No need to worry. They'll like you plenty. This can be your new home. I hope you'll want to stay. Hey, is that your stomach growling? You hungry?" Mark teased.

Mark stopped the wagon by the well and they both hopped down. He understood the risk. One wrong word about the attempted stagecoach holdup and Sarah would figure out he lied again. He promised Sarah no more lies.

"Mark, you're back! We worried about you." Jack ran to greet him.

"Yes, we expected you last night," Lydia added, running to hug him while glancing at the boy who stood beside him.

"Well, I'm back now, and I have a friend with me. Billy, this is my family, my wife Mrs. Hewitt, Jack, and Lydia."

"Hello, I'm Billy Henry." Billy smiled, and took a step closer to Mark.

Sarah extended her hand for Billy to shake, "Welcome, Billy. Supper is almost ready. Give me a half hour."

"We'll tend to the horses and clean up. Jack, can you give us a hand with the horses?" Mark said.

"Sure, I'll help." Jack began unhitching the horses.

Billy helped.

Jack tended to one horse and Billy the other while Mark drew water and fetched oats.

"Where you from?" Jack asked.

"Kansas City. I lived there all my life. Well, most of my life. I was never on a farm before."

"You going to stay with us a while?"

"I'm willing to stay if you'll teach me farming." Billy stretched his hand out.

Jack shook his hand and said, "Then I guess you're staying a while, because you have a lot to learn."

Mark walked over and asked, "Everything all right?"

"Yup. It's okay if Billy stays a while isn't it, Mark?"

"Well, I hoped he'd want to stay and make this his new home." Mark picked up two sacks of supplies to carry to the house.

"I'll stay a while. You need help building the barn,

and I'd like to learn farming."

Heading to the house, Mark called back over his shoulder, "I'll send Lydia out, and you can show Billy around a little until supper's ready."

"How'd you meet Mark?" Jack inquired.

"Well, he kind of saved me. I was in a bad situation, and he helped me out."

"Mark's a good man. He and my father were best friends. Then my father died on a hunting trip, and Mark stayed on and helped us plant the crops. Then he and my ma fell in love and got married, making us a family again."

"You don't mind if I stay, do you?"

"Do you like to fish and go hunting?" Jack scratched behind the horse's ear.

"I like to fish, but I've never been hunting. In Kansas City we didn't raise any animals."

"I never lived in a big city. Come on. Let's get these horses over to the corral."

Lydia ran out the door, calling, "Wait for me." She hurried to catch up. "Mark said to show Billy some good hiding places so when we play hide and seek he'll have good spots."

Inside the house, Mark wasn't sure what he would say, but Sarah deserved some sort of explanation for another mouth to feed. Everything he would tell her would be the truth.

As Sarah sliced the bread, Mark explained, "Sarah, I had to fetch Billy home with me. He's the orphaned boy from the stagecoach robbery." Mark wouldn't lie. He couldn't lose his family. *All true so far*, Mark sighed.

"The boy was helping a peddler in Dead Flats

selling wares out of a wagon. His shoes were tied to his feet with rawhide. The man trussed him to the wagon at night, and I witnessed him begging for food at the back door of the hotel." *All still true.*

"The poor boy." Sarah sighed, her eyes filled with tears.

"Billy told me the sheriff in Marysville gave him to the peddler and told him to do what the man wanted. If you'd seen the clothes he wore, you'd agree he was treated poorly. You can see how thin he is, and he told me he is sixteen.

"Please understand, Sarah, I couldn't leave him with that old man. He'll be another mouth to feed and more responsibility, but—"

Sarah put her finger to Mark's lips. "I'd have done the same thing. We have enough love to go around and enough work, too."

"Then you understand?"

"Of course I do. You have a good heart, Mark Hewitt. You always have. Billy's welcome to live with us. I don't think the children will mind having someone to help with the chores and talk with, especially Jack. But let me talk to them."

Mark kissed Sarah's cheek, thankful she understood but fearful Samuel's secret might soon come out in the open. He didn't want to think of Sarah's reaction.

Just then, the children rushed in. "I'm hungry, Mother," Jack announced, "and I heard Billy's stomach growling. He's hungry, all right."

Sarah set the kettle of stew in the middle of the table, and Lydia carried the plate of sliced bread and the crock of butter.

"Billy, you can sit next to me." Jack nudged the chair.

Mark then took the chair at the head of the table.

Jack recited the meal's prayer with haste. He couldn't wait to tell Mark everything that happened since he left. They got the garden planted, he'd caught a rabbit in his snare, and Lydia finished sewing a new apron.

Alone with Mark for a moment after dinner, Billy asked, "Do you think they like me—Jack and Lydia, I mean? Do you think they want me to stay?"

"I don't think you need to worry about Jack. And Lydia will come around. She's a little shy."

"She already told me I could help her gather the eggs tomorrow."

"Well, that's a good sign." Mark patted him on the back. "You'll sleep with Jack in the loft. He'll make room for you."

****

Inside, Sarah shared a quiet conversation with Lydia and Jack about Billy staying.

Jack offered, "I don't mind sharing my room. It'll be nice to have a friend. He already told me he likes to fish. And he said he's grateful to Mark for all his help."

"What do you think, Lydia?" Sarah took her hand. "Be honest."

"It'll be all right, I guess. As long as he has to do chores too. He'll be someone else to talk with, and if he can't play chess, we could teach him."

"It will take time to get acquainted. He lived in a town most of his life, I think," said Sarah. "So we'll have to teach him what it's like to live on a farm."

"Yes, he wants to learn about farming," Jack

added.

"Please don't say anything to Billy about making this his forever home. That's his decision to make.

"Also, you should know both his parents have passed away. You understand how hard it is to lose someone you love. If he wants to talk about them, he will, but until then all we can do is make him feel welcome."

****

That night Billy snuggled under the wool blanket Mark bought him. This blanket he could call his own. *I don't have much, but now I have a roof over my head and a family who will let me live with them.* He'd take life one day at a time. He closed his eyes and said a prayer of thanks for the Lord bringing Mark into his life.

Chapter Seven

After one of Sarah's hearty breakfasts, the children were eager to have Billy help them with the chores, but Mark needed to talk to Billy privately.

"Billy would you mind giving me a hand with unloading the lumber?" Mark asked.

"Sure, I'll help."

Out of earshot, as they unloaded boards and stacked them on the pile to dry, Mark said, "Living with Rusty was no life for a boy. He treated you terribly. My wife and I and the children want you to stay with us. We want you to live here and let this be your home. Would you like that?"

"Well, your family seems real nice."

"Jack and Lydia showed you around. Any questions?"

"Not right now. Jack said he'd let me help with the morning chores and show me how to milk the cow. Miz Hewitt's cooking is great. Best food I've eaten in a long time. I'm not sure about Lydia, but I haven't had much time to get to know her, and besides, I'm not used to young girls. She did say I could play with her cats, though."

"You'll have three meals a day. I'll teach you how to hunt, and you and Jack will be fishing every free minute you get. There are fish in the creek we crossed on the far side of the property and a few real good fishing holes. You'll have daily chores and you'll be riding a horse in no time."

"Farming is hard work." Billy wiped his brow. "My father wanted me to go to school and become a lawyer. You know, follow in his footsteps. But I told him I didn't want to go to college. If you teach me about farming, I wouldn't have to go to college, would I?"

"No. You don't have to go to college to run a farm, but you must know arithmetic and how to read and write."

"I can do all of that. I completed most of eighth grade, in Kansas City."

"How old are you?"

"My birthday was in April, so I turned sixteen last month. I'm old enough to live on my own now."

"Well, I wouldn't want Jack on his own at sixteen. But yes, by some folks' standards you're old enough."

"I don't mind hard work, but I have a question. Why did Rusty turn me over to you?"

"Let's say he knew I could take better care of you than he could. I told him I'd get you to your uncle, and remember, he thought I knew your parents."

Mark picked up more boards. "Could you tell me a little about life in Kansas City, Billy?"

"Were you ever there, Mark?"

"Yes, a couple of times." Mark lifted another board.

Billy grabbed the other end. "Then you probably passed my father's office. His name was Paul Harrison Henry. He was a lawyer. A good one. My father called my mother Ada, but her real name was Adeline. She enjoyed reading and music, and loved to dance. She wanted me to learn the piano, but I wouldn't practice, so she gave up. I really miss her."

"Sounds like they were wonderful folks."

Just then one of the horses nickered in the corral.

"Jack and Lydia told me they lost their father too. We have a lot in common."

"Yes, you do," Mark agreed.

Billy stopped and shook Mark's hand. "Thanks for what you did. I mean lying and everything for me. If you hadn't come along, I realize now, I'd still be with Rusty. I'm ready to give farming a try."

Mark smiled from ear to ear. "That's great, Billy. Why don't you find Jack and help him with the rest of his morning chores? I'll finish with the lumber. And if you need anything, let me know."

Pausing to wipe his brow, he reached into his coat pocket and discovered the letters he picked up at the postal office. He hurried to the house and gave them to Sarah. "Sorry, darling. In all the excitement yesterday, I forgot to give these to you.

"And good news, from now on, you and Lydia will no longer be helping in the fields. We have another mouth to feed. Billy said he'd stay and try farming for a while. I still worry I might wake up one morning and he'll be gone, but he's here for now."

Sarah gave him a warm hug before he went outside.

****

Sarah recognized her mother's handwriting on two letters, and the other was from Mark's mother. *I'll read them and share the news at the dinner table.* Precious valuables from home were welcomed reading.

Then Sarah settled with a cup of tea and opened the

earliest postmarked letter from her mother.

January 10, 1859

Tidioute, Warren County, Pennsylvania

Dearest Sarah,

The holidays are over and a new year brings new challenges. The town was quite festive. The church was decorated with evergreens and the church choir sang in the streets. We put up an evergreen this year and decorated the living room. I was not going to bother, but the girls talked me into a tree and I am glad they did. The smell of pine filled the house. Your father even enjoyed the holiday, especially the food.

The reason I am penning this letter is because I am sure you are remembering and missing your son Walter today. Your heart must ache. I so wish I could be with you, but I am glad you have the comfort of Mark in your life.

I miss spoiling my grandchildren especially during the holidays. No doubt you had a memorable time as a new family. I hope you still read the Christmas story to the children. Why, I bet Jack or Lydia read from the Bible to you this year! My, how quickly the time has passed. I still remember the day you left on the wagon train. I cannot believe five years have already passed since you left home. The time seems longer. So much has happened.

I always miss you and the children the most this time of year. Give them each a big hug and kiss from me and your father and let them know how much we love and miss them.

You probably will not receive this letter until the spring, but when I am thinking of you I like to write. Take care of yourself, my dearest Sarah, and know that

I love you.

   Prayers and blessings,

Mother

She returned the letter to the envelope. *I can share all this news with the children.* Then she read the second letter:

March 1, 1859

Tidioute, Warren County, Pennsylvania

Dearest Sarah,

   Happy Birthday my sweet Sarah! I was thinking of you and the children this morning because of your birthday and the next thing I knew, I had pen and paper in hand to write.

   As always, my darling daughter, I pray this finds you in good health and good spirits. I worry about you and the children even though you have Mark to help with the farm.

   Matilda, Emma, and Matthew are not little children as you remember. They are growing up so fast, as I am sure Jack and Lydia are.

   Matilda is now working with Doc Davis. She has helped deliver several babies since she started, and Doc is pleased with her skills. I am amazed that she enjoys learning about the human body and the power of medicine. She always has a story to tell around the supper table.

   Abel Evans is courting Emma now, and she spends most of her free time trying to impress him. He is a nice young man. Emma is also waiting tables for the dinner crowd at the hotel. She says she wants to save her money, and that surprises me. I hope she is not saving for a wedding right away.

   Matthew's interest is writing and someday

journalism. He is an apprentice with Mr. Reed at the newspaper and learning the trade. I will send you a clipping of his first article, which he hopes to have published soon.

I can tell old age is catching up with me. Some mornings my arms and legs do not want to work like they did a few years ago. It takes me more time to go up and down steps, and whipping the mashed potatoes makes my arms ache. I am not really complaining; a few aches and pains are natural. Maybe the cold weather is the problem. Thankfully, warmer days are around the corner.

Give my grandchildren big hugs and kisses from me and your father and tell them their grandparents love and miss them. I will write again soon.

All my love and prayers,

Mother

Sarah debated for a moment whether to open Mark's mother's letter or not, but then thought, *He wouldn't have given the letter to me if he didn't want me to read it. I'm sure letters from his mother mean as much to him as letters from home mean to me.*

February 9, 1859

Tidioute, Warren County, Pennsylvania

Dear Sarah and Mark,

The news of your wedding brought tears of joy to my heart. The only thing that would have made me happier was if I were standing there with you on your special day. I'm delighted for both of you.

You have my blessing and best wishes for a happy life together, although I was sorry to read about the circumstances with Samuel that enabled your union.

Sarah, thank you for writing all the details a

mother wants to hear. In your next letter, I hope to read that a baby may soon be on the way.

I so wish I could meet your new family someday, Mark, but I am sure a trip east is not possible. I talked to your mother and father in town, Sarah, and we all rejoiced in knowing your union was of mutual needs and wants.

Most of my holiday was spent in bed with a fever and chills, and I am just now starting to recover. We are having an exceptionally cold winter, and I am looking forward to spring.

Mark, even though your birthday is not until next month, I am not sure how often you pick up the mail. While I am thinking of you, I want to wish you a Happy Birthday. Do you remember the year it snowed on your birthday and you built a fort? I had to bribe you with cake to get you to come in the house. You wanted to sleep in the fort that night. You must have been six or seven, I do not recall exactly.

Please send me the dates of the children's and Sarah's birthdays. I will be sure to write and send them birthday notes, and enter this information in our family Bible, which will one day be yours, my dear son.

I will stop now and place this in the mail my next trip to town. Please know my thoughts are with you often, and I hope you will write again soon.

All my love,

Mother

That evening Sarah shared all the news from both grandmothers and caught Billy looking sad a few times as she read aloud. She was certain hearing about family was difficult, with his own parents gone. He could be resenting the fact that Jack and Lydia had parents and grandparents and he didn't. She would wait and talk alone sometime with Billy to see if she could do anything to make him feel more at home.

****

Saying his prayers silently that evening, Billy asked God, *Why did you take my parents away from me?* He asked this question every night since he lost his father. Tonight he also asked, *why did you lead Mark and his family into my life? Is this where you want me? Is this my second chance? I prayed you'd take me away from Rusty, and you brought me Mark.*

****

Billy awoke with a new outlook on life. He was eager to learn, and Jack seemed grateful for his companionship. Working in tandem, the boys sowed a plot of rye grass, one of buckwheat, and a mix of alfalfa and oats. Come sundown, the four-acre field was three quarters planted.

The next day, the boys finished the field, and Jack let Billy take the reins of the plow horses. Billy plowed only a small area to plant pumpkin seeds Jack and Lydia had saved from last year's harvest, and his shoulders already ached.

Billy sat in the grass to take a break. "What if we get hundreds of pumpkins? We planted at least a hundred seeds."

Jack flopped down beside him. "Then we can sell them at the Harvest Festival this fall, and we'll be rich."

"Lydia will want a cut of our profits, won't she?"

"Yeah, probably. We could split the money three ways."

"I was thinking more like forty, forty, and twenty."

"Yeah, that sounds better. But we better wait and

see if they grow first."

****

As the weeks passed, Mark heard Billy tease Lydia like a sister and Jack as a brother and vice versa. Jack and Billy were racing each other from the house to the barn, arm wrestling on the kitchen table when Sarah wasn't watching, and always eager to play a game of checkers or chess, with Lydia taking on the winner.

Mark could see Jack and Billy becoming lifelong friends. The boys were inseparable, almost as if they could read each other's minds. They were as close as birth brothers the way they teased, wrestled, and challenged each other all the time. Jack taught Billy things around the farm, and Billy helped Jack and Lydia with reading and arithmetic, giving Sarah a break from time to time. Jack even taught Billy advanced chess moves his father taught him, and the boys enjoyed a game in the evenings.

"It seems like the farm is on track for a good year as long as Mother Nature cooperates," Mark said one night. "We need to fetch another load of lumber. Then we can begin the chicken coop and start the barn the following week. The new barn will have a door on each end so you can drive the wagons in and out, be four feet wider, and eight feet longer, making space for storage and two more stalls." Mark was proud of the new design and was sure, come fall, he and the boys would have no problem finishing the work.

"It's Jack's turn to help with a load of lumber. Do you think you can handle the chores, Billy?"

"Sure I can. I can do everything, and Lydia will tell me if I do anything wrong." Billy chuckled.

Mark grinned in response. *If I leave Billy alone*

with Sarah and she learns the truth about how his father died, the information could end our marriage. I guess it's a chance I must risk unless I break my promise to Samuel. I've come this far, I can't go back on my word now. Please God. Help me be a good husband and do right by Billy. Don't ever let Sarah find out the truth.

Chapter Eight

Mark and Jack left for lumber, leaving Billy the man of the family for a few days. Playing with Lydia's cats after chores one afternoon, Lydia and Billy discovered they had something in common; they both liked animals.

Lydia's inquisitive side began asking Billy questions to get acquainted better, such as: "What was Kansas City like? How many kids went to your school? When's your birthday? And when she found out Billy didn't celebrate his last birthday, she rushed to share an idea with her mother.

Sarah sat mixing lye water with wood ash to make soap when Lydia rushed over. "Did you know Billy's birthday was last month and he never got to celebrate? Could we fix him a special meal? I'll make him a cake. Perhaps a celebration would make him feel more like family. We could make a special day just for Billy and give him presents and everything."

"That's a wonderful gesture." Sarah gave Lydia a hug. "A two-month belated party would be fun. If we hold the big event in June, we would all have time to make him a present."

When Mark and Jack returned, Lydia explained the surprise.

Mark agreed. "Great idea. I have an idea for a present, and I'll pick it up in town on my next trip. I'd also like to use some of the lumber and buy rope to make him a bed."

"Oh, he'll appreciate his own bed. Momma and I will start working on a quilt," Lydia said.

"His bed should fit right next to mine. Space will be a little tight, but we'll make do. And I know what I'll make him for his birthday. I'll whittle him something Father taught me how to make." Jack climbed up the ladder to the loft to measure for the bed.

****

The following week everyone except Sarah pitched in to get the foundation of the old barn cleared so construction could begin. They cleared the site and hauled the last of the ashes to the fields. The chicken coop took only two days to build with three people working together. The windowpane from the old coop was salvaged, cleaned, and used again. With two more wagonloads of wood to retrieve and one more trip to town for supplies, they would have everything needed to finish the barn project.

This time Billy would ride to the lumber mill and town for supplies. Mark hoped the subject of the stagecoach robbery would never be mentioned again, although deep down he knew the conversation surfacing was only a matter of time.

This trip to town lent the perfect diversion for the family to plan Billy's surprise party. While there, Mark took Billy to the hardware store to look in the knife case.

"Which one would you buy if you had the money?" Mark asked casually.

After studying the different knives displayed, Billy finally said, "I really like the one on the end, with the sheath. Jack showed me his father's. This one looks a lot like that knife. The blade is about five inches, with a nice curved tip, and I like the wooden handle."

Mark nodded at the sales clerk, who took the knife from the showcase and handed the shiny blade to Billy to look over.

Billy slid the knife in and out of the sheath a few times and checked for sharpness the way Jack showed him.

"Well, maybe someday when you earn enough money, you can buy yourself a knife." Mark walked over and asked the clerk for a box of ammunition.

Billy walked to the rack of rifles. "I'll buy one of these one day, too, when I earn enough money."

While Billy turned away from the counter looking at the guns, Mark asked the clerk to add the knife to his bill along with a ratchet and rope enough to string a bed. After they loaded the supplies, they headed to the sawmill.

Mark hoped the three-day trip gave Sarah, Lydia, and Jack an opportunity to finish their birthday presents. The party would take place the evening they returned.

On the return trip, the wagon bumped in and out of ruts along the path. Most of the conversation was Billy asking questions. He inquired about when and how the crops would be harvested, how long baby chicks took to hatch, and why were they only milking the one cow? He was full of questions but never mentioned the one topic Mark hoped to talk about—would Billy stay permanently and be a part of the Hewitt family?

The house in sight, Mark asked, "Billy, if you could have anything to eat for supper tonight, what would you pick?"

"That's strange you should ask. Lydia asked me about my favorite meal right before we left. I told her I didn't have just one. I like baked fish, beef steaks, and her fried chicken."

"All good choices," Mark agreed.

As soon as the wagon stopped in the yard, Jack ran out, gripped the horses' harness, and led the horses to the new hitching rail and watering trough built right after Billy's arrival. "Mother said to wash up before you come in tonight. Did you get everything we needed?"

"Yup, we can start framing tomorrow." Billy and Mark had discussed the construction process most of the way home.

Mark let Billy enter the house first. The table displayed the good linens, and the smell of fresh baked fish Jack caught that morning wafted in the room. Then Billy gazed at Lydia holding the pedestal cake plate topped with a two-layer confection.

"Chocolate with white icing," Lydia said. "Your favorite, even if it is two months late."

Everyone said, "Happy Birthday," at the same time and Billy stopped cold. He looked at each of his new family's faces and suddenly missed his own family; his mother's face, his father's air of confidence. They were so happy the last time they were together, before the baby took everything away.

His mind flashed to his last birthday with his parents. They gave him a fancy blue suit which they expected he'd need at college. The suit was left behind because his father made him pack so quickly.

"Come sit down, Billy." Jack's words startled him

back to the present.

After dinner, Sarah served the cake while the others brought out their surprise presents. Billy couldn't believe the family surprised him without him suspecting a thing.

Lydia gave Billy her present first, a pillowcase with his name embroidered on the opening end and a drawstring pouch with his initials, to keep small things in.

"Thanks, Lydia. Gosh, that's real nice handwork."

Next, Mark handed him the knife wrapped in paper.

"Wow! Thanks, Mark, I never owned my own knife. Momma always said I didn't need a knife, and in town I guess she was right, but on a farm you need one. Look, Jack, it's like yours." Billy jumped to his feet to show Jack. "I thought I'd be waiting a long time before I could get my own."

"You're right. On a farm you do need a knife. Isn't that right, Jack?" Mark said.

"Yeah, a knife comes in handy," Jack agreed. He tested Billy's blade for sharpness, slid the knife in and out of the sheath a few times, and handed it back. Billy's knife may have been new, but Jack's was special because it had been his pa's knife.

Sarah and Lydia showed him the start of a scrappy quilt they were making with squares cut out of fabric from the sewing basket.

"Thank you, Miz Hewitt and Lydia. I love all the colors."

"It will look good on your new bed," Mark said.

"Really? My own bed? Thanks! I can't wait."

"The rope is in the wagon." Mark motioned toward

the barn. "All we need to do is build the frame and we can string the bed together. We'll work on it in the evenings after supper."

"Thanks, Mark," Billy said. "My own bed."

Jack finished Billy's present that morning. He started whittling while Billy worked on the chores. They traded off every week, one doing morning chores, the other doing evening chores.

"You made this out of one solid piece of wood?" Billy asked, thrilled Jack cared enough to make him a special gift. Billy knew he would treasure the whistle forever.

"Yup, I made it myself. My father used to whittle them for me all the time." Jack puffed out his chest. "I'll show you how to whittle, if you want."

"That'd be great," Billy exclaimed. "And thanks for the cake, Miz Hewitt."

"I can't take credit for the cake, Billy. Lydia made this one."

"I baked your favorite." Lydia beamed.

Everyone sat ready to dig into the cake when Billy surprised them and stood. "Wait a minute. I need to say something." Billy looked around the table. "First, I want to thank you all for my presents." He smiled and put his hands in his pockets. "I know I haven't been here long, but you folks treat me real good." Looking down at his piece of cake, he said, "I hadn't thought about my birthday and everything I missed for a while now. I guess I kind of gave up while with Rusty." He looked at Mark. "Thanks for taking a chance on me and thanks for making me feel like family. I wasn't sure at first if I'd like life on a farm, but I sure like having a sort of brother and sister." Billy's eyes teared, but he

Judy Sharer

brushed them away quickly so no one would see.

"Mark asked me if I would stay and make this my new home. I'd like that very much."

Jack jumped from his seat and gave him a hug. "Now I'm not sort of your brother. I *am* your brother."

"And I'm your sister," Lydia added.

"It's your decision, Billy, and I hope you don't think I'm being too presumptuous, because I'm not trying to take away your mother's memory, but it might be easier for you to call me Mother or Ma rather than Miz Hewitt."

"I used to call my mother Momma, so calling you Mother or Ma would be all right. I'd like that," Billy replied.

Mark said, "You can keep calling me Mark, if you like. That's fine."

Billy shook Mark's hand, then sat back down, and everyone enjoyed the cake.

****

A week later, the boys hauled the completed bed up the ladder to the boys' side of the loft. The quilt wasn't quite done, but Lydia worked every spare minute she could find to finish the task.

One day, Mark and the boys took a break from construction to check on the fields. Rain passed by a few days before, and Mark took pleasure in the plants' new growth.

On their way home, Mark stopped the wagon and dug out fishing poles from behind the wagon seat.

Jack remembered the story about his father and Mark's fishing competition and said, "Mark, could you tell Billy the story about you and my pa's competition to see who could catch the most fish before dark?"

66

While Mark recalled the story, Jack helped Billy find worms and baited their hooks. "The first one to catch three fish wins," Jack challenged.

They raced to see who would catch the first fish.

It had been a long time since Billy held a rod in his hands. Memories of skipping school with George Weber and some of the other boys and heading to the creek in his home town of Kansas City rushed back. His mother only found out once and didn't tell his father, so he never got in trouble. He didn't go every time the other boys skipped school for the day, but he always enjoyed the challenge of catching a fish.

Billy's thoughts kept returning to his home in Kansas City, his parents, his mother's death, and the events that led him to Mark. He'd go back one day, but there was no one there he'd want to live with, so he'd stay with his new family for now.

After hauling in three fish each, the happy trio put their poles in the wagon. Mark won the contest, snagging in his third fish just minutes before Jack, and Billy wasn't far behind.

"The only thing better than catching fish is eating them," Jack said. He'd heard his father say the same words many times.

"And you know my rule when it comes to fishing and hunting." Mark looked at the boys.

The boys said it in unison, "If you catch it or kill it, you clean it."

Jack and Billy didn't mind, because everyone enjoyed the eating. Fish were always a welcome change.

On the way back to the house, Mark commented, "The barn is progressing nicely. The framed sides are completed, and it'll soon be time to raise them."

"I'm learning a lot about farming and building," Billy commented. "Maybe I'll have my own farm someday. A little hard work never hurt anybody, and around here everyone pitches in and does their share."

Jack repeated what Mark and his father always said when the work got tough, "Many hands make light work."

After that day, fishing was all the boys wanted to do with their free time. A standing competition continued between them to see who could catch the most.

Chapter Nine

With Independence Day only a few weeks away, Lydia asked, "Will we go to town for the festivities this year?"

"Only if your mother is feeling up to traveling." Mark looked at Sarah. Already in her sixth month, her health was Mark's primary concern.

"If we take the covered wagon for shade and a bed of quilts to ease the bumps, I'm game for a weekend in town." Sarah rubbed her belly. "Everyone will enjoy the time away. You've been working hard rebuilding the barn and the children deserve some fun and a chance to see their friends."

"Well, we need a few things to finish off the barn, and Ruby and Button could each use new shoes." Mark added, "They don't like pulling the wagon, but they can."

"What about Daisy? We'd have to see if Seth Frazer can come and milk her, but with Emily staying with him now, they may be going to the festivities themselves." Sarah often wondered how that relationship was coming along. The family hadn't seen them since Seth brought Emily home from town to live with him last October.

"Only one way to find out," Jack interjected. "Billy and I can ride over and ask them. Billy hasn't met Mr. Frazer and Emily. I'll make the introductions and ask if they're going to town or if he'd be willing to come over and help out. We can go tomorrow."

"Sure, I'll go," Billy agreed. "How far away do they live?"

"Their place is about twelve miles west. We can get there and back in a day. Don't worry, we'll be back in time for supper," Jack explained.

Mark looked at Sarah, who said, "All right, you boys can go tomorrow, but promise you'll be careful and don't stay too long. And be back before dark. I can't let you go empty-handed, so Lydia, I'll need help to make pumpkin bread to send along. Oh, and we can send the newspaper. We've all read every page several times. I'm sure news from town would be welcomed."

The next morning the boys headed west toward Mr. Frazer's place with pumpkin bread, the newspaper, and a midday meal Sarah packed them, tucked in the saddlebags. Jack led the way, riding Button, and Billy rode Ruby. Along the path, Jack pointed out places of interest and property lines.

The boys ate their meal at the place in the bend of the creek where Jack and his father always stopped. When they arrived at the house, Jack called out, "Mr. Frazer? Mr. Frazer, are you home?" The boys dismounted, drew a pail of water from the well for the horses, and Jack called out again, "Mr. Frazer... Ma'am...Anyone home?" Not seeing any activity at the house or outbuildings, his stomach did a little flip-flop. *What if we rode all this way and nobody's home?*

Then the door opened a crack. A woman's voice called out, "Who are you and what do you want?"

"Ma'am, is that you? I'm Jack Clark from down the creek a ways. My mother's name is Sarah, and my father is Mark Hewitt. We met last year. Remember you stopped at our house to meet us when you first arrived in Kansas with Mr. Frazer?"

"Who's that with you?"

"This is my good friend, Billy. We're like brothers. He lives with us now. Is Mr. Frazer home? I wanted to ask him a favor from my family." Jack rummaged in his saddlebag and held out the pumpkin bread and newspaper as a peace offering. "This is from my mother. She sent bread for you, and thought you might enjoy an old newspaper."

The door opened wider, and Emily stepped out. She rested the butt end of a muzzleloader rifle she carried on the wooden stoop and gestured for the boys to come in.

Once inside, Jack gazed around the room at the changes. An addition to the back wall he assumed was a bedroom was new. Emily motioned them to the sitting area. There sat a rocking chair, a two-seater backed wooden bench with a small table and oil lamp beside it, and an oval braided fabric rug on the floor. Jack and Billy sat together on the two-seater bench with their feet flat on the floor and hats in their hands. A quilt draped over the back, and they were afraid to lean against the beautiful hand-stitched fabric with their sweaty shirts.

Emily asked the boys, "Would you like a piece of pumpkin bread and a glass of tea?"

After accepting, Jack asked again, "Is Mr. Frazer around, ma'am? We rode over to ask if you're planning on going to town for the Fourth of July festivities. In the past, Mr. Frazer would come over and help with the animals while we were in town."

"Mr. Frazer is away hunting for a few days. I'm sorry I didn't come to the door when you first called out, but we haven't had company since the traveling preacher visited and married us last November, and I hesitated to answer without Seth here."

"I understand. You're not used to company. We don't get much at our house, either," Jack replied.

Emily handed the boys their plates of bread, and Jack suggested, "We'll sit at the table to eat, if that's all right, ma'am. I wouldn't want to spill anything. Besides, Momma always makes us eat at the table."

"All right, I'll get the tea and join you."

"I like what you did around here. We passed the garden on our way in. You must water yours every day like my momma does ours. We've been praying for a good soaking rain like the storm that burnt our barn down back in March."

"Oh, my, you lost the barn? Did you lose any animals?"

"No animals, but we did lose the hay in the loft and some grain," Jack said.

"We've been working hard to rebuild," Billy added.

"I don't know what to tell you about the Fourth of July, boys. I think if Seth wanted to attend, he would have mentioned the trip, seeing as it's only a few weeks away. I don't expect him home for two more days. I'll tell you what. If he does plan to attend, we'll ride over and tell you so you can make plans for someone else to do the chores."

Although disappointed, Jack said, "That'll be great." He added, "Sometimes we pick up supplies for Mr. Frazer when we go to town. If you need anything you'd like us to get you, you can make a list."

"You'd do that for us?"

"Sure, my father has done that for years for Mr. Frazer. After we're back, he comes and fetches them when he has time, stays for dinner and breakfast the next morning, and comes home. Or sometimes we haul him the supplies. We're only a day's ride away, round trip."

"That sounds wonderful. We don't need much, but we could use some provisions." She made a list and fetched the money jar Seth always used. "This should cover the cost. We'll come for the supplies after you return, and settle the bill." She added, "I'm not sure I'm ready for Mrs. Seth Frazer to meet the townspeople just yet."

"Well, congratulations on your marriage," Jack said. "I'll be sure to tell my folks the good news."

The boys finished their bread and tea, thanked Mrs. Frazer, and then Jack asked, "Is there anything we can help you with before we leave?"

"I'll feed and water the chickens and fetch the eggs for you, if you'd like," Billy offered.

"I can milk the cow and feed and water the cows and horses for you, if you want. And I'll fetch you a bucket of water," Jack added.

"I'll take you boys up on those offers," Emily said.

The boys hurried out the door and soon returned with a basket of eggs, a pail of milk, and a bucket of water.

"Thank you, boys. I appreciate your help and generosity. When Seth returns, I'll ask him about our Fourth of July plans. I so appreciate you taking my list and your family's willingness to fetch things back for us. That saves us a lot of time and traveling. I hope I gave you enough money. We can settle when you get back, if I didn't. Please tell your folks I say hello and, if Seth wants to go to town, we'll ride over and let you know. If he doesn't, I'll look forward to seeing your family again."

The boys mounted their horses as Emily waved and called out, "Thank your momma for the pumpkin bread and newspaper. I'll save some bread for Seth."

With that, the boys gave a nod, headed home, and returned in time to sit down for supper.

Talking around the supper table, Jack couldn't wait to tell about their time with Mrs. Frazer. "Mr. Frazer and Emily got married," he began, then described some of the changes made in the house and the rest of the conversation about them riding over if they couldn't take care of the animals.

Billy filled in parts Jack left out.

****

Almost a week passed. Seth hadn't ridden over to let them know of his plans for the Fourth of July, so Sarah started getting things ready for the family's trip to town. The children were excited. Jack practiced his dance steps and learned Billy was a good dancer. They took turns dancing with Lydia and Sarah, polishing their steps in preparation for the big dance. Even Mark got in on things one evening, and they shoved the kitchen table to the side for more space.

The evening before leaving, Jack yelled down from the loft, "Ma, Billy doesn't have any old pants for swimming. What should he pack?"

The day the boys rode over to Mr. Frazer's place, Lydia and Sarah began sewing a pair of cotton pants with a drawstring at the waist. Lydia finished them only the day before the question.

"Lydia," her mother called.

"I have them," Lydia called back.

"Billy, come here, please," Sarah said.

Both boys bounded down the ladder.

Lydia held out the swim pants. "Here, Billy. Mother and I guessed at your waist size, but I'm sure they'll fit."

"You made these for me?" Eyes wide in surprise, Billy held them to his waist. "Oh, they'll fit all right. Thanks, Lydia."

"You're welcome. I'm glad you like them."

"They're great. Now I can go swimming too!"

Chapter Ten

Mark was uncertain about leaving the farm for four days not knowing for certain if Seth would come to feed the animals, but Sarah assured him Seth would hold true to his word. He wrote a brief thank-you note and left the note on the table, hoping Sarah was right. Sarah added to the note about the food she prepared, and Lydia wrote a reminder to give her cats some milk.

With the wagon packed and Emily's supply list tucked in the basket with Sarah's prize-winning blueberry pie, the family piled in for the long day's ride. Mark didn't take his rifle for the Best Shot Contest this trip. "Maybe this fall I'll try again," he told her the night before, but Sarah wanted Mark to have a chance at the prize and told Jack and Billy to sneak the gun into the wagon. Sarah hoped this would be his turn to win. They could afford the entry fee, and they could use another gun in the house.

Knowing they would be swimming that evening made the ride more bearable for the young'uns. Mark even took a turn riding in the back of the wagon with Sarah, under the canopy, and let the two boys and Lydia handle the wagon for a few miles, giving everyone a break and change of scenery.

When they stopped under a shade tree at midday, temperatures were so high Mark rushed to fetch Sarah a cool drink and offered to help any way he could with the meal. Everyone needed a rest, water, and a bite to eat.

Although uncomfortable, Sarah never complained.

****

Back on the trail, time passed quickly with the children talking about seeing their friends, who they'd dance with, all the good food at the picnic, and their favorite—going to the stores. Billy seemed especially excited. This time he'd be free to join in the fun instead of being trussed to the sideboard in the back of Rusty's wagon, watching the events going on around him. With the loving care of his new family surrounding him, he hadn't thought of Rusty in a long time, and the memory of the abuse he suffered was thankfully fading.

Arriving at the old oak tree campsite in the late afternoon, everyone pitched in and made light work of setting up camp so the children could get to the swimming hole as soon as possible. On the ride, all the children talked about were the water games Jack and Lydia would show Billy, and the challenge they made to see who could hold their breath the longest under water. Sarah and Mark insisted on going along to watch, and the children didn't argue. They were hot and wanted to cool off.

Walking the path, Jack explained to Billy, "The swimming hole is straight ahead."

Billy, eager to get wet and cool off, dared, "I'll race you. Last one in is a rotten egg."

Jack had never been challenged like this before, but knew smelling like a rotten egg couldn't be good, so he tore off like a bobcat was trailing his heels. He beat Billy fair and square and leaped in first, with Billy on his heels. Lydia didn't want to race with the boys or smell like rotten eggs, so she walked with her momma and father until they reached the water, then jumped in with the boys.

"You should come in, Ma. The water is nice and cool," Lydia teased, then scooped a handful and flung the water in her mother's direction.

After spreading a blanket in the shade of a tree, Sarah and Mark talked while the children swam and played water games. An hour passed, and Mark finally called the children out of the water. "All right, now, it's your mother's and my turn to swim. Jack and Billy, you're on fire detail. And Lydia, you get what is needed ready. We won't be long."

The children raced each other back to the wagon. Once they were out of sight, Mark gently helped Sarah out of her dress and stripped as well.

"This water feels heavenly. Lydia was right." Sarah lay back and floated in the calm stream. "I can't remember the last time I swam here."

"Then we should make this a tradition," Mark replied. He cradled his cherished wife in his arms and rocked her gently, letting the water flow over her. A proud husband and soon-to-be father, he lovingly kissed Sarah and then her belly.

A few stolen moments of delight and then the couple reluctantly climbed the bank to pat each other dry. Mark helped Sarah with her dress and donned his pants before they strolled back to the wagon arm in arm, cooled and refreshed.

After a light supper and some rollicking campfire storytelling, Mark announced, "It's time for bed. The women will sleep in the wagon, and the boys and I will bed underneath."

****

Billy awoke first the next morning and rekindled the fire. Mark and Sarah soon stirred about and started breakfast before sending the children to wash.

When Lydia finally arrived back at camp, she slowly approached her mother.

"What happened to you, Lydia?" her mother asked. "You're wet from head to toe."

Lydia looked down and replied, "I slipped and fell in the creek."

"Are you hurt?

"I'm not hurt. Just embarrassed."

"Well, get dressed in the wagon. With this sun, I'm sure your wet clothes will dry before tonight."

After dressing, Lydia used her mother's brush to smooth her hair, twisting the wet strands into several knots so when her hair dried, she'd have curls for the dance.

The family enjoyed breakfast before packing up and heading for Dead Flats. The slight breeze on her wet hair reinvigorated Lydia, but the relief wouldn't last long. Once the clouds burned off, another scorcher of a day threatened.

Chapter Eleven

Settled into the church grove for the stay, the children wanted to find their friends. Jack especially wanted to introduce Billy as his new brother. Once they left, Mark and Sarah took the wagon to the dry goods store, picked up the items on Emily's list, and gathered a few staples to last them until fall.

Sarah waved her letters and said, "I'm going to walk to the postal office to mail these."

Mark jumped up onto the wagon seat. "I'll meet you at the bank after I return the wagon to the campsite and unhitch the horses. Now's as good a time as any to open our bank account."

****

Sarah's letters to her mother, Mark's mother Ruth, and Betsy, Samuel's mother, shared news about Billy joining their family and how the barn rebuilding was coming along. A letter from her mother and one from Mark's were waiting. She eagerly ripped open her mother's letter and read:

May 18, 1859

Tidioute, Warren County, Pennsylvania
Dearest Sarah,

I am so sorry to read about the barn and the loss of the chicken coop. Thank God you and your family were not injured and no animals were lost, especially Muzzy for Lydia's sake. Rebuilding will be difficult, but the good Lord will be right there with you giving your family the strength needed to carry on. Your faith will help see you through these rough times and make your family stronger. I know you believe this to be true and pray Mark has the same strong faith as you and the children to help him through as well.

Mark made the right decision, Sarah decided. Rebuilding the barn is essential to survival. She also knew that, without Mark's money, holding on to their dreams wouldn't have been possible. Calmness surrounded her.

Please remember, although at times you may feel like God doesn't understand your needs, He is beside you always, and when you need a helping hand, you can always turn to Him and He will listen.

Once again Sarah gave thanks that Mark's stability in her life answered her prayers.

Our family is praying for you and you are in the prayer chain at church. People still ask me all the time how you are doing and if I have heard from you. I spoke with Mark's mother in town recently and we had a nice talk. She is a lovely person and is so glad Mark found you and your children. We both agreed we cannot wait to read the news in October about the birth of our new grandbaby. I am hoping for a little girl, while Ruth wants a boy for Mark. Please do not overdo helping with the barn. Let Mark and the boys handle the lifting and hard work.

Sarah turned over the paper and continued reading.

Your father's health has improved to the point where he can do the daily chores around the house again. Of course, your brother Matthew helps when he can, but it seems like all the children have their own lives now, and your father and I find ourselves home alone more often than not.

With Matthew working at the newspaper office, we read the news of the political unrest still happening in Kansas. I pray you are safe and far enough away from the violence that it doesn't affect your daily life.

This is all for now. Please take care of yourself and my grandbaby. I'll write again soon.

All my love and prayers,

Mother

Delighted to have news from home to share with the children, Sarah caught up with Mark as he entered the bank. "We received two letters." She handed Mark the letter from his mother. "I thought you might want to read your mother's letter first."

"No, you can read it to me later."

"I already read my mother's letter. She was thankful none of us were hurt in the fire and that all the animals were saved, especially Muzzy and Momma Kitty."

At the bank, the couple asked to combine their accounts into one with both names so either could make a withdrawal.

The clerk said, "Are you sure this is the way you want this account to read?"

Mark answered a resounding, "Yes," and put his arm around Sarah's waist.

Sarah always left money matters to Samuel. She never realized they were in so much debt at the stores. But Mark paid off that debt last year and they were now in good standing again. As she signed her name on the legal document, she knew Mark wanted to do right and make up for his lie about how the money came about.

She appreciated his honesty and had forgiven him but often replayed the details of the attempted stagecoach robbery in her mind. Now reality struck her conscience. They had been living on money Mark received for killing two men, but he did save Billy and the driver's lives that day, and some of the money was from the bank for saving the payroll.

How Billy viewed the event she wasn't sure. Billy never talked with her about the day he lost his father. But Mark chose to take two lives that day. She wondered if he'd made peace with the killings she could not forget.

****

Back at the church grove campsite, Mark gathered the horses to take them for new shoes at the livery. He called to Sarah, "When I return, I'll meet you in the grove under our tree."

When Mark joined her there, he explained, "When I was at the livery, two men tore into each other. If the sheriff hadn't come and broken up the fight, the scene would've turned into a free-for-all. Evidently the Free State Constitution is written and coming up for adoption. It's being sent to Washington this month. Finally, after all the meaningless bloodshed, Kansas will be admitted to the union as a free state. Tensions are high. Fights are bound to break out tonight, so we better keep a close eye on the children. Ask Lydia to check in with us from time to time."

Sarah closed her eyes and said a quick prayer that the state would soon join the Union and bring political rest to the territory. Opening her eyes, she said, "That's wonderful news and a good idea. I'll speak with Lydia and the boys." Then Sarah read aloud Mark's mother's letter of how happy Ruth was that Mark had a family to love and a baby on the way. Mark stretched out with his hands clasped behind his head and soon dozed off.

While Mark napped, Sarah took her pie to the judging table for the baking contest. *Who will judge this year? Will there be another blueberry pie?* She signed her name and took her number as she looked over the table of entries. *Maybe this time.*

Strolling back to the blanket, she walked past a group of women gathered to sew. She stopped to say hello, and Sylvia Turner glanced up from her stitching.

Sarah smiled as one woman asked, "Do you want a boy or a girl this time, dear?"

"A boy would be nice, but either, as long as the baby's healthy."

"Have you picked out names yet?" asked another.

Sarah patted her belly. "Not yet, but I guess we better soon."

Looking at the other women in their fancy dresses, she suddenly was aware her clothes were not in fashion, but she didn't let outdated clothing bother her. She was with child, and the clothes she wore were the least of her concerns right now, although she made a mental note to add lace to the sleeves, collar, and waistline of her next dress, and she would buy enough for Lydia to add to one of her blouses and skirts also.

When Sylvia Turner spoke to Sarah last, she let it be known she never approved of Sarah's marriage to Mark, her first husband's best friend. Sarah was waiting and ready with an answer for whatever comment Sylvia slung her way, but Sylvia never said a word, and never looked up from her needlework again.

Nearing time for the Best Shot Contest, Sarah

excused herself. "Good to see you, ladies, but I must go wake my husband. He's taking a nap. He'll be shooting in the contest today."

She woke Mark as the boys walked around the corner and Lydia ran down the hill to meet them.

"We packed your gun and ammunition so you can shoot in the competition," Sarah explained.

"But I haven't practiced enough." Mark shook his head. "We should save the money, with the baby coming. The barn still isn't finished, and we may need extra supplies. I already spent enough money this trip. "I'll sit this one out. Maybe next time."

"No." Jack handed Mark his rifle. "Come on, Mark. I know you can win this time, and we can use the rifle. Let's get to the sheriff's office right away."

"Yeah, the competition starts soon, so there's no time to waste." Billy threw him a box of ammunition.

"All right. Let's go. You make it hard to say no." Mark grabbed his hat.

"Lydia and I'll find a good spot," Sarah called out. "When you're done registering, you boys find us, and we'll all watch together."

****

Mark noted there weren't as many shooters this year. *My odds of winning are better. I should have practiced more. Some of these men are professional men for hire.* Finally, his turn. Sweat formed on his brow. He stepped to the line and shot the paper target bull's eye, dead center. Next three bottles were placed at one hundred, two hundred, and three hundred yards. He broke the first bottle and sent glass flying. The second bottle shattered to pieces. The third bottle. Bang! A gasp rose from the crowd. The bottle wavered but didn't fall.

Jack slapped him on the back. "Good shooting."

Billy shook his hand. "Yeah, you only missed one bottle."

"Thanks, boys, but one miss can cost you the contest." Mark ran his fingers through his hair.

Mark leaned in and whispered in Sarah's ear, "A kiss, sweetheart? I must have pulled the last shot. Maybe next time luck will be on my side."

"Of course, my dear." Sarah pecked his cheek. "Not maybe. Next time for sure."

Mark clapped after every shooter finished. Two contestants shot perfect scores. The sheriff made the final decision and looked over the paper targets one last time before he quieted the crowd to make the announcement. The winner stepped forward to claim his new gun.

Mark gave Sarah's shoulder a squeeze when the sheriff awarded the prize.

"Sweetheart, I know you can win. We'll come back in the fall, and you can try again."

September would be close to Sarah's delivery date. If there were complications, the baby could come early, or there was a chance she wouldn't be up for traveling. "We'll see," was all Mark said.

A small band marched down the center of town. The mayor followed, waving a flag, and other politicians passed out campaign flyers and flags. Most of the town clapped and cheered, but angry boos were also shouted from some people in the crowd. Mark, Sarah, and the children stood quietly and enjoyed the festivities. The church choir with people singing hymns came down the street in a wagon, and Sarah swayed and hummed along. A few clowns juggled their way past; one dropped a ball right in front of Lydia. The fire wagon ended the parade.

Afterward, the children asked to find their friends. Sarah cautioned the boys, "Stay together, don't go far. And Lydia, stay with the Spencer girls and only go to town if an adult is with you. There is unrest in town this weekend, and some fighting has already taken place. It's not that we don't trust you; it's that we don't trust others. Don't mention anything political, and stay away from those who are."

"Come on, dear. Let's go see if my pie won a prize." Sarah took Mark's hand and they strolled to the judging table to see if Sarah's blueberry pie won a ribbon. Looking down the table, she was hopeful. Then she spied the first place ribbon. The plate wasn't hers. When she found her plate, the pie was gone, but not even a second or third place score to show for all her efforts.

"No ribbon again this year." Sarah sighed. "I guess I'll try apple next time." Noticing the name on the winning entry was Sylvia Turner, she vowed next time to enter and win.

"Your pies are the best in my book, no matter what kind." Mark chuckled.

Sarah's face brightened. "Thank you, dear. But next time, I'm adding two tablespoons more sugar than the recipe calls for."

The boys returned and told about the guns and knives in the case at the hardware store, while Lydia shared that she and the Spencer girls discovered a new dress shop with Mrs. Spencer.

The clouds cleared, and the weather held fair for

the picnic and into the evening for the dance, with a bonfire-lit night. Sarah enjoyed watching her children dance, knowing their social skills were acceptable, and although they didn't get to town often, they still had friends and fit in with others.

After a few dances with boys, Lydia rushed over. "A boy named Ben asked me to dance, Ma. We talked, and he lives with his grandparents a half day's ride out of town on the same road we come into town on. He's real nice. You'd like him."

"I'm sure I would, sweetheart. Now go enjoy the rest of the evening. Just stay in the firelight where I can see you."

"I will, Ma. I promise." Lydia ran off.

As Jack glided across the dance platform with Abby Proctor, Sarah realized Jack was dancing to songs he never heard before, not missing a step. His movements flowed. He stopped second-guessing himself. The lessons with his sister paid off.

Sarah met Abagail and her family at last year's Fall Festival, so she wouldn't worry about Jack tonight. But where was Billy?

A slower song began. Mark took her hand and led her to the dance floor. Cheek to cheek, her belly protruding between them, they stepped to the music, and when the song ended, they headed to sit down. One song at a time was the most she could take, but she enjoyed every minute.

****

Billy found a pretty, brunette gal he got the courage to ask to dance. Palms sweaty and stomach churning, he blurted out, "Would you like to dance?" The prettiest gal there, in Billy's eyes, and to his estimation pretty close to his age.

She took his hand. "Sure, I'll dance with you. You must be new in town. I've never seen you before."

"Our farm is a day-and-a-half's ride from here. Where do you live?"

"I'm from Dead Flats. Our house is a few streets over from the church. What's your name?"

"I'm Billy Henry. What's yours?"

"Elizabeth Parker."

The song ended, and they walked off the dance floor. Elizabeth commented, "You're a good dancer. Can you dance to all the songs?"

"I learned to dance at town dances, birthday parties, and holiday events when I was younger." In a soft voice he admitted, "My momma taught me."

The two of them spent most of the evening together dancing, talking, and watching the flames of the fires burn lower. Billy, more at ease with Elizabeth now, asked more questions. He found out she loved the color blue and her father bought and sold cattle.

Finally he said, "It doesn't really matter, but how old are you?"

"I'll be sixteen in November. Why? How old are you?"

"I turned sixteen in April."

The dance ended, and Billy walked Elizabeth over to introduce her to Sarah and Mark. "This is Sarah and Mark. They sort of adopted me, and I live with them now."

"It's nice to meet you," Elizabeth said, and shook their outstretched hands.

"It's nice to meet you, too," Sarah said, placing her hand on Elizabeth's shoulder.

"I'm going to walk Elizabeth home now. I won't be long," Billy said.

Mark gave a wink.

Billy winked back.

While walking down an alleyway, a cat jumped from a woodpile. Elizabeth sidestepped right into Billy who wrapped his arm around her waist and held her tight. "Don't be afraid. I'll protect you."

Standing at the door on the front porch, he gazed into her eyes. "I had a great time tonight. Can I call on you again?"

"How often do you get to town?"

"Hopefully we'll be back for the Fall Festival, and I'm sure I'll be back in the spring, when we pick up our seed."

"The festival isn't that far off." Elizabeth twisted from side to side.

"I'll come find you as soon as we get to town. I won't be seeing anyone else between now and then. Will you?"

"I won't make any promises, but I'd like to see you again. I had a good time tonight, too."

Hands sweaty, he pulled them from his pockets and took her hands in his. Then he pecked her on the cheek. "I hope you'll think of me, because I'll sure be thinking of you." He took a step closer, squeezed her hands, and kissed her right on the lips.

"I'll think of you, too, Billy." She took one of her hands and twirled her curls around her finger. "I'll write you letters. Of course, you won't get them until you come to town, but I like writing. I'll tell you what I do every week."

"I'll write you, too," Billy promised. "And I'll tell

you about the farm." He stepped closer, pecked her on the cheek, and said, "I have to go, but I'll think about you until I see you again." With that, Billy ran down the street, back to the wagon. *This must be what love feels like.*

Once Billy arrived back at the wagon, Mark announced, "I have a surprise for your mother. On my last trip to town, I made a reservation at the Wild Rose Hotel for tonight. So Lydia will sleep in the wagon, and you boys will sleep underneath. Don't stay up talking all night, because your ma wants us all to go to church tomorrow. We'll be back in the morning in time for breakfast."

"Be good, and we'll see you in the morning. You're old enough to stay the night alone. If you need any help, ask Mr. or Mrs. Spencer," Sarah said. Then Mark extended his arm and they walked to the hotel to spend a special romantic night together. Mark's justification for spending the money was a night in a real bed would be better for the baby.

"You shouldn't have, Mark. I could have slept in the wagon tonight."

"I know you could have, but I want you all to myself tonight, sweetheart."

****

Billy reached for the checker board and asked, "Anyone want to play a game?"

"Sure. I'll play." Jack lit a candle.

"No, I'm going to get ready for bed." Lydia climbed into the back of the wagon and emerged in her nightdress. "Did you ever see a star fall out of the sky before? I did one time, on a night just like this."

"I remember that," Jack added. "It left a streak of

91

light behind."

Billy said, "It's like a star is falling from heaven. I read about them. They're called shooting stars, and people say if you make a wish when you see one, your wish will come true."

"Poppa taught me a little about the night sky and how to figure out directions," Jack said. Staring at the night sky, he pointed at a group of stars. "You know the directions North, South, East, and West. You look for the little dipper—seven stars that make a picture of a ladle or dipper, like we use at the well. The North Star is the brightest star in the sky. Poppa taught me that the old-timers would set their course using the North Star, each night pointing their wagon or spotting a landmark, and then in the morning they'd know exactly which way to travel."

"Boat captains depend on the stars all the time to tell them where they are and which direction to go," Billy added.

Lydia gazed at what seemed like millions of twinkling stars. She said, "Think about it. We miss seeing this every night because we're inside doing things. We need to sit outside more often."

A star streaked across the sky, then another, and yet another.

"Did you see them?" Lydia shrieked, arm shooting straight up.

"Yeah." Billy jerked his head upward.

Jack spoke up. "Sure did."

"Quick, make a wish." Lydia squeezed her eyes together.

"Let's make three wishes," Billy said. "One for each star."

They closed their eyes and made wishes.

"Don't tell what you wished for, or your wish won't come true," Billy told them. He believed his words for a moment. Maybe his wish would come true. Then he thought back to his last year with Rusty. If wishes and prayers did come true, Mark would have found him sooner.

Billy knew what one of his wishes would be, but wasn't sure his wish would ever happen until he could earn some money.

"Well, we better heed Father's reminder of not staying up too late," Lydia said, then crawled up into the wagon.

The boys finished their game of checkers, then stretched out under the wagon with their heads peeking out, looking up at the starry night sky.

Chapter Twelve

The same night sky streamed through the window of the hotel where Sarah lay contently in Mark's arms. Her breathing matched his in harmony. Time alone with Mark this way was special. A soft bed after the long journey to town was most welcomed.

"We are the luckiest parents to have such great children." Sarah lifted her head to gaze into Mark's eyes.

"We are fortunate, Sarah. Jack and Lydia are very loving and caring. Billy is fitting in nicely and is grateful for his new home. Giving him a family and a place to live changed his life forever." Mark tucked a strand of hair behind Sarah's ear and kissed her, holding her close.

"And now, with a baby on the way, I couldn't be more proud of our family. We have new dreams. I was hesitant to give up Samuel's dream, but turning the farm into a ranch makes sense. We have the land, the barn will be completed by fall, and a good herd should come next." Sarah lay back and stared at the ceiling.

Mark rested his head close to Sarah's belly for a few moments and was surprised. "Sweetheart, I hear him," he whispered. "He can't wait to meet us, so we can both take care of him. Don't worry, darling, I'll take care of you and our family. You are the most important people in my life. There isn't anything I wouldn't do for you, and this child will have a home where he'll feel safe and loved."

Sarah turned and gazed into his eyes. "You mean *he* or *she* will feel safe and loved." She smiled.

****

Sunday morning, after a quick breakfast, everyone helped clean up and pack the wagon before heading to church together for the first time as a family.

When the minister, standing at the front of the church on a raised podium, spotted them in the congregation, he offered a special prayer of unity, and the entire congregation wished them well, encouraging them to attend more often.

A lengthy rendition of the story of Moses and the Ten Commandments spewed forth, with the Sixth Commandment, Thou shalt not kill, standing forthright in Sarah's mind. Her thoughts returned to the two lives Mark took the day of the attempted stagecoach robbery. She glanced at Mark during the sermon. His solemn face told her he must be thinking the same thoughts.

Mark took Sarah's hand and squeezed as the minister finished the sermon, and Sarah squeezed his hand in return.

What remorse Mark must feel every day. How can he live with himself? Sarah prayed Mark could heal from his experience.

After the service, the family set out on the long ride home.

"We received a letter from Grandma, and I'll tell you right away that Grandpa's heart is much better and he is getting stronger," Sarah said. "We also received one from Grandma Hewitt." She read aloud the special parts the children always enjoyed about what their aunts and uncle were doing. They especially liked the part where Grandma said she loved and missed them and Mark's mother said she hoped to meet them someday.

As usual, Billy became quiet when she read family mail or when conversation concerned relatives. While Jack and Lydia laughed and joked about the contents, Billy stared off in the distance. When Sarah finished reading she said, "Billy, why don't you tell Jack and Lydia about your parents and things you remember about your family? I'm sure you've shared some stories, but we have plenty of time, so why not use this time to get better acquainted with one another?"

Mark straightened in his seat and ran his fingers through his hair.

By the time they arrived at the farm the following afternoon, Billy was more at ease talking about his old friends and his life back in Kansas City. Mark was relieved Billy hadn't shared details of the farmer who saved him the day his father was killed.

The children helped unload the supplies. Jack grabbed three items, and Billy, trying to outdo him, scooped up four. Lydia took her things in the house while Mark unhitched the horses and Sarah checked on the garden. Inside the house she read the note Seth left.

Thanks for picking up our supplies. We'll come to settle with you in two weeks. The barn is coming along well. I'll give you a hand when we come. Emily said she'd bring dessert. Oh, and tell Lydia I fed her cats. Seth.

"Well, looks like we're getting company," Sarah said. "Now that Seth and Emily are married, maybe they'll come around more often."

****

That evening, as Mark passed the bowl of mashed potatoes, he mentioned, "The herd has almost doubled this year. We're at nine head and should be able to sell a few in town this fall. We'll definitely need a fenced-in pasture soon." He rubbed his hands together. "But first things first. Let's start cutting and stacking the hay to dry tomorrow so we can get back to work on the barn next week. We can turn this farm into a ranch yet. We just need good breeding stock.

"The barn needs a few more boards to enclose the two side walls, so Daisy and the horses will have to wait a while before they settle into their new home. Then comes the work of stacking the hay in the loft." Mark looked at the boys, who were excitedly exchanging comments, smiles on their faces.

Jack spoke up. "Does selling a few cows mean another trip to town?"

"Does it mean we get to ride herd and sell them at the stockyard?" Billy asked.

"Only if you learn to rope and herd them properly," Mark replied. He knew four cows were manageable, but roping lessons wouldn't hurt the boys and would give them something new to learn.

****

Sarah and Lydia worked hard all day while Mark and the boys were in the fields. Lydia hoed and Sarah replanted two rows of peas, two of beans, and one of lettuce before they plopped down in the grass to take off their shoes and shake out the dirt and pebbles. Sarah was tying her shoes when she heard a covey of quail take flight on the top of the knoll. Seconds later, she heard horses' hooves pounding dirt. She looked up to see three Indian boys riding in. "Quick, Lydia, in the house! Barricade the door, and hide where I've shown you. Quick! Go! Now, and no matter what happens, don't come out."

Sarah grabbed the shovel and started walking toward the well, positioned between the house and the barn. If all they wanted was to water their horses, she would let them and they could be on their way. As they rode closer, she could see they were young braves, about Jack's and Billy's ages, maybe a little older. "Please God, let them pass by." She dropped the bucket down the well and hauled up water to offer them a drink. Two of them got off their horses and walked to the well. Sarah backed away, still holding the shovel as they both drank deeply of the cool water. She had never been this close to an Indian before. They motioned for the third boy to come, but instead he rode his horse to the garden, trampling through the rows she and Lydia just planted.

Raising the shovel in the air, Sarah yelled, "Stop!" But he didn't. She brandished the shovel about, yelling, "Get out of my garden!" The other boys were mounted and rode away yelling and motioning to the third to follow.

Sarah smacked the horse with the shovel. The boy looked her directly in the eyes and raised his fist in the air before he rode off in a cloud of dust.

Heart pounding, Sarah took a moment to catch her breath. She would not soon forget this experience. Indians rode past at a distance last year, and now this. She wasn't afraid of the three boys, but the situation could have turned out differently. A prayer and a shovel saved her. The Indians never bothered them before, but since more settlers arrived and took over the land they once called their own, they might retaliate.

Once the three young braves were out of sight, Lydia ran out and gave her mother a big hug. "You were so brave, Ma. I was scared. They could have come after you when you raised the shovel, but you scared them off. Wait until I tell Father and the boys."

"Lydia, if you were hiding where I told you, you couldn't have seen what happened. Why didn't you mind me and do as I said?" She took Lydia's arm and turned her, so they were face to face. "What if they caught you looking out the window? They could have come after you." Thinking of this, Sarah suddenly shook with a delayed reaction.

"But Momma, what if they had been men, a raiding party, and you needed my help? I didn't want them to hurt you, Ma."

Sarah gripped Lydia's arm tighter. "I needed you safe, Lydia. I didn't want your help. Your safety is more important to me than anything. I can take care of myself. God was with us." Sarah released her grip. "From now on, you must obey what I tell you, and if I say to hide, you hide. Do you understand?"

"Yes, Momma, I promise." Lydia took a step back.

Sarah took a deep breath, calming herself as she looked into her daughter's tear-filled eyes. "Come on. Let's straighten the rows that got trampled, the best we can. Your father and the boys will be home soon."

****

When Mark, Jack, and Billy finally rode in, Lydia was waiting at the door to tell them what happened. "Indians were here," she yelled.

By the time Sarah welcomed back the threesome from their long day in the fields, they were already fully informed. Mark rushed to Sarah's side, wishing he had been home to defend her.

"They were young boys," Sarah explained. "They only wanted a drink of water. If the one hadn't ridden his horse through the garden, the encounter would have been peaceful."

"You were lucky this time." Mark paced back and forth in front of the stove. "Next time they could be braves, wanting more than a drink. You need to learn how to handle a rifle and defend yourself, Sarah, and I'm not taking no for an answer."

Sarah sighed. "Well, maybe just the sight of a gun might scare them. All right, I'll learn, but I could never use a gun to kill anyone."

"I'll buy a rifle next trip to town. Having another one around isn't a bad idea. The boys can use the rifle for hunting, and we can keep it loaded in case we have other encounters. For now, I'll teach you how to load and shoot my rifle, and I'll leave it here at the house and take my pistol to the fields. Lydia should learn too. Tomorrow we'll take a break from working on the barn in the evening, and you'll have your first lesson."

****

Lydia looked out the window the next morning with a long face as the men prepared to leave for the fields.

"Lydia, I'll add to the basket for the midday meal, and we'll help in the fields today, if you'd like. Why don't you go change into your work clothes?"

A smile flashed across the young girl's face.

Sarah rode in the wagon with Mark, and the boys and Lydia walked alongside. She wasn't sure how much she'd be able to help, but she'd do what she could.

Mark got the boys started on their tasks, then said, "We need firewood for the winter. There's a load already cut from a fallen elm and a few cottonwood trees near the wagon. We cleared them this spring. We'll work on getting the rest of the hay stacked and the wood loaded today, but please don't overdo. There's also a few berries in the hedgerow. Probably enough for a pie." Mark slapped his hat across his legs to knock off the dust. "Lydia, please keep an eye on your mother."

With the sun at its peak, Mark wanted to get home and get Sarah out of the hot sun. After everyone helped finish loading the wood in the wagon, Lydia suggested, "How about we take the rest of the day off and hit the swimming hole on the way home."

With hopeful smiles on their faces, they awaited a reply; they all looked at Sarah. Sarah looked at Mark. He winked, and the corner of his lips turned up.

"Sure, let's go," Sarah said. Even though nobody brought clothes for swimming, they would make do.

Everyone jumped in the water this trip, even Sarah, clothes and all. The water was cool and refreshing.

Finally emerging after a few games of drop-the-rock, nobody cared that they were soaking wet. They were almost dry by the time they got home.

****

That evening Mark set up targets and showed Sarah and Lydia how to load the gun, and they took turns and shot the target a few times. The boys looked on and learned a few things too, such as how holding their breath gave them better control over their aim. They would practice more, but for now Mark was sure

Sarah and Lydia knew how to load and fire the weapon. Mark was confident his family could handle a gun safely if they ever needed to use one for self-defense.

The next evening, sitting alone at the table, Mark and Sarah took time to look back over the past year. So much had happened. September would be upon them before long, and again time for the Harvest Festival.

"We need new breeding stock," Mark said. "The boys will have fun keeping track of four head of cattle this trip because I plan to ride in the wagon."

"Are you sure we should spend the money on new stock?" Sarah asked.

"I think it's time to grow the herd and turn this farm into the ranch it deserves to become. We'll clear more pasture and cropland in the spring, and cattle could be our means to make money in the future. We have the land. We need to use more of it for profit. I'd like to buy fruit trees next spring and start a real orchard, too."

"I like your ideas, Mark, but can we afford them?" Sarah remembered Samuel's dreams to make the farm self-sufficient.

"If we manage our money, we can. With our child on the way, I've been thinking a lot about the future. Kansas may enter the Union as a Free State, but there is still talk of war between the North and South. We must be prepared for whatever happens."

"Speaking of being prepared, don't forget you promised to win the rifle in the competition this fall, sweetheart." Sarah took a sip of tea. "I know you can do it."

"Yes, I hope to win, but even if I don't, we're still coming home with another rifle for protection. I'll teach you more tomorrow. I'm not leaving you alone again until I'm sure you feel safe. You can load the gun and shoot, but now you have to hit the target."

Chapter Thirteen

Two weeks to the day, as promised, Seth and Emily rode in. The children ran out to greet them and Jack helped Mrs. Frazer down from the wagon.

"My, you've done a lot of work on the barn since I was here last," Seth called to Mark as he walked over to shake hands. "Why, the roof is on and the sides are coming along."

"Yes, we've been busy, between getting the hay stacked and rebuilding. Now that you're here we can get the ends enclosed."

"Well, then, we better get started." Seth grabbed his tools.

Wiping her hands on the apron Sarah could barely tie around her swollen tummy, she emerged from the house. "Emily, please do come in. I'm mixing a batch of muffins and steeping tea for us. We expected you'd get an early start. It's so good to see you again. Come, let's chat, and leave the men to the barn. Lydia, are you joining us?"

"In a little bit, Ma," Lydia called, as she ran out the door.

Once inside, Sarah quickly finished mixing, and slid the muffin pan in the oven. "Can I pour you a cup of tea, Emily?"

"Tea would be lovely. We really appreciate your willingness to pick up our supplies. Neither Seth nor I are interested in going to town unless we absolutely must. We enjoy our privacy. We don't bother anyone, and we're left alone. The farther from others the better is how we both feel. I don't know anyone in these parts other than your family." Emily took a sip of tea.

"I'm sure you've been wondering why I would travel all the way to Kansas from Pennsylvania when I didn't even know Seth," Emily began. "What kind of a woman would give everything away and travel across the wilderness to live with a man she'd never met?"

"Well, I have wondered, yes."

"At least you're honest." Emily grinned. "I went through a rough time in my life. My parents died in a house fire, leaving me alone, angry at God for taking them from me, and with nothing in my life to care about." Emily sighed and sank back in her chair.

"A few months after the fire, a dear friend dragged me to church. I didn't want to go but couldn't think of an excuse quick enough. I already put her off for weeks. After church, the pastor approached me." She straightened. "He read me Seth's letter asking the preacher's help in finding a companion. Seth would pay the fare for my travel with no expectation. I knew of him, but never met him before. I did some digging and discovered Seth's mother still lived in Sheffield. I visited her and explained I was thinking of taking him up on his offer and wondered if she could tell me more about her son."

"You were brave, leaving everything you knew to travel all this way." Sarah checked on the muffins' progress, warmed their tea, and sat down to let Emily continue her story.

"Brave or stupid. I'm not sure which. Seth's

mother was so kind. We connected right off. We talked all afternoon and into the supper hour, losing track of time. She is a dear, sweet lady, and everything she told me about Seth turned out true." Emily smiled and looked down.

"Both Seth and I needed companionship. After spending time with him, I've come to find him a gentle and understanding man.

"Living together in the same house was a little awkward at first. The house is small, and we found to survive last fall we had to work together. We hadn't known each other long before we made the commitment to wed, but we worked together well. We each had deep feeling for the other and we understood developing our relationship would take time. Once I said my wedding vows, my life changed. Seth and I both agreed to be with each other for the rest of our lives, and we began showing each other, in our own ways, how much the other meant."

"Yes, the boys told us your good news. Congratulations. You both look very happy. I haven't seen Seth smile or look at another woman like he looks at you in a long time. Losing his wife on the journey from Pennsylvania devastated him. I'm glad you found each other and everything worked out so well."

"Yes, everything has worked out well. I believe I'm with child, and we are praying it is so."

"Oh, Emily." Sarah leaned forward to hold Emily's hands in hers. "I'm so happy for you. This is wonderful news. How are you feeling? Any sickness?"

"Some days are worse than others. Seth helps with some of my chores now. I've only had a few days I didn't feel like getting out of bed." Emily rubbed her belly.

"Do you want to wait and make sure before you share the news with my family, or would you like to tell them today?"

"I told Seth I'd tell you today. We'll let him make the big announcement in his own time. If I'm right, this means the baby will come the end of February or beginning of March. I wish I could have Seth come fetch you when the time comes, but the weather will be terrible right then, and I couldn't stand to be alone, in case something happened."

"Are you sure about your time frame? If the weather isn't too bad, I could try to come sometime in March. Even if you already had the baby, I could help out a few days. I'm sure Seth would appreciate another woman's presence, and I'd like to help."

"I'd love to have you come, weather permitting, of course." Emily touched Sarah's hand.

"Would you like to come when my little one is born? Mine's due in early October. We're hoping for a boy. How about you?" Sarah took the pans of fragrant trays from the oven, serving Emily and herself.

"I'd love to come. Then I'd have an idea what to expect. And, yes, a little boy would make us both very happy."

Just then, Lydia arrived. "Are the muffins done yet, and is there any tea left, Ma?"

"Sure, dear, help yourself, and when you're finished you can take muffins out for the others."

****

Outside, the men nailed siding in place and were half way done when the ladies called them to supper.

"We got a lot of work done today. Some of that

work really required four men. I'm glad we're staying the night. We can finish tomorrow." Seth took a bite of stew.

"I appreciate the help. I hope Emily doesn't mind." Mark turned to face Emily.

"I don't mind. Sarah and I can swap a few more recipes. I'm enjoying some woman talk for a change," Emily replied.

While eating slices of Sarah's pumpkin pie, Seth proudly shared the couple's news with everyone about their hopes for the baby.

Mark and the boys stood to shake Seth's hand and Lydia ran to Emily and asked, "Has the baby kicked you yet?"

"I know he's there, but no kicks yet," Emily said.

****

Work began the next day bright and early. By midday, the only work left to complete were the doors on each end, which needed to be built and framed, and the inside work of laying out the stalls and a tack room.

While the women set dinner on the table, Seth asked, "Are you going to the Fall Harvest Festival this year? I'll be glad to feed the animals for you."

Mark looked at Sarah for a response.

"If I think I can make the ride, I'll go. Mark wants to sell some cows and get better breeding stock as well as put in the seed order. Oh, I'm sure we'll probably go. The children look forward to seeing their friends and taking a break from farming for a few days."

"If the boys could come let us know if you're going, I'll have our list of seeds and supplies ready, to save us the trip." Seth looked over at Emily and smiled. "And as I said, I'll be glad to take care of the livestock."

"You've been a good friend over the years, helping when needed," Sarah said. "And, Emily, I'll send for you when I have my little one." Sarah smiled, and touched Emily's clasped hands. "Having another woman here to assist would be nice."

Mark shook Seth's hand and helped him pack his tools. "Thanks for everything. We couldn't have gotten as much done without you." Mark wiped his brow.

"Glad to help. I know you'd do the same for me." Seth helped Emily up onto the wagon seat and then sat beside his wife, took the reins, and they both waved good-bye.

Chapter Fourteen

"If you boys are going to drive four cattle to town, you're going to need riding and roping skills. Herding cattle is one thing I know." Mark grinned. "Get a good night's sleep, because come morning we'll get up early and work. Then in the afternoon you'll start learning to rope."

"I've seen cows roped a few times." Billy stood and mimicked the motions of swinging a noose over his head.

"Those cows won't get away from us, will they, Billy?" Jack joined in and they both swung their arms, pretending to rope everything in sight.

"Can I try too?" Lydia asked.

"We'll watch for a while, dear, and then you can decide if you want to try. I'm not sure you're cut out for roping cattle." Sarah kissed her cheek.

"See you in the morning, boys, bright and early," Mark stressed.

After breakfast and the morning chores, they worked on the barn. In the afternoon, the boys were eager to start roping and Lydia wanted to watch, so she and Sarah sat on the fence for a while.

Mark started simply, demonstrating how to tie a Honda, coil the rope so it wouldn't knot, and release in one fluid motion. Then he re-wound the rope, making everything look simple as he roped the heifer in the corral. He handed rope to each of the boys as he demonstrated the movements, explaining step-by-step what and why he did everything. "You could lose your thumb real easy if you don't follow every step carefully."

"Let's go, Ma." Lydia took her mother's arm. "I don't want to lose my thumb. I'd rather help you in the kitchen."

Mark retreated to the barn. With the boys occupied and the women cooking, he'd put his time to good use and start the project he'd been thinking about for some time. He selected several pieces of prime walnut from Samuel's stash of furniture wood, as he used to call it, from the storage shed. Then he laid out a cross and marker to place on Samuel's grave.

Completion of this project was important. He wanted the cross and marker in place before the baby arrived, hoping this would give Sarah final closure with Samuel and allow the baby to come into the family as a Hewitt.

Mark started to sand the boards and prepare them for carving.

****

The boys practiced on fence posts, throwing nooses several times before the loops landed correctly. They made roping the post a competition. After hours of practice, the motions got easier. They got better at shaking the twists out of the rope and faster at re-coiling it in their left hands. They weren't missing as often but still needed practice.

About to give up for the day, their ma called to them. "Time for supper, boys."

Billy dusted off his pants and gathered up his shirt

he took off earlier when he worked up a sweat. "Where'd the day go?"

Jack grabbed his hat and brushed himself off. "I don't know. You hungry?"

"Starving! I hope Ma fixed something good for supper and lots of food."

At the table, Billy asked, "Did you fix the roast different today, Ma?"

"Yeah, the meat tastes really good." Jack took another bite.

"No, this is the same roast, fixed the same way as always," said Sarah. "You boys must have worked up quite an appetite."

"I'm going to bed as soon as I have my chores done," Billy groaned, "and I'll be asleep before my head hits the pillow." Billy rubbed his right arm.

"Me too." Jack looked down at his rope-burned hands.

"Good, because you'll need your strength tomorrow when you practice on a live calf." Mark chuckled.

****

When they finished with the barn for the day, the boys jumped onto their horses to begin training while on horseback.

"Practicing with a moving horse triples the difficulty," Mark had told them that morning.

Both boys, stiff and sore but not letting on, sat ready on the horses for Mark's next lesson. But Mark didn't come out of the house as the boys expected.

Mark could tell from the sky that a rain shower would be coming through and so stayed in the house, accepting another cup of coffee as he talked with Sarah.

In their excitement, the boys hadn't taken note of the sky until the rain pelted them. They rode for cover inside the barn.

"Why'd the rain have to come today? Now we can't practice." Jack swung down from Button.

"Yeah, we may as well unsaddle the horses and run them out to the corral." Billy took off Ruby's bit and bridle.

They walked the horses to the corral, then dashed for the house, walking in dripping wet.

Mark laughed out loud. The sky was brightening and sunlight was peering through the window. "You boys need to learn how to read the sky and take note of the weather. Knowing how to predict rain will serve you well in life." Mark took a sip of coffee. "You could have left the horses saddled and waited out the rain in the barn. But instead, you're soaked to the skin." Looking out the window at breaks in the clouds, he added, "Looks like the weather is going to turn into a beautiful afternoon." Mark finished his coffee and headed for the door. "I'm going out to separate three calves from the herd for you to practice roping. They'll be waiting for you in the corral."

After changing clothes, Jack tried first and soon found out Mark was right. Roping a fence post while standing still on the ground was a lot easier than from astride a moving horse. Several times he swirled the rope and tossed before he achieved success, then landed on his face when the calf jerked one way and the horse lurched the other. Dusting himself off, he looked at Billy, who was stifling a laugh.

"All right," Jack scoffed. "Let's see you try."

Billy wanted to impress Mark and be one up on

Jack. On his first try, he hit the mark and didn't fall off. His second toss also looped around the calf and, although still a little unsteady in the saddle, he didn't fall. But his third toss landed successfully, and off the horse he flew.

Dusting himself off, he heard Lydia call, "Time for supper."

Jack and Billy dragged themselves to the table.

Mark wiped his plate clean with a crust of bread and said, "You'll probably be a tiny bit sore in the morning, boys."

Neither Jack nor Billy were willing to admit, but they ached from head to toe after just two days of practice. No matter. During any spare time, the family knew where to find them.

****

That evening, sitting in front of the fire with Sarah, Mark found himself staring into the embers and thinking about Samuel. He recalled the terrible day and circumstances of Samuel's death. That day brought Mark and later, Billy, into the family. Mark was sure Samuel would be pleased with the way everything turned out.

While the fire on the embers danced, the movement and warmth soothed him. Then he heard Samuel's voice in his head calling his name. At first he thought he was dreaming. He looked at Sarah. She was sewing patches for the baby's quilt, unaware anything was happening.

The voice said, "*Mark. Thank you. Thank you for not telling Sarah the truth. You're a good father to Lydia and Jack. You did right by Billy, accepting him into the family. I'm happy for you and Sarah. I know how much this child means to you both. Take care of her, old friend, and thank you for the cross and marker.*"

Mark had been thinking about Samuel a lot lately. Was this his mind playing tricks on him? The fire cracked and popped, shooting a burning ember onto the edge of the hearth. Mark jumped to his feet to step on the dim glow with his shoe. When he raised his foot the black ash on the hearth was in the shape of a knife.

Samuel's voice whispered in Mark's ear again, *"Thanks for making sure Jack got my knife and for teaching him how to hunt."*

Mark knelt to look at the charred image more closely and suddenly found himself flat on the floor.

The cross and marker now had new urgency. Mark would send the boys hunting right after chores in the morning so he could work on his tribute.

Sarah looked up from her sewing and asked, "What are you doing down there?"

He knew exactly what he was doing, as he heard Samuel's laugh fade. "I bent over to put another log on the fire and tripped over my own two feet." Sarah would think him crazy if he let on any differently. Grinning from ear to ear, he picked himself up off the floor. Cupping her face in his hands, they kissed. "We're lucky, Sarah. We have each other, Jack, Lydia, Billy, and now our little one growing inside you."

Sarah put the baby quilt down and returned his kiss. Taking his hand, she led him to the bedroom.

****

"How about a break from work and roping cattle today, boys? Why don't the two of you get your fishing poles and take the snare with you to catch a rabbit?

We've not eaten fresh fish or a good rabbit stew in a while. Then, take a swim. How's that sound?" Mark motioned to the door.

"Hurry, before he changes his mind." Jack poked Billy's shoulder and rushed out.

Billy was right on his heels.

Sarah and Lydia planned to spend most of the day in the kitchen baking, so Mark would have the entire morning to work uninterrupted.

He wanted the cross and marker to last a good long while. He gathered Samuel's tools and skillfully carved a vine around the center post and on the cross bar. Next he carved the marker. He centered the following inscription on the square plaque: *Samuel Lucas Clark, Born July 21, 1827 - Died March 24, 1858, Husband, Father, and Friend.*

He prided himself on his carving. Tomorrow he'd finish gouging out the wood around the letters, sand them, and rub each with oils to help preserve the wood.

****

After supper, he brought Sarah and Lydia out to the corral, carrying a chair so Sarah could sit while she enjoyed the boys' show. She was moving slower and resting more often. He found her in bed a few afternoons. As Sarah's belly grew larger, Mark's concern grew as well.

Jack and Billy took turns roping and reeling the calves and leading them to the edge of the corral before jumping off their horses and freeing them unharmed for the next time.

"Not bad, not bad at all," Mark said as Lydia and Sarah clapped and cheered the boys on. Roping from the saddle got easier, and the horses were getting used to the new commands and maneuvers. The boys would sit a long day in the saddle driving the cattle to town, but Mark knew they were prepared, and he'd be there if needed.

****

The following morning, when the boys checked the snare, Mark went to finish the cross and marker. He wanted to surprise Sarah and the children.

The boys returned home and found Mark working in the barn. They couldn't wait to show off their haul. Jack held up the rabbit and Billy held up a pheasant in each hand.

"A good day's catch," Mark noted. "Now all you need to do is clean and prepare them for your ma."

"We'll take them out back. We know how." Jack took out his knife.

"Then we're going to ask Ma if we can have rabbit stew for supper!" Billy added.

"What you working on, Mark?" Jack asked.

"I'll show you, but this is a surprise for your ma, so no telling." Mark raised his figure to his lips. "I made a cross and marker for your father. I hope your mother will like them."

"She'll like them, all right." Jack picked up the marker for a closer look.

"After supper, I thought we could all walk up to the gravesite and put them in place. Remember, don't tell your ma."

****

Sarah set a pot of rabbit stew on the table, sure to taste good with fresh corn muffins. "You can go back out and practice after you eat if you want, boys."

"We'll see, but I think I've had enough for today."

Billy yawned.

With full stomachs and sore backs and legs, the boys limped out the door to complete their evening chores. When they returned, Mark announced, "I'd like everyone to join me in the barn."

The cross and marker lay on Mark's makeshift workbench. He was a little nervous Billy might take note of the date and say something about his father's death on the same day, but no mention was made.

Lydia picked up the cross. "I miss Poppa and how he always teased me about my cooking." She wiped her eyes.

"We all miss him, sweetheart," replied Sarah, tracing her fingers over the carved letters.

"I think about him often. He teased all of us about one thing or another and always had a smile on his face," Mark added.

Jack agreed. "It's been difficult without Father. I miss him every day. I wish we could go fishing together again. And I wish he could meet Billy."

Billy looked at the cross and marker, but never really read the inscription. He took Lydia's hand. "I wish I had met your pa. I can see how much you all loved him."

"I wish we could have met your pa and ma too. I'm sure you miss them just as much." Lydia squeezed Billy's hand.

They walked to the old elm tree together to set the marker and cross in place. Lydia picked wildflowers to place on the grave. The boys carried the pick and shovel, Mark carried the wooden marker, and Sarah the cross, held close.

Once the items were in place, Sarah said a prayer

and Lydia led them in song. The sun dipped below the horizon as they headed down the hill to the house.

The children walked ahead.

Jack patted Lydia on the shoulder. "We miss him, don't we?"

Lydia's eye teared. "Every day."

"You were right, Lydia, I miss my ma and pa too, and I think of them all the time." Billy swiped his hand across his eyes.

Mark walked with Sarah, putting his arm around her shoulder. "I'm at peace now." Mark leaned over and kissed her cheek.

"The marker and cross are beautiful. They're perfect, Mark. Thank you so much." Sarah cupped her hand over Mark's. "Everything is as Samuel would have wanted."

****

The Fall Harvest Festival was approaching. Jack and Billy loaded their saddlebags and prepared to ride to the Frazers' place to pick up their supply and seed orders and make sure they could still come care for the animals. While they prepared to leave so they'd be back in time for supper, Sarah said, "Be careful and watch for Indians. I doubt they'd bother you, but keep an eye out." Sarah tucked the cornbread she made in Jack's saddlebag.

As Jack and Billy crossed the creek for the fourth time and linked up with the old path that led to the house, they heard what sounded like a baby crying. No, more like a whimpering sound and coming from a clump of brush ahead.

The boys jumped from their horses and ran toward the sound. Billy put his arm out to stop Jack, right beside him. Billy pointed and asked, "What is it?"

"Why, it's a little dog," Jack replied. Something much larger and more powerful had attacked the poor creature.

Pieces of missing fur exposed flesh. Blood covered the neck and belly. The dog crawled toward them, but one front and one hind leg appeared broken.

"The best thing we could do is put the poor thing out of his misery," Jack said. "Living on a farm you learn not to get attached to animals and not to let them suffer if in pain. He looks in bad shape and probably won't survive."

"No, we can't, Jack," Billy pleaded. "He might live. We can't just kill him or leave him to die. Let's take him to the Frazers' place. Maybe Mrs. Frazer can help." Billy took off his shirt and carefully approached the dog. Gently he covered the suffering creature with his shirt and scooped the limp body into his arms. "Get on your horse and I'll lift him up to you, Jack."

Jack, careful not to squeeze too tight, cradled the wounded animal in his arms and they headed to the Frazers' farm.

There, Billy jumped from his horse and ran to knock on the door. "Mr. and Mrs. Frazer, come quick."

Seth opened the door. Jack held out something small and bloodied. "Hurry, Emily. Grab bandages and come to the barn."

Jack handed the dog down to Billy, who rushed to the barn and carefully laid the animal on some hay Seth readied.

Emily ran to assist. The condition of the poor thing broke her heart.

"Boys, did you see how this happened?" Emily

asked.

"No. We heard a whimpering noise and followed the sound to find the poor thing lying in a pool of blood. We brought him straight here. Please help him." Billy swiped his hand across his eyes.

"Can I do anything to help?" Jack asked.

"Yes, get the scissors from the drawer to the right of the sink."

"Sure will, Mrs. Frazer." Jack set off to the house.

"Seth, can you dig out the liniment we use on the horses? That's the only medicine we have. Liniment might help the little fella."

Soon Jack ran into the barn with the scissors, and Emily cut bandages and got to work on the dog's deep wounds. She finished cleaning and bandaging the injuries, and splinted the legs, but worried her efforts were in vain. The little dog lay shivering and whimpering but seemed appreciative of the attention. Stepping back finally, Emily wiped her hands on her apron. "He's lost a lot of blood, and his wounds are deep."

"Let's give him water, food, and time to rest. We can check on him again before you leave." Seth took Emily's arm, led everyone out of the barn, and closed the door.

In the house, Seth fetched an old shirt for Billy, while Emily offered the boys a cool drink.

Jack ran out and got the cornbread from his saddlebag. "Ma sent this for you, Mrs. Frazer."

Emily sliced the bread and set the plate on the table.

"Here's the provisions and seed list, with enough money to cover the cost." Mr. Frazer handed them to

Jack. "Make sure this gets to Mark for me."

Jack tucked everything in his pocket.

Seth asked, "How's the barn coming along?"

"All right," was all he got out of Billy before the conversation quickly returned to the little dog.

"Maybe a wagon train passed through and left the poor thing behind," Jack mused aloud.

Billy added, "His body sure has a lot of curly white fur. Hey, you'll be coming to pick up your supplies in a couple of weeks, won't you, Mr. Frazer? You could return him to us then."

Jack patted Billy on the shoulder.

"You'll make him better, won't you?" Billy pleaded.

Seth spoke up. "Yes, boys, rest assured. If the little fella pulls through, we'll bring him along when we come to pick up the supplies."

Before leaving, the boys peeked in on the dog. He wasn't whimpering as often and his breathing was calmer, so they didn't disturb him.

"We'll see you in two weeks," Jack called to the Frazers, standing in the yard to wave good-bye.

"Take care of our dog." Billy waved back.

The boys headed home and arrived just in time for supper to share all their news.

Chapter Fifteen

Knowing they were leaving in the morning for town, the family got a good night's rest. Jack and Billy awoke, dressed, and had all the morning chores done before their ma put the morning meal on the table. Their first cattle drive, as the boys liked to call it, although they were taking only four beef cattle to town to sell. The pumpkin patch produced well, and the boys loaded sixty of the nicest pumpkins in the wagon to sell, careful not to jostle Sarah's blueberry pie wedged in the back corner, ready for this fall's contest. She had thought about an apple pie, then decided on blueberry and added two additional tablespoons of sugar.

With the wagon overflowing, the family headed to town. Billy and Jack nudged the cattle along in front of the wagon. About two hours into the journey, Billy's horse reared up. Billy held on, and when the horse's hooves hit the ground, the coiled rattler's tail sounded. Ruby's hind legs kicked out, his head bobbed, and Billy flew over the horse's shoulder to lie on the ground motionless. The snake was behind him when he heard the rattle again.

Jack shouted. "Are you all right, Billy?"

Billy didn't answer. He didn't dare move.

Jack quickly rode back toward the wagon and screamed, "Billy fell off Ruby and he isn't moving. I called his name, but he didn't answer." Jack jumped off

Button and Mark jumped on.

As Mark approached, Billy's stiff and pale body gave concern for caution. In a low voice, he said, "Are you all right, Billy?"

Billy didn't answer. He didn't even blink.

Then Mark heard the rattle, and the tail movement caught his eye. There lay the coiled snake in the grass, head poised to strike. There was no time to waste. Mark drew his pistol and shot instinctively. When he let out his breath, the snake still squirmed on the ground and the tail rattled. He shot again. The snake lay still and dead.

The terror in Billy's eyes gave way to relief and gratitude.

"The snake is dead." Mark put the gun away. "Are you all right, Billy?"

Billy turned toward Mark, sighed, and a tear rolled down his cheek.

Mark picked up the snake and hurled the sleek body into the brush. He knelt at Billy's side, helped him turn and sit on the grass, and then gave him a bear hug, being careful not to squeeze too hard, then motioned for Sarah to come.

Sarah hurried to Billy. "Lie still." She ran her hand over his already swollen ankle and asked, "Can you move your legs and wiggle your toes for me?"

Billy did as asked.

"Don't try to get up. Where else do you hurt?

"I'm all right, Mother," Billy insisted. "Just a little sore, and I think my elbow is bleeding. I landed hard and twisted my ankle."

Sarah checked him over. "Good, I don't think anything is broken. We'll put your elbow in a sling and wrap your ankle."

When Mark heard Sarah say she didn't think anything was broken, he took off after Ruby. The family couldn't afford to lose a good horse and saddle.

Sarah stood. "Can you stand, Billy? Let's get you up."

Sarah and Jack helped Billy into the back of the wagon, where Sarah, with Lydia's assistance, worked with bandages to wrap the bruised and swollen ankle.

"I'm all right, Mother," Billy insisted. "I'm sorry I couldn't hold on when the horse kicked."

Jack said, "Don't worry about the horse. And I'm sure the cattle didn't stray too far."

Soon, Mark returned, holding Ruby's reins.

"Is Billy all right?" he called out.

"He'll be fine," Sarah answered.

Mark rode up, and Billy shook his hand. "That snake could have killed me. You saved my life again. A thank you doesn't seem like enough. Maybe someday I can save your life."

"If I ever need saving, I hope you're there." Mark grinned. "You rest now."

Mark and Jack drove the cattle the rest of the day, until they stopped for the night at their usual oak tree campsite. The cattle slowed them, and they arrived later than usual. Everyone pitched in and made camp. While Sarah unpacked and fixed supper, Jack acted as a crutch for Billy and helped him back to the swimming hole. Mark, Jack, and Lydia took a quick dip in the creek while Billy soaked his ankle in the cool water.

Annoyed with himself for letting Mark down, Billy was determined to recover and be as good as new in the morning. He didn't want all his hard work and practice to go to waste and not get to finish the cattle drive. After supper, he soaked his ankle in the creek again to relieve the pain and reduce the swelling.

The next morning, Billy's whole body ached. His elbow and ankle were both black and blue, and he limped, trying not to put too much pressure on his ankle.

"I'm good enough to ride. Please, can't I take the cattle down Main Street with Jack?"

"All right, you can drive them through town," Sarah agreed.

They got an early start and, without much rough terrain, managed to arrive in town late morning. Mark stopped, and Lydia helped Sarah down from the wagon at the dry goods store and fetched the eggs and fresh vegetables to sell and the blueberry preserves to trade with the store owner for honey. Mark escorted the boys in the wagon as they drove the cattle through town. The boys sat tall in their saddles, as proud of the four beef cattle as the big ranchers they'd watched several times herding hundreds of cattle down Main Street.

Mark took over at the sale corral, where the stench of cow manure lingered and buyers and traders made fast deals. He haggled a fair price on his four head of cattle, then turned around and bought a good bull and a springer, a first calf heifer, for breeding. There were still a few dollars left over.

****

Once finished at the dry goods store, Sarah and Lydia walked to the post office to check for mail from back east. Sure enough, two letters were waiting, one from Sarah's mother and the other from her sister, Emma.

"Open them now and let's read them. Hurry, Ma." Lydia grabbed to open one.

"No, we don't have time now. Let's wait until later, when everyone is around." Sarah slipped the treasured communications into her pocket as they walked to the sale corral.

When Mark and the boys turned the corner coming their way, Sarah called, "How'd you make out?"

Jack grinned. "Mark is quite the haggler."

"He made a good deal," Billy agreed.

"We'll tell you later, Ma. Mark has to register. The Best Shot Competition is starting soon." Jack slapped Mark on the back. "He'll win this time for sure."

The fall day was warm and the sun bright. Mark remembered a few men he competed with before, shook their hands, and wished them well.

The sheriff announced, "This here's a Volcanic .38 caliber, lever-action rifle, and comes with five tins of self-primed lead projectiles guaranteed waterproof. This Volcanic Rifle was made in Norwich, Connecticut, and shipped to us special for today's event. This gun has a pretty walnut gunstock with engraving on the receiver, trigger guard, and the butt plate. And this can be yours if you have the highest score."

Mark waited until the sheriff's call, "Contestant twenty-one to the line." Nobody shot a perfect score yet. Maybe this would be Mark's year to win after all. He cleared his mind, breathed in and exhaled slowly. Then he took a breath and held it as he squeezed the trigger. The first shot took out the small center dot on the paper target. With a clean sweep on the first two bottles, his last shot—the farthest and the hardest bottle to take down—made him nervous. He missed this bottle

127

the last time. He held his breath and squeezed the trigger. The bottle shattered. The crowd cheered. No doubt about the perfect score this time.

There were eight more shooters after Mark. Would someone else tie his score? He'd been in a shoot-off before. He stood to the side and patiently waited as each man approached the firing line. Mark, eager for the competition to end, cheered on each of the contestants. Nobody matched his perfect score. The crowd cheered as Mark made his way to pick up his prize.

"You won fair and square." The sheriff handed Mark the gun. "This rifle is all yours, mister."

Mark shook the sheriff's hand and some of his competitors', held the gun high in the air, and said, "Thank you." The crowd cheered again as he made his way back to his family. The gun meant an extra rifle in the house, one Sarah could use for self-defense and the boys for hunting.

A shrieking whistle got the crowd quiet. "Attention, attention please," the mayor called to the crowd. "The picnic will now commence in the church grove."

Instead of going to the saloon with the other men to celebrate, Mark walked with the family to the grove for the picnic feast.

After adding the pumpkin pies and cabbage salad to everyone else's contribution to the picnic, Sarah placed her blueberry pie on the contest table and took a number.

A line quickly formed to enjoy the feast.

****

Afterward, with stuffed bellies and empty plates,

Jack and Billy set out the pumpkins for sale. The sign read *Pumpkins 3 Cents*. "If you help us sell them, we'll each give you ten cents, Lydia," Billy offered.

"If we sell them all," Jack added.

Lydia and her sales pitch turned out to be their biggest draw. She explained to the women what wonderful pies, cakes, and muffins they could make if they took home a pumpkin. In two hours they sold out.

Lydia ran to show the Spencer girls her coins and catch up on the latest news.

Jack asked, "What are you going to buy with your money, Billy?"

"I don't know yet. Maybe something for our new dog. I can't wait until the Frazers come and he's ours. Just think, we'll have a dog to teach tricks and play with. Maybe we can even teach him how to herd cattle. Have you thought of any names yet? You think of a couple, then we can pick one."

"All right. I'll think of a few, but I wouldn't get my hopes up. That little dog may not live. He was in rough shape."

"Oh, he'll survive. He has to live." Billy straightened. He couldn't bear the thought of another death in his life. Deep down, he was still grieving for his father and mother.

"Hey, how about you? How're you spending your money, Jack?" Billy asked

"I'll buy some candy, but I'm not sure after that. We better save some. I want to buy my own rifle someday." Jack jingled the coins in his pocket.

"Yeah, me too. But a few cents on candy would be all right," Billy agreed.

"Well, I'm going to find Abby. I want her to save

me some dances and I want the first one of the night. See you later." Jack ran off.

****

Billy limped to Elizabeth's house, thinking of names for the dog. Elizabeth was home but busy getting ready for the dance, so they didn't talk long. Billy handed her three letters and promised to write more. Then Elizabeth fetched her letters and handed him a fistful.

"Gosh, I promise to write one a week from now on. I can't wait to read all of yours."

"And I'll cherish each of yours too." Elizabeth hurried him out the door. "I'll look for you when the first song starts."

"I'll be there looking for you too." Filled with determination, Billy walked to the creek to soak his ankle, which throbbed a little. He'd dance tonight even if his ankle hurt.

****

Alone, Sarah opened the two letters from home. When she and her brother Richard left Pennsylvania five years ago, their sister Matilda was sixteen, Emma thirteen, and little brother Matthew only twelve. *I wonder what they look like now.*

Emma wrote:
July 18, 1859
Tidioute, Warren County, Pennsylvania
Dear Sarah,

I am sure you are surprised to see a letter arrive from me. I wanted to write and tell you myself. I plan to marry come next May. I have met a wonderful young man, named Abel Evans, whom I can't wait to marry. We have been courting since December of last year and

*I finally agreed to his proposal on the Fourth of July
after he told me he took a job working for a logging
company here in Tidioute. He makes a trip a week to
Pittsburgh, so I don't get to see him much.*

*I am sure Mother told you I am working at the
hotel dining room in town, but I am looking for a better
job. I have been saving and now have enough money to
buy the fabric for my wedding dress.*

*We hope to buy the old Goss farm about six miles
west of town and will live there once we marry. We both
want to start a family right away. Three or four
children would be perfect, God willing.*

*Although the wedding is not until spring, I am
writing in hopes that you and the children might be able
to return home and attend my special day. I know it is a
lot to ask and you'll have the new baby and all, but we
would all love to see you. You will not believe how we
have all changed in the last five years.*

Oh, Emma, Sarah mused, *I'd love to be there but I
cannot leave and take a stage back to Pennsylvania.*
Everything depended on money and the farm.

*We are all happy that Mark and Billy are in your
lives now and I'm sure you are anxious for the baby's
birth. We would all love to meet them. I hope you will
give the wedding some thought and write as soon as
you know if you can come.*

Give my niece and nephew a big kiss for me.

Your loving sister,

Emma

Sarah opened her mother's letter next.

August 12, 1859

Tidioute, Warren County, Pennsylvania

Dearest Sarah,

131

We are all pleased to read the baby is doing well. Everyone is happy for you, darling. I rest easier knowing Mark is there to take care of you and the children. And now with another child on the way, I am sure Mark is proud and excited.

I invited everyone to dinner and we read your letter at the dinner table just like we used to when you children were little. Emma invited Abel to join us and everyone enjoyed the details as I read about your joyous baby news and about the progress on the barn.

I am delighted that Emma has found a man that will take care of and can provide her a good life. She is so excited about the wedding. His parents, James and Isabella Evans, are good people. They have the means to watch out for the young couple until they get established. She would like you here to share in her excitement; we all would love to see you again. But I also understand coming will be impossible.

Matthew is doing very well at the newspaper. Enclosed is an article he wrote on the church box lunch social. He asked me to send it. This job is good experience and gets him out more. He is maturing and turning into quite the young man. Still no girls in Matthew's life, but I am not too concerned.

Matilda is still working for Doc Davis. She met a young man. They are friends right now, doing things together when they can find time.

I imagine you are in the peak of harvest season. I hope your crops fared well this year, but please do not overdo. I am proud of you, Sarah. I hope you know that. You have gone through some hard times, but you survived and are now a stronger person.

I love and miss you, my darling daughter.

My prayers and thoughts are with you,
Love, Mother

Folding the letter, Sarah turned to Mark. "My sister Emma is getting married next May and would like us to come for the wedding. Of course, returning east is out of the question. May is our planting season. Besides, we couldn't afford a trip like that."

"You're right, but I'm sure you'd like to visit."

"I'd love to see Emma get married and visit the family, but getting the fields and garden planted are more important." She sighed.

"Come on. While we have time, let's pick out a few surprises for Christmas morning and make the day extra special."

Sarah selected calico fabric with matching buttons, lace, and thread, then selected two patterns for Lydia and found fabric to make an outfit for the baby.

Mark picked out bows with arrows and extra strings for the boys. New books for the children topped off the gift pile. As planned, they added a piece of glass for another window in the front of the house. The store clerk wrapped the pane corners well with paper.

"What a difference another window will make," Sarah said. "Samuel and I intended on adding the window but never had the money to afford the glass."

As they carried the presents to the wagon, Sarah marveled at the new storefronts that had sprung up since her last trip to town. A new dress shop in particular caught her eye. She hadn't bought a store dress in a long time. Maybe next summer when she had her figure back she'd treat herself. Then she thought better of the idea. Her home-sewn dresses were just fine.

Emma's letter still lingered in her mind. Although they couldn't attend the wedding, perhaps a photograph of the family would show she was thinking of them. Earlier in the day she happened upon a wagon vendor taking a picture of a family.

"Mark." Sarah stopped walking. "Do you think we could afford to have a family photo taken? I'd like to send one to the folks back home. This way, even though we can't be there for the wedding, they will know we are thinking of them."

"That's a great idea, Sarah," said Mark. "In fact, if we are going to have one taken, let's splurge and get four. We can send one to your mother, my mother, and Samuel's mother, and keep one for ourselves. Photographs will be costly but would be a wonderful surprise for our families."

Sarah brightened. "Oh, could we? I'll see if the photographer can work us into his schedule right now and then have the tintypes ready in the morning so we could put them in the mail before we set out for home."

Moments later, Sarah walked toward Mark with a smile on her face. "If we come right away, he can take the photographs. Hurry, we must find the children."

"You gather everyone. I'll get money from the bank, and take the wagon back to the church grove," Mark called over his shoulder as he walked toward the bank.

Coming out of the bank, Mark caught sight of two men watching him from across the street. He thought he recalled shooting against the one with the beard and buckskin pants. The other wore a hat with a tear on the brim. There were many people in town for the festival, and he was sure he didn't know these characters, so paid them no mind.

Sarah located the children at the creek looking for crayfish under rocks. "Hurry!" she called to them, "Get cleaned up and changed into your good clothes, for a photograph to send to our family in Pennsylvania."

Sarah and Lydia rushed to the church to change into the dresses they brought for the dance. Mark and the boys dusted off their pants, put on clean shirts, and slicked down their hair.

****

"Now, stand still and try not to blink or change your facial expression," the photographer explained to the assembled group.

Sarah and Lydia sat, and Jack and Billy stood behind, one on each side of Mark. The backdrop was a piece of medium blue fabric to block out the busy street behind. "Each half plate tintype takes about a minute or so of exposure."

Sarah anticipated the delight seeing the group photograph would give their families. She ordered four half-plate tintype photographs, each measuring approximately four and a half inches by five and a half inches, small but large enough so everyone's face was clearly visible. Each photo cost fifty cents. Quite an expense, but well worth the price, in Sarah's mind.

Mark paid the vendor, who agreed to have the tintypes ready for the morning.

The boys returned to the creek to find crayfish, Lydia walked to town with the Spencer girls to window shop, and Mark and Sarah spread a blanket in the shade.

A gentle breeze blew as Mark napped. Sarah walked to the store to buy ink, a pen, and writing paper. She would write her mother a letter to accompany the photograph and respond to Emma's request for the family to return for the wedding.

Relaxed but a little self-conscious of her bulging belly, she leaned against Mark's back and began her letter. When she finished, she had filled two pages front and back. Sarah also wrote shorter letters to Mark and Samuel's mothers, catching them up on news.

I know staying in Kansas is right for us. This is our home now, she wrote in all three letters, *and we will survive any bad times we may face because we have each other.*

Although Sarah wasn't having cramps or pains, she told Mark when he awoke, "I'm going to walk to Doctor Glasgow's office and see if he's in."

Still sleepy, Mark bobbed his head.

She carried the coins from her money jar to pay the doctor in a handkerchief, tucked in her pocket.

"Do you have time to check my baby's heartbeat and tell me if anything is wrong, Doctor? My mind would rest easier knowing my baby is all right. I lost my last child at birth, and I'm concerned. My husband and I so want this child healthy and happy."

"Of course, my dear. Come in. You look as though you're ready to deliver any day now."

"Why, yes, I'm large, but the baby isn't due for another month."

"Let me listen." Doc Glasgow placed the stethoscope and moved it from one location to another, asking Sarah to breathe in deeply and exhale slowly.

"The heartbeat isn't as strong as I'd hoped, but I do hear movement, so the baby is progressing, but this better be your last trip to town for a while."

"What do you think, Doctor? A boy or a girl?"

"I'm not good at telling. I'd say my predictions are only correct fifty percent of the time. How about we leave that up to the good Lord and worry about you having an easy delivery?" Doc Glasgow said.

"You're right. The sex doesn't matter as long as he or she is healthy and whole. Thank you, Doctor. Is there anything I can do to help the baby?"

"You need to rest and don't over exert." The doctor put his stethoscope away. "Will anyone be with you during delivery?"

"Yes, the neighbor lady said she'd come help. This will be my fourth delivery. My last child miscarried at birth, so I know what to expect." Sarah stood. "What do I owe you, Doctor Glasgow?"

"Not a thing, Mrs. Hewitt. You take care and rest easy going home. The bumpy ride won't be comfortable," he said as he showed her to the door.

Returning to Mark, Sarah shared only the good news. "Doc Glasgow assured me the baby is fine and he heard some movement." Sarah didn't want to worry Mark. She would rest and only dance a couple dances tonight.

Mark's arms embraced her in a cocoon of love and understanding. They kissed, and he held her face in his hands and gazed into her eyes. "That's great news, sweetheart. I can't wait until this baby calls me Poppa."

Chapter Sixteen

While window shopping with Mrs. Spencer and her friends, Lydia ventured into the new dress shop, saying she'd catch up with them later. In the back of the shop a woman sat at an unusual machine, pumping the foot peddle while sewing the outside leg seam of men's pants. Lydia never observed such a sight before and stepped closer.

"May I watch?" she asked politely. "I've never seen a needle move that fast."

"Of course, you may, my dear," the woman replied.

Lydia couldn't take her eyes off the shiny needle that glided over the fabric. The speed and ease finished the straight seam on the pants the lady was making in no time.

Lydia offered, "I made the dress I'm wearing. I enjoy sewing and making my own clothes."

"Would you like to try the machine?" asked the woman.

Lydia smiled and blurted out, "Can I really?"

"Yes, dear," the woman answered. "Let me finish this seam, and I'll help you. What's your name?"

"I'm Lydia Clark. I'm almost twelve. My family lives a day and a half ride away. We come to town twice a year." She patiently waited for the woman to finish.

As promised, the woman soon guided Lydia through the steps of operating the sewing machine. She showed her how to lift the pressure foot, and then release it to secure the fabric. After rocking the foot peddle in a rhythm to make the needle go up and down, she demonstrated how the pressure foot pulled the cloth forward under the needle. The sales woman even showed Lydia the bobbin and how to make the machine go in reverse to tack the ends of the seams. With scrap fabric, Lydia was encouraged to make a drawstring pouch.

"You're a natural, Lydia," the woman told her, "very patient, and precise."

"I made that pouch in less than five minutes using this machine. Sewing the same seams by hand would have taken me at least a half hour. Lydia's eyes widened. "Can I ask how much money a sewing machine like this costs?"

"New, one would cost about thirty-eight dollars," the woman told her as she inspected the seams.

"It will take me forever to save that much money," Lydia said. "But maybe someday I'll have enough. Thanks for letting me try the sewing machine." Lydia stood.

"You can keep what you made, dear," the woman handed Lydia her prized pouch.

Excited and pleased with her accomplishment, Lydia expressed her thanks again and couldn't wait to show her mother. *Someday maybe I'll be a seamstress and own my own dress shop. Then I can make Momma and myself the most beautiful dresses in town.*

With the twenty cents in her pocket, she stopped at the dry goods store, even though she knew she wasn't to be in town by herself. She bought fancy lace to sew on the sleeves and collar of her old blouse. One yard of lace cost eight cents. She added two cents' worth of candy and saved the rest of the money for the next trip to town, then ran all the way back to the church grove.

****

That evening, the weather held for the square dance. With a beautiful moonlit sky overhead, Lydia danced several times with different boys, but the one she liked the best was Ben, whom she met at the last dance. "You're a good dancer," Lydia said after their third dance.

"So are you. And you're pretty," Ben added.

Lydia blushed. "Thanks, Ben." She knew her dress wasn't as fancy as the girls', but she stitched every inch herself and boasted, "I made my dress. Do you like it?"

"Yes, it's very nice. My grandmother sews her own dresses, and makes some of my clothes, too," Ben admitted.

Then they talked about the farms they lived on, their daily chores, and when they thought they'd see each other again.

****

Jack danced all evening with Abby Proctor, except when he got them punch and returned to find her dancing with another boy. Jack stood there with two drinks in his hands. Didn't she think he'd see her? She appeared to know the boy and smiled at Jack when she spotted him and then frowned. Jack turned to walk away.

Abby ran after him, calling out, "Please, let me explain." When she caught up to him she took his hand and said, "He's my cousin. My mother told me I had to dance at least one dance with him, so now the rest of the evening I can spend with you."

After Abby's explanation, Jack laughed, and they drank their punch, sat, and talked. After seeing Billy writing his girl letters a few times, Jack asked Abby, "If I write you letters until we see each other again, and tell you about living on a farm, would you write me some letters too?"

"Of course, I will." Abby took Jack's hand before he could take hers, and they talked and danced the rest of the evening.

****

While Mark talked with Joe Spencer, Sarah caught Martha up on news. "Seth and Emily got married last fall. The happy couple came over to help with the barn, and I got to know Emily better. She's a real sweet woman and really loves Seth." Then, of course, the women talked about the baby and caught up on other news.

Sarah even found her way to Mark's arms on the dance floor a few times. Being with child slowed Sarah somewhat, but not to the point of saying no to a couple of dances.

The children were having a good time and Sarah and Mark agreed this had been a great way to celebrate their first anniversary. "Coming to town allowed our entire family to enjoy time away from the farm." Sarah rubbed her belly.

****

Billy spotted Elizabeth just in time to dance the first song together. Then he walked her to a quiet location and said, "You look very nice tonight."

She squeezed his hand. "And you're the reason

why. We're the best looking couple at the dance."

Billy gazed into her eyes. "Well, you're certainly the most beautiful girl here, and the only one I'll be dancing with this evening."

They caught up on her life first. "I'm singing in the church choir now, and Mother is teaching me how to embroider so I can attend her women's group meeting. She says I need to become more involved in organizations and attend more social events."

"Yes, that's important when you live in town. That also means other men will ask you to attend these events with them."

"I suppose so. Mother said it's time for me to start looking for a beau. She didn't like the fact that I want to dance with you all night, but I told her you only get to town once in a while, and the time we spend together is special."

"I lived in Kansas City, until a year and a half ago. My father was a lawyer, and your mother sounds like mine would have. She would want me to meet girls and find one suitable for marriage. We're of the age where that's important to parents. I miss my parents and think of them often, but the family I live with now is real good to me. I realize living a day and a half ride from town is difficult. There's no way to know when social events are happening and no way for me to get to town. Then once I'm here, I don't have any place to stay."

"I understand you can't get to town for all the social events, but you're here now, so come on, let's dance again."

Song after song, they enjoyed each other's company. When the dance ended, they walked, arm in arm, back to Elizabeth's house.

"I promise to write more letters. I even bought paper and ink so I have my own. I'll fill them with everything I do. I won't be attending social events, but you'll learn more about farming, like I have. Farming is different from living in the city—you work with animals and get your hands dirty. Did I tell you Jack and I found a little dog? The poor thing was in pretty bad shape, but Mrs. Frazer is taking care of him, and in two weeks she's going to return him to us."

"You really have a soft spot in your heart for animals." She stopped outside her front door. "Where did the night go? I don't want it to end. When will I see you again?"

"I don't know, but hopefully before next spring. I'll try to get to town again if I can, before Christmas. I have a surprise in mind I'd like to make for you. I might just show up one day."

"Oh, I hope you do. I'll keep writing you letters."

"And I'll keep writing you, too." Billy kissed her.

This kiss wasn't a quick kiss on the cheek or forehead. This kiss was meant to last a good long time, so he took his time and held her in his arms tighter and closer than they had ever been before. And when he released his lips from hers, he said, "That won't last me." And kissed her again, mouth wider this time, giving them a chance to explore and take their time.

Breathless she gazed into his eyes and whispered, "Nobody has ever kissed me like that before."

He cupped her face in his hands. "Good, and don't let anyone but me kiss you like that again." He held her close one last time. "I've got to go. I'm sure my family is waiting for me." He kissed her neck; the smell of her perfume lingered. He wanted to remember that smell.

He took off down the street, but turned and looked back when he got to the alley. Elizabeth waved. He waved back and kept running until he turned a corner. He had totally forgotten about his sprained ankle until that moment. Throbbing with pain, his ankle would no doubt ache all night, but for now all he wanted to remember was Elizabeth... He was in love.

Chapter Seventeen

Clouds like bales of dirty cotton filled the morning sky while Sarah and Lydia packed the wagon, careful to secure the pane of glass for the new window. The supplies were covered to protect them from the imminent rainstorm looming overhead.

Meanwhile, Mark and the boys headed to the corral to pick up the new bull and springer, purchased for breeding stock. The boys left immediately, driving the animals out of town, to get a head start. The family would catch up soon enough.

Earlier, Sarah picked up the tintypes from the photographer's wagon, three packaged for safe travels to Pennsylvania and the fourth for the Hewitt family. The pictures were perfect. Everyone was smiling and Sarah was proud of the family she and Mark were nurturing. She couldn't wait to show them. She addressed the parcels at the postal office and sent them on their way, hoping the letters and photographs would help everyone back home understand her need to stay in Kansas, even though her heart ached to return east for a visit. She tucked the other photograph in the wagon to share with the family that evening.

****

Rain began falling outside of town, a gentle rain, but a soaker nonetheless. Mark, drenched to the skin, sat on the box seat of the wagon and carefully guided the team along the rutted, puddle-laden road. Sarah, cumbersome with child, and Lydia wrapped themselves in blankets, trying to keep dry under the canvas.

Steady rain drumming on the tarp of the wagon masked the approach of two strangers on horseback who quickly flanked the wagon team. One rode a Morgan and wore a torn hat like the man Mark caught watching him in town. The other character rode a pinto and hid his face with a hat pulled low. He matched the other person in the pair from town that watched him come out of the bank. Uneasy, Mark brought the wagon to a halt, hoping the boys had ridden far enough ahead that the two strangers didn't know they were there.

"What can I do for you gentlemen?" Mark said loud enough that Sarah might hear him, and she and Lydia would be quiet and stay out of sight.

"We're heading north to Nebraska for a spell, and that rifle you won in town sure would come in handy. We were wondering just how good a shot you really are," said the older man.

"I shot against you," the younger man continued. "And the way I see it, you should hand over that rifle if you want to live. With that gun, I could win every competition."

In unison, both men drew their pistols, cocked the hammers, and pointed them at Mark.

These men wouldn't stop with taking the rifle. They'd want his money and would surely ransack the wagon. He didn't have a choice. He couldn't let them find Sarah and Lydia. No telling what they'd do.

"Okay, you fellas win, two against one. I'll give you the rifle if you'll let me go on my way," Mark said to the older man.

"Sure thing," the young stranger with the torn hat replied. "We'll let you go. Just hand over that rifle, real slow like."

"The gun is in the wagon right behind me." Mark leaned back slowly.

Concealed under a blanket, Sarah put her finger to Lydia's lips as she guided Mark's hand to the rifle she had cocked and ready to fire.

Mark had to wound or kill at least one of them and hope the other wouldn't get a shot off. He couldn't let them find Sarah and Lydia. A rumble of thunder murmured in the distance.

As Mark prepared to hand off the gun, the young man glimpsed movement in the wagon and leapt from his horse to the wagon seat.

Mark struggled, using the prize rifle to shove him away.

The young man's pistol barked and a bullet shot past Mark into the wagon. Mark heard Lydia scream. *Were Sarah and Lydia all right? The baby?*

Mark thrust the rifle barrel up, catching the young man in the throat with enough force to knock the man off balance. Mark kicked him hard and sent him flying from the wagon.

The older man was unable to get a clear shot until that moment. The bullet ripped through Mark's left arm, the searing metal burned the cold flesh, and blood seeped from the wound.

Mark recoiled and got off a shot, hitting the older man in the chest. The man fell to the ground as a bright flash of lightning made his horse rear and run off.

Mark worked the gun's action again and looked to his left in time to see the other assailant ready to shoot.

Without hesitation, Mark shot, and the man lay limp.

"It's safe now. Are you both all right?" Mark jumped down and checked. Two lifeless bodies lay on the ground. "It's all right to come out. Both men are dead."

"We're good, Mark. That bullet passed over our heads." Peering out from the depths of the wagon at Mark standing over the dead men, Sarah held Lydia, who shivered with shock.

Then Sarah spotted Mark's bloody shirt. "Mark you've been shot."

"I'm fine. The bullet only grazed my arm," he said as he climbed back into the wagon to enfold Sarah and a trembling Lydia. "The boys! They could have hurt the boys!" Mark jumped to the ground and ran, calling, "Jack! Billy! Are you all right?"

Ahead, the boys heard calls coming from a silhouette, barely visible in the downpour, running toward them.

When Mark got closer, he shouted, "Are you both all right?"

"We're fine. What happened? We thought we heard shots, but then figured the noise came from the storm."

"Two men ambushed us. They wanted the new rifle. Don't worry, Ma and Lydia are safe. We'll need the outlaws' horses, so round 'em up, if you will. They haven't gone far."

"Sure, I'll get them and meet you at the wagon," Billy said and rode off.

Jack located the cows and started them back toward the wagon.

When Mark got back to the wagon, Lydia was still

recovering. "Don't worry, sweetheart, the bullet just grazed me." Mark gave her a comforting hug. "Could you make sure the dry goods aren't getting wet? We can't afford to lose our supplies."

Lydia kissed him on the cheek and turned to do the task Mark asked.

"The boys are fine," Mark said.

Sarah let out a long sigh. Tears welled as she tore her petticoat for bandages.

The boys soon returned with the horses and cows in tow. Sarah and Lydia were calmer, and Mark's arm was expertly wrapped. With everyone gathered around, Mark explained, "Those men gave me no choice. I shot in self-defense, and that's what I'll tell the sheriff when I take the bodies to town."

They bowed their heads in silent prayer for the two men, and then the boys helped Mark sling the bodies over the horses and tie them securely. "I saw these men in town at the celebration. I'll turn them over to the sheriff. Jack and Billy, see that the family gets to the campsite, and I'll meet you there as soon as I can." Mark took the reins and headed back to Dead Flats.

****

The family and cows arrived at the campsite with rain still lightly falling. Grateful to stop for the day, Lydia and Sarah huddled in the wagon to keep warm until the boys could gather wood and start a fire. A hot drink would help settle them all.

Soon, the rain stopped, the boys fed and watered the animals, and everyone enjoyed steaming mugs of tea and a light meal.

While everyone sat around the campfire, Sarah brought out the family photograph to help take their minds off the day's events.

Billy said, "I didn't realize you're almost as tall as me, Jack."

Jack poked Billy in the shoulder. "Yes. And I'm twice as good-looking."

Billy poked him back.

"Boys!" Sarah scolded.

"I don't like the way my hair looks," Lydia said. "There aren't enough curls."

"Yes, there are, Lydia," Billy said. "You look beautiful."

"I'm glad we had the photograph taken. Maybe we could get one taken every year. Then, when you children have your own families, your father and I will have them as memories to look back on.

"Come on, everyone. We better get some sleep. We've had a long day. One I'm sure we won't soon forget. I've never been so terrified in all my life."

"Me too, Ma." Lydia exhaled. "Today was worse than when the Indian boys came to the house."

"Today's been hard on all of us." Jack sighed. "I know Father didn't want to kill those two men."

"This is the second time I've seen men killed, and both times there was no other choice." Billy added another log to the fire. "The sheriff will understand. Mark won't be in trouble."

There was silence for a few moments and Sarah stood. "If I know your father, he'll want to get an early start in the morning. To bed with you now. He'll be back soon. I'm going to wait up so I can check his wound. Home will surely be welcome tomorrow."

Chapter Eighteen

Soaked to the skin, cold, and hungry, Mark guided his grisly cargo along Main Street to the sheriff's office. He tied the horses to the hitching post and walked in.

"What can I do for you?" the sheriff asked, looking up from his desk. "Mark, isn't it?"

"Yes, I brought you two dead men. They ambushed me." Mark recalled the story, ending with, "I had to shoot them in self-defense."

The sheriff was on his feet. "Let's go have a look."

"The young man shot in the Best Shot contest. He itched to get his hands on my new gun." Mark raised the man's head.

"If he was in the contest, maybe we can figure out who he is. Did he shoot before or after you competed?"

"Before me, I believe, but I can't say for certain."

The sheriff examined the two bodies for distinguishing marks. "Yes, I remember this man."

"I caught them watching me yesterday. I thought it odd, but with so many people in town, I didn't pay them much mind. I guess they followed us," Mark mused aloud.

Inside, the sheriff picked up a pile of wanted posters. "If they were willing to kill for a gun, maybe they've killed before. Let's see if we can find them." He took half the wanted notices and gave the rest to Mark.

Surprised by the number, Mark checked each carefully and read some that caught his eye for the crime committed. Mark finally identified the younger man's photo first. "This is one of them, sheriff. This is the one who shot in the contest." The next photo was the face of the older man. "And here's the other man, too."

"Looks like you got yourself some reward money. These posters each say, 'Two hundred dollars reward, DEAD or ALIVE.' You'll need to fill out paperwork, and I'll send it off in the morning. The mail will take a few weeks, but the four-hundred-dollar reward's all yours."

"Sheriff, will you be selling the horses to pay for their funerals?"

"Why do you ask?"

"I'd like the pinto for one of my boys." *Maybe the pinto would help ease the pain of losing the little dog if it doesn't live.* He had promised Billy a horse of his own one day.

"That's not a problem. That Morgan should sell for enough to bury both of them."

"Can I have both saddles and gear, too? Oh, and what about their pistols? I have two boys who could each use one. Could I buy them cheap?"

"Buy them, nope, but you can keep them, the saddles, and the gear too. My report will say self-defense, but I don't need their firearms as evidence."

"You just made two young boys very happy, sheriff."

"Can you help me drop the bodies off at the undertakers and take the horses to the livery?"

"Sure, I can do that. After, I'll get something to eat

at the hotel, and then I'll come back to sign the paperwork."

Outside, people gathered to find out what happened.

"Go home, folks. No news here."

The crowd dispersed as Mark and the sheriff took care of the bodies and the horses.

"I'll sign the papers, sheriff, but I'll only take half the money. The horse, saddles, gear, and pistols make up for the other half. Would you see that a hundred dollars goes to the town church and the rest to support the abolitionist movement? Oh, and no mention of my name, please."

"Whatever you say. That's mighty generous of you." The sheriff patted him on the back.

Mark walked to the hotel, ate, and returned to sign the papers.

"I'll see that your wishes are met."

Mark shook the sheriff's hand, put the pistols in his saddlebag, and rode out of town leading the pinto laden with extra gear.

****

When Mark arrived at the campsite, he tethered the horses and slipped past the boys sleeping under the wagon.

Sarah greeted him with a kiss. "How's your arm, my brave hero?"

It was throbbing dully, but Mark said, "It's good enough until morning."

Sarah poured him a cup of tea.

Mark explained about the reward posters and money, pointed out the pinto, and mentioned the two pistols he negotiated for the boys. From Sarah's expression, he'd keep the gun conversation for another day. But at least they were in his possession, and someday he'd give them to the boys.

****

As they sat around the fire, eating their morning meal, Mark noticed long faces trying to avoid eye contact. He said, "You must know how badly yesterday's events pain me. Taking a life is a horrendous choice." Silence filled the air. "As a family, we are blessed. Always remember, your mother and I love you, and we would do anything to protect you."

Sarah added, "Fighting and killing is a sin, but if Mark hadn't killed those two men, I fear what they'd have done if they found Lydia and me in the wagon." Sarah moved closer to Mark. We're lucky the bullet only grazed your arm."

A tear glistened on Lydia's cheek as she ran and gave Mark a hug. Jack and Billy each patted him on the back.

Jack pointed to the pinto. "Wasn't that one of the men's horses?"

"Yes, and now he belongs to Billy." Mark stood. "He seems real gentle."

"Really? You mean he's mine to keep? But how?"

The sheriff let me keep him for bringing in the two men. Turns out, they were both outlaws. We found Wanted posters.

"Now the pinto is your responsibility, Billy. And, Jack, Button is all yours. No more sharing or taking turns. Ruby and I've been together for over six years. You get attached to a horse. Treat them good and they'll treat you good." Mark gave him a nudge toward the animal, and Billy and Jack checked out the horse, saddles, and gear.

"Thanks, Mark. I don't know what to say but thanks." Billy stroked the horse's neck and scratched him behind the ears. "I'll take good care of you, boy. Now all you need is a name. Don't worry. I'll come up with a good one. Have you thought of a name for the dog yet, Jack?"

"No, not yet," was all Jack said.

Heavy clouds lurked overhead, so the family headed out quickly. Mark wasn't sure how much the cows might slow them. Today they would concentrate on getting home.

****

A few hours later, Sarah called to Mark. "I think we better stop, sweetheart. I need to stretch my legs. I'm having some pains and need a change from the wagon's rocking."

Mark helped Sarah out of the wagon and cradled her arm as they walked. "Are the pains any better?"

"No. Actually, I think they're worse."

"How's the baby? Are you all right?"

"Let me keep walking for a few minutes. Maybe the pains will pass."

The boys, who were out ahead, stopped and returned to the wagon, letting the cattle graze.

"The pains aren't sharp like the last time. Perhaps if I sit and rest a spell..."

Mark grabbed a crate for Sarah to sit on. "Should I go for the doctor in Dead Flats?"

Sarah breathed in deeply and let the air out slowly. "The doctor said soon, but I thought I had another month."

"You've been through a lot the last two days. I'm

going to send one of the boys for the doctor."

"Maybe that's best. I don't want to lose this child."
I can't lose this child. This is Mark's chance to become a father. He so wants a child of his own.

"Can I do anything for you, Ma?" Lydia asked.

"Maybe a cup of tea would help."

"Jack and Billy, please tie the cows, the bull in the front and the other to the side of the wagon, then one of you needs to ride to town and fetch the doctor," Mark said.

"I'll go," Billy offered.

"Go now. I'll take care of the cattle," Jack said.

Billy took off on the pinto, calling back, "I'll hurry, Ma."

"Jack," Mark said, "can you fetch wood for a fire so Lydia can make your ma some tea?"

"Sure, right away." Jack found enough burnable material to get a fire started.

Lydia dipped water from the barrel to brew tea.

"I need to walk some more," Sarah said.

Mark helped her stand, and they walked back and forth until the tea was ready. Sarah sat and took a few sips.

"Thank you, Lydia. This tastes good."

"Can I do anything else for you, Ma?" Lydia asked.

"Why don't you help Jack find more wood? We might be here a while, and we'll need a fire to keep warm." Sarah took another sip. "Those clouds are going to cut loose sooner or later."

Mark asked, "Sweetheart, do you think the baby is coming?"

"Yes, with all the excitement yesterday and the bumpy ride, I do think the baby is on its way. I'm all right, but I think he or she is trying to tell me one of them is coming soon."

Mark took her hand. "Billy better hurry and get back here with the doctor."

"And if he doesn't, don't worry. I'll talk you through each step. You'll do fine. I can't do this without you. Lydia will want to help, but I'd just as soon she only watch from a distance in case, God help us, something goes wrong. You've delivered foals and calves before. You can help me."

"Not quite the same, sweetheart, but I'll do my best." He chuckled and kissed her cheek. "I'm here for you, darling. Let me know what you need."

"Right now, I need to walk."

Mark helped Sarah to her feet, and they paced back and forth on the path until she needed to rest again.

Glancing at his pocket watch, he noted the time. "Nine twenty-five. Billy and the doctor should arrive in six hours or so."

"I'm not sure I'll last six hours. This could be an eventful day."

Jack and Lydia returned with only an armful each of burnable material. "Jack, why don't you and Lydia ride back and gather wood along the creek." Mark patted Sarah's shoulder. "If your mother is going to have the baby today, we'll need lots of wood. From the looks of those clouds, if you hurry you can make the trip and be back before the rain starts. Take the extra saddlebags to keep the wood dry."

Jack hoisted Lydia up behind him in the saddle, and they rode off.

****

"We haven't settled on a name for this baby yet,

Mark." Sarah took a deep breath. "I definitely believe we'll need a name, and soon. Help me to my feet again. I can't seem to get comfortable."

As the couple walked arm in arm, Sarah reminisced, "We sure have come a long way, haven't we? Are you happy, Mark?"

"Of course. Why do you ask?"

A tear threatened to spill. "If anything should happen to me…"

Mark cut her off, clasped her hands in his, and said, "Nothing's going to happen to you or the baby. I'll be right here every minute."

"That doesn't mean something couldn't happen. I pray it won't, but there's no guarantee. If anything does happen, promise me, please promise me, you and the children will be all right."

"You know I'd never leave them. I love Jack, Lydia, and Billy as my own." Mark kissed her tears away.

"I'm at peace now. I guess I needed to hear those words. I love you, Mark Hewitt. You're a good father and loving husband. I love you with all my heart."

"And I love you, sweetheart, but nothing bad will happen. We'll bring this baby into the world together. Maybe the doctor will arrive in time, but no matter what, I'm here. I won't leave."

"I can't ask for anything more, Mark. You share your love with all of us every day. Now, take me back, please. I need to sit. What about names? We really need to settle on two names. One for a daughter and one if it's a son."

"I've given this some thought. How about Richard James Hewitt? Richard for your brother and James was my grandfather's and father's name, and my middle name."

"Perfect. I love Richard James, if it's a boy. And if it's a girl, how about Johanna Verena, after my two grandmothers?"

"We could call her Hanna," Mark suggested.

"No, I like Johanna. The name means 'Gift from God.' Grandpa would call Grandma 'Hanna' when he was upset with her. We'll call her Johanna if we have a daughter."

"Johanna is a sweet name for our sweet little girl. Well, that wasn't difficult." Mark placed his hand on Sarah's belly, leaned in, and whispered, "Lord, please help Sarah have an easy delivery and let Richard or Johanna be healthy and whole. We have so much to be thankful for, Lord." Taking Sarah's hands in his, he added, "And please let the doctor get here in time." A smile lifted his face.

Sarah gasped as pain enfolded her entire body. "That is, if the doctor is available. He might not be able to come. And I doubt he'll arrive on time. Sorry, time to walk again. The pains are getting more regular and more intense."

After several rounds of walking and resting, Sarah's time came. "You'll have to fix a space in the wagon and help me up the step," she said between deep breaths.

Sarah propped herself with blankets. The pain eased off briefly, and they heard Jack and Lydia ride in dragging four tree limbs and with the saddlebags brimming with dry moss and twigs. "Good, you're back. Jack, can you get that fire going again, and Lydia, can you put more water on to boil?"

"Sure, Mark," Jack said, and added, "Lydia's going to help me build a lean-to with the cook tarp."

"You thought ahead. Good idea." Mark smiled, then glanced at his watch. *Only ten-thirty*.

Chapter Nineteen

"I'm afraid our baby isn't going to wait much longer." Sarah took in a deep breath, the pains more intense now. *But isn't this too early? Is it possible I misjudged the date? I could lose our baby. There could be complications. Please, God, don't let our baby die.*

Staying calm, taking deep breaths, and trying to stay focused, Sarah endured the intense pains as they swept over her in waves. They weren't close enough yet for her to push, but they were becoming more regular, reminding her of giving birth to Lydia and Jack.

Hearing the fire crackle, she asked Mark to suggest Lydia get a pot of soup going. When the rain arrived, at least they would have something hot to eat, and being busy would be good for Lydia.

Sarah caught Mark checking his watch again. "How long now?" she asked.

"Too long, I'm afraid, another three or four hours at the earliest. Don't worry, Sarah. I can handle this, so anytime you're ready, let me know."

Mark took her hand, and she squeezed hard to relieve the intensity of her pain.

"Quick, find the flannel cloth I bought for the baby quilt."

Mark searched in the sacks, found the piece of soft material, and gave it to Sarah.

"Mark, you'll wrap the baby in this cloth to keep it

warm." Sarah took another deep breath and exhaled slowly. "It won't be long and I'll need to start pushing. You must help me." Sweat beaded on her brow.

Soon Sarah couldn't hold back the overwhelming urge to push.

Lydia poked her head under the tarp. "Anything I can do to help? Are you all right, Momma?"

Between contractions, Sarah managed, "I'm fine, dear. If you want to come in, you can, but you might be in Mark's way."

"How about you stay outside, and when the baby arrives, you come in." Mark kissed his daughter's cheek and gave her a hug.

"Is your knife clean, Mark? Maybe we should have Lydia wash it and bring a basin of hot water," Sarah said.

"I'll clean it, Mark." Lydia held out her hand.

"Use hot water and clean the blade real good. Don't run, but do hurry," Mark said, handing her the instrument.

Back after a few minutes, Lydia said, "Here, be careful. The blade is clean. I'll bring some hot water right away." Returning seconds later, Lydia handed the bowl to Mark.

Sarah clutched the blankets. Intense pain enveloped her. The pressure became a force of its own. She looked to Mark for assurance. She was close to exhaustion.

Mark wiped the beads of sweat from Sarah's forehead with his handkerchief. "If I could take your pain away, I would."

Sarah clenched her fists, took a breath, and pushed. After a few more deep breaths, she pushed again.

"I see the baby's head! You can do this,

sweetheart."

Sweat rolled down Sarah's face. She was completely focused on the task at hand. Nature took over, and all she could do was follow its direction.

"That's it, Sarah! You're doing great, sweetheart. Another push should do it!" Mark coached.

Sarah took a deep breath, puffed out air, waited until the urge to push overwhelmed her, and bore down with all the strength she possessed. She felt the release as the baby left her body, and she breathed a sigh of relief. Exhausted, she gazed at Mark holding the little form. Expecting to hear a cry, she looked as Mark held the tiny life in his huge hands. "Show me the baby. Please show me!" Mark offered the baby, but the limp body wasn't moving. The baby hadn't taken a first breath and now lay blue and lifeless.

"No God, not again," she cried out.

"Quick, unbutton your shirt and hold the baby against your bare chest. Keep it warm while you rub it all over. It has to breathe, it has to live."

Mark had the newborn against the warmth of his body. He briskly rubbed the back and little legs, feet, and arms all wrapped in the soft flannel, repeating the words, "Breathe, come on, little one, breathe."

No cry. No response. *Will this precious life be taken from me too?* Seconds seemed like hours. Mark gently attended to the baby.

Sarah feared the worst. Instinctively she reached for the infant and, at that moment, they heard a faint mewing. The little body squirmed, and the bluish skin tone melted into the pinkness of health. "Oh, Mark, you brought our baby to life."

Then out bellowed a cry, and they knew the child

would live.

She held out her arms. "Thank God, thank God. Mark, please, let me hold our baby."

"Meet your mother, Johanna."

Lydia, peeking through the flap of the wagon shouted, "It's a little girl! Her name is Johanna. We have a little sister!"

****

Billy arrived in Dead Flats and headed directly to the doctor's office and rapped on the door, then read the sign, *Out to Eat.*

The sheriff, maybe he could help me find him. He tore across the street just in time to catch the sheriff coming out the door.

"Where's the doctor?" Billy panted. "Mrs. Hewitt's going to have her baby any minute, and we need the doctor."

"Mrs. Hewitt? Sure, come on, son. Doc's probably at the roadhouse down the street, or maybe at the hotel. You take the roadhouse, and I'll check the hotel. We'll meet back at his office." The sheriff slapped Billy on the back, and they took off.

Billy swung open the door of the roadhouse. "Is the doctor here?"

A man stood. "I'm Doctor Glasgow."

"My ma's having a baby, and she needs you right away," Billy said, and the doc gulped down his coffee and hurried to his office while Billy filled him in.

"I remember Mrs. Hewitt. I saw her the other day. I knew her time was close, but this seems a bit early. My horse is at the livery. You fetch her for me while I get my bag and some supplies." Doc Glasgow pointed to the door for Billy to hurry.

Outside the office, two men eyed Billy's horse.

"We know this horse," said one man.

"He belongs to a friend of ours," the other man chimed in.

"Not anymore," Billy said as Doc Glasgow stepped out of his office.

The two men left, heading toward the saloon.

Soon the doctor and Billy were riding hard, west out of town.

****

Sarah let out a sigh of relief as she held the baby close, then immediately counted fingers and toes and ran her hands over the rest of the little body that was warm and wiggling. "She's perfect!" she said, tears of relief slipping onto her cheeks. She took a cloth and cleaned Johanna and herself to look presentable for the children.

"You can come in now, Lydia," Mark said. "And Jack, you, too."

Lydia climbed into the wagon and asked, "Can I hold her, Ma?"

"Of course, dear." Sarah placed Johanna in Lydia's waiting arms.

"She's smaller than I expected." Lydia kissed Johanna's forehead and turned her to show Jack. "Isn't she tiny?"

"She sure is," Jack said. "I prayed the whole time, Ma. I prayed the baby would live this time, and she did."

Mark put his hand on Jack's shoulder. "Yes, she lived, and now you have a little sister. I know you and Billy were hoping for a boy, but a little sister is all right, isn't she?"

165

"Yeah, another sister is all right." Jack chuckled.

Mark motioned for Lydia and Jack to leave. "Let's give your ma time alone with the baby."

Mark sat beside Sarah, tucked a stray strand of hair behind her ear, and kissed her forehead. "We did well, sweetheart. We have a beautiful little daughter who needs her momma right now." He lightly placed his hand on the baby's belly and gazed into Sarah's eyes. "Call me if you need me. I'm going to have a cup of Lydia's tea. Would you like some?"

"Yes, and a bowl of soup would taste good, too." Sarah rocked the baby in her arms.

"When the doctor arrives, I'm sure he'll tell us everything is fine." He looked at his watch. "It's almost one o'clock. I'll fetch the tea and soup. You rest now."

****

When Billy and the doctor rode in, Mark looked at his watch again. "About three-thirty, you made good time, Doctor, but the baby was born more than two hours ago. They're in the wagon resting. Sarah will be glad to see you. Go right in, Doc."

"Is Ma all right?" Billy asked.

"We have a little sister," Lydia announced. "And I got to hold her. Her name is Johanna."

When Doc Glasgow emerged from the wagon, he said, "Mother and baby are doing fine."

"Good news, Doc. How about some soup?" Mark offered.

While Lydia dished up steaming bowls, the doctor took two jars out of his saddlebag. One held peaches and the other applesauce. Handing them to Mark, he said, "Here. I wasn't sure about your supplies and knew the children would enjoy these. They will be a treat for

Sarah, too." The doctor finished his soup and said his good-byes.

"What do I owe you, Doc?" Mark reached in his pocket, for his coin pouch.

"We'll settle the next time you're in town, but I will say I do enjoy pies and sweets." He patted his stomach. "I figure I'll ride into town in time to eat a late supper at the hotel." Doc mounted his horse and rode east back toward Dead Flats.

Mark took the boys aside and explained, "I want your ma to rest before traveling, so one of you needs to leave right away so the animals at home don't go without feed and water. If you go right now, you'll still have some daylight and can ride the rest of the way in the morning. We'll catch up when we can. Your ma may not be able to travel tomorrow. We may not get home for two or three days."

"I'll go," Billy said.

"No, I'll go," Jack demanded. "You rode to town for the doctor. I'll ride home to take care of the animals."

"We could both go and take the cows with us," Billy offered.

"No, the cows will slow us down. I'll go myself," Jack insisted.

Jack's face showed determination, but Mark asked, "Are you sure, Jack? You'll be alone until we can get there."

"I can do this, Father." Jack puffed out his chest. "Let me do this."

"All right, Jack, you can go. I'm proud of you, son. Be careful.

Lydia handed the bucket to Billy, to draw water,

and Billy said, "Yeah, be careful, Jack."

"Lydia, please fix your brother some food to take along." Mark helped Jack saddle Button. "There are apple trees along the trail. Feed one to Button every so often. No need to run him hard. He'll get you there in time."

"Tell Momma not to worry. I'll be careful." Jack strapped on his saddlebag and set out for home.

****

Sarah called for Mark to ask, "How are the children doing?"

"Jack's gone ahead to feed the animals at the farm. Please don't be upset with me for sending him." Mark helped Sarah sit up, tucking a blanket behind her for support. "Jack's old enough to take care of himself."

"I'm not upset. A little worried for Jack, but not upset." Sarah handed Mark the baby, who snuggled contentedly in Sarah's shawl.

The baby cooed, and Sarah's face glowed.

"I'm so happy, sweetheart. I know how much this little one means to you." She rubbed his knee and said, "I think I'd like some more hot soup. Please tell Lydia her soup sure tastes good."

****

Jack rode until darkness made the path ahead difficult to see. Not taking the time to start a fire, he hobbled Button so he could graze and fed him an apple he'd picked up earlier. Figuring he was within a half day's ride from home, he dug a biscuit from his saddlebag, munched on an apple, then laid out his blanket and settled in for the night.

The sounds of the wild were vivid, filling his mind with worst-case scenarios. He told himself, *I can do this*. This was his first night all alone, depending on nobody but himself. He was sure he could put the strange sounds out of his mind, get a good night's sleep, and awake refreshed and ready to take on the day. Then an owl screeched. Jack knew an owl when he heard one, but he moved his blanket closer to Button, in case he needed to make a quick getaway. After a few minutes, his nerves eased and he fell asleep.

Awakened by a noise, he was rested enough to continue his journey. Dawn was about to break as he gathered his things and hopped on Button. On the path again, he spurred Button into a jog for a ways, then eased off for a few miles. He did this until they crossed the creek on their property. He let Button drink while he splashed water on his face, and then headed home.

There, the first thing he did was fetch the bucket and draw water from the well. He fed and watered all the animals, including Button. Then he milked Daisy, giving Lydia's cats a few squirts into open and waiting mouths.

Inside he discovered the note Seth left on the table.

Please tell the boys the little dog did not survive. Honestly, the poor animal didn't have a chance. I know Billy was praying for a different outcome. Please help him understand we did all we could, but saving the dog's life wasn't meant to be. I fed Lydia's cats, and the rest of the animals were fine when I left.

Emily and I will come in two weeks to pick up our supplies. Emily said to send one of the boys if Sarah needs her sooner. Her bag is already packed.

Seth.

Jack knew how hard Billy would take the news, and a wave of sadness washed over him. Billy really looked forward to the dog being well, and this news would be hard to bear.

More at ease since he arrived home, Jack fended for himself with raw vegetables from the garden and cooked-up eggs for supper. He slept in his ma's rocking chair all night; just in case something happened, he'd be ready.

He tackled the chores the next morning and, with free time on his hands, set the snare behind the root cellar to hopefully catch a rabbit. He'd check in the evening to see if he had any luck. Maybe the family would come home today and he could surprise them with a rabbit stew.

The house was quiet, too quiet, and soon Jack got bored. He hoped everything was all right with his ma and the baby. Mid-afternoon, while Jack sat in the sitting room reading a dime novel he'd read at least four times, he heard the cattle and ran to the window. Billy and the cattle rounded the barn. Quickly, he put the note from Mr. Frazer in the cupboard so his parents could read the news first, then ran out to greet Billy.

"Are Ma and the baby all right?" Jack called.

"Yes, they're coming, but Mark's going slowly on account of the baby. They'll arrive about suppertime, and we need to have some food ready."

Chapter Twenty

The next day, the Dead Flats sheriff greeted the two men who approached him on the street. "What can I do for you, gentlemen?" He could smell booze on them and figured they'd come from the saloon.

The older man asked, "Who was the boy who rode with the doctor out of town the other day?

"I don't know his name," the sheriff replied. "He said he needed the doc right away."

The younger man raised his voice and added, "Well, he was riding the horse of a friend of ours. A pinto. He even had our buddy's saddle. I'd know that horse and saddle anywhere."

"What's your friend's name?" the sheriff asked.

The old man scratched his chin; the other let out a long sigh. They knew the man was a wanted outlaw, and they weren't sure if they should say his name or not, for fear the sheriff would ask for their names and look into their past.

The older man spoke. "We were wonderin' if you knew what the boy needed the doc for. Maybe our friend is hurt and needed help?"

"No, I don't think it's your friend the boy wanted to help. How long are you planning on staying in town?"

"Not long. We were just curious how the boy got that horse," said the older man.

"Is there anything else I can help you men with today?"

"No, guess not." The younger man glared at the sheriff, and they turned away.

"You could always check the hilltop cemetery for your friend. He might turn up there," the sheriff called to the men crossing the street.

"If Victor lives around here, he'll come to town. We'll wait around for a while and see if he shows up. Sure could use the money he owes us."

At his office, the sheriff checked his stack of posters, but didn't find either man who questioned him. The following day, the same two men passed his window, so he knew they didn't ride out to find the boy. He'd make sure to mention the men to Mark the next time he saw him.

The following day, the town undertaker loaded his wagon with the two men Mark shot. At the cemetery, the men were laid to rest with markers pounded in the ground, telling the men's names, taken from the wanted posters.

****

When the wagon arrived, Sarah carried the baby into the house, gratefully aware of the rabbit stew simmering on the hearth. She laid the baby on the bed and opened the trunk tucked in the corner of the room. The baby clothes were on top. She washed, then dressed Johanna in a clean gown before placing her in the cradle that Samuel made for Jack.

By then, the wagon was unloaded, and Jack and Mark brought in the pane of glass for the new window. When they unwrapped the three-foot-square glass pane, the family received a bonus. The clerk used a few old newspapers to protect the corners, and they would be able to catch up on some old news.

"Let's eat," Sarah suggested, "while the baby is napping. The stew smells wonderful. You boys may end up helping Lydia in the kitchen if you're not careful. After supper, you can each hold Johanna, if you'd like. I'm sure everyone is weary, and our own beds will feel good tonight."

****

During the morning meal, Mark suggested that he and the boys put all their energy into finishing the barn, at least to the point that when Seth Frazer visited in two weeks, he could help with heavy lifting and final finishing. Plus, Mark would welcome Seth's help installing the new window.

Mark looked at the children and said, "With only one good arm, I can do only half my work. Billy's still limping, so he's moving a little slower, too. If we all pitch in, we'll get the chores done sooner and give your ma time with Johanna."

Later, as promised if he won the gun, Mark gathered everyone behind the barn to practice shooting. Safety lesson first, then the features, loading, and shooting the new rifle. They each took a turn looking down the sights. Once Mark was sure they could handle the gun, they practiced until they could hit the large target at twenty feet.

Soon Sarah could hit the target and was confident she could defend herself if ever necessary. Lydia overcame her hesitancy and learned not to flinch when the gun fired. The boys got so good that Mark challenged them with a smaller target placed farther away. They turned target practice into a competition to see who shot best out of three. Mark mused, *There might be a three-way tie one day at the Best Shot contest.*

Mark placed the rifle in the corner of the bedroom, where the gun would be loaded and located from now on. Sarah dished up Indian pudding, rich with molasses, then read aloud the letters she received from Emma and her mother. With so much turmoil over the course of the last week, she'd forgotten to share the news.

"It would be so nice to go back east for Aunt Emma's wedding and see everyone again." Lydia closed her eyes and tried to picture everyone's faces and the old house they left behind.

"That's why we sent the photograph, sweetheart, so they could see us even though we can't be there in person." Sarah placed the tintype on the side table by her chair, so she could see her family whenever she wanted.

Lydia frowned. "But they won't get to see Johanna in this picture. We should have waited and sent one next July."

"We'll have another photograph taken next year, with one more addition." Sarah sat holding Johanna.

****

Billy had trouble sleeping that evening. The stagecoach robbery, the death of his father, and thoughts of Mark killing the two men for trying to steal the rifle kept running through his mind. Mark was a hero, just like the farmer who helped them during the stagecoach robbery.

Lying in the bed he helped build, Billy could no longer picture his mother and father and the home he left behind in Kansas City clearly in his mind anymore.

He wanted to go back home. No. He had to go back to find the portrait of his parents that hung in the sitting room behind the piano. Since Rusty threw the photograph of his parents in the creek, their faces were fading in his mind. He needed that portrait desperately.

I know Father told the banker to sell the house, but what about all our belongings? Were they sold too? If I could just get back there. Would my friends still remember me? How about my friend Lillian? Surely she would remember me. Our families were friends, and I liked her a lot. It's only been a year and a half.

Billy would talk to Mark soon. Confident in his quest to return, he'd make Mark understand.

****

After a week, all injuries were well on the mend. Mark and the boys were working on the barn every day, finishing the board-and-batten sides. Sarah and Lydia were busy caring for the baby, and everyone eagerly awaited Seth and Emily's visit to pick up their supplies. Billy couldn't wait to greet the dog they had found and give him a name.

Mark knew he needed to tell Billy the truth about the dog before the Frazers arrived. When the family was all gathered together, he read aloud the note Seth left.

Lydia had never seen the dog, but she started to cry when Mark recounted Seth's words, "I know Billy was praying for a different outcome. Please help him understand we did all we could, but saving the dog's life wasn't meant to be."

"I'm so sorry, Billy." Lydia stood and rushed to his side.

Billy sniffled, and tears ran down his cheek. Lydia

put her hand on his shoulder and patted softly until he suddenly jumped up from the table and ran out the door. Lydia ran after him.

Sitting on the back of the spring wagon, Billy said, his voice quivering, "I lost my momma and the baby. Then my poppa was killed. Mark had to kill those two men the other day. I understand that, but why did God have to take that poor dog? The little thing never did anything to hurt anyone. You'd have liked him, Lydia, even if he might have chased Muzzy and Momma Kitty. He wasn't much bigger than the two of them. I wanted something to love and be mine to take care of, to play with, and teach tricks."

Lydia took his hand. "But you do have something to call your own, Billy. You have the pinto. Pa said he's yours, your responsibility. You can give him a special name and take care of him and teach him tricks." She squeezed his hand.

"Yeah, you're right. Mark didn't know the dog died when he gave me the pinto. That horse is mine. Maybe I can teach him some tricks. But I still don't understand why the little dog had to die."

"You're right. Life isn't always fair. I lost a little brother before he took a breath, then my father's accident. An accident took his life. Nobody to blame. Things just happen. I was mad at God for a while, but God wasn't to blame."

Billy squeezed Lydia's hand. "Thanks for understanding, Lydia."

Lydia squeezed back. "You're welcome."

Chapter Twenty-One

Sarah had Johanna in a basket on the ground beside her in the garden as she picked the last beans of the season. In the distance she heard a horse snort and looked up to see Seth and Emily about to cross the creek. She scooped Johanna's basket in her arms and picked up the basket of vegetables, then called to Lydia in the house, "The Frazers are here."

Mark and the boys also heard and walked from the barn to the well, where the wagon stopped.

"You had the baby, Sarah!" Emily hurried to Sarah's side as she handed a basket to Lydia. "I so wanted to be here for the birth."

"She wouldn't wait any longer, Emily. And she's perfect. Meet Johanna." Sarah handed the infant to Emily. "The doctor gave her a clean bill of health. We couldn't be happier. Come, I'll tell you the whole story."

The two women walked to the house with Lydia close on their heels, carrying Emily's basket.

Inside, Sarah served tea and muffins made fresh that morning. Sarah recounted the story, beginning with the snake and Billy and ending with the baby's birth and the doctor's words, "The baby is fine." Lydia also chimed in from time to time with her account of the events.

"What an experience. One you'll not forget, I'm

sure, but some things are out of our control." Emily searched her basket, and handed Sarah Billy's shirt, now clean of the little dog's bloodstains. "I hope Billy can forgive us, but the poor dog was too far gone to recover."

Lydia spoke up. "He ran outside when he heard, Mrs. Frazer. But he's all right now."

****

Outside, Mark told the same story minus the delicate details to Seth as he and the boys showed off the progress they'd made on the barn.

"While we were in town, I bought a pane of glass so Sarah could have another window." Mark looked at Seth. "I sure could use your help. If we don't hang the window now, I'm afraid it'll have to wait until spring. The boys already have the pane framed. What do you think?"

"Sure, I'll help. Let's get started." Seth motioned to the house and asked, "Where's the window going?"

"Sarah would like the window on the kitchen side, to brighten the room. Boys, grab the tools. I'll show Seth the exact location."

As they entered the kitchen, the fragrant smell of simmering soup filled the room.

Seth glanced at Emily holding baby Johanna in her arms. "You look natural holding her, dear."

"I can't wait to hold our own child, someday." Emily answered with a smile and patted Johanna's back.

Mark fetched the framed pane of glass and held the window in the location under discussion. "Right here is where Sarah thought best." The outline was already scribed on the log wall. The boys brought in the tools, and the men got started.

Sarah bundled the baby in a quilt and offered, "We'll take Johanna for a walk and let you men work."

"We should have the worst of the mess cleaned up and finished before dinner. I'll keep the fire going to keep the house warm enough for the baby." Mark took the ax Jack handed him and started chipping away the existing wall.

****

The ladies walked up the knoll to sit under the old elm. Lydia picked wildflowers along the way and placed them on the graves while Sarah told Emily of the loss of her last child and the effect the bereavement had on her decision to conceive Johanna. Tears welled in both their eyes.

Lydia glanced at the two women crying. "I'm going back to the house so you can talk."

Sarah shared the story of Samuel's untimely accident and how they dug up the baby's coffin and buried the little blanket-wrapped form in Samuel's protective arms, giving her great peace of mind.

"You're a strong woman to endure all this pain and heartache in one year." Emily rested her hand on Sarah's shoulder.

"Yes, and Mark was right beside me giving me the strength I needed to make it through those rough patches. I didn't realize at the time, but I couldn't have survived without him. We're together today because we worked ourselves through our losses and realized how much we shared together. Our beliefs, our goals, and our dreams are the same. Mark and I were friends for years. He even spoke of marriage with another woman, but when we discovered we had feelings for each other, everything changed."

"You really love him don't you, Sarah?"

"Yes. I thank the Lord every day that Mark is in my life."

Emily sighed. "At first I wasn't sure if Seth loved me or if he wanted to fill a void after losing his first wife. Please tell me about Anne. What was she like?"

"Are you sure you want to know? You don't need to live up to anyone else. Seth loves you for who you are. I haven't seen him this happy in a very long time. I'm sure he's not comparing you to Anne. She was a good person, friendly and outgoing, just like you, but there's no need for a comparison. Be your sweet self and get on with life. Let the past be the past. You've got your whole life ahead of you, and now with a baby on the way, what a blessed way to start anew."

Emily sighed again. "You're right. Seth loves me, but he doesn't talk about Anne."

"Maybe tell him how you feel, that you don't mind if he talks about her. But make sure that's what you want." Sarah took her hand. "I think you're worrying for no reason."

Emily looked at the ground and then up at Sarah. "If he doesn't want to talk about Anne, I shouldn't force him." She gave Sarah a hug. "Thanks for another woman's point of view."

After their talk, they returned to the house for a diaper change and so Sarah could feed little Johanna. The men were making short work of the project, and with the fireplace glowing, the house stayed warm. Sarah invited Emily into the bedroom. The noise wasn't as loud, and they could talk while Johanna napped. Lydia stayed with the others, curious to watch the progress of the window installation.

Sarah was glad for Emily's company. She finally had a friend she could trust and share personal conversations, plus another woman's opinion and confidence reassured her. Sitting on the bed and talking reminded her of sharing talks with her mother and sisters. Now Lydia would also have another woman to talk to and share her thoughts and opinions.

"Please try to come over again before the snow flies, Emily. After that we probably won't see each other until you have your baby." Sarah patted Johanna on the back. "It's nice having another woman to talk to, and I'm sure you get lonely for conversation too."

Emily smiled and leaned forward. "Oh, I hoped you'd ask us over again, but I hate putting you out when we spend the night. And making you cook for extra people is a chore. I do so enjoy our time together. Next summer you and the family must come for a picnic."

"I enjoy our time together too, and a picnic sounds like fun," Sarah agreed. "Our little ones will grow up together, and I'm sure they will want to visit every chance they get."

Emily took Sarah's hand. "The men get along well, too. Helping each other is part of survival out here. You're better than a friend. You're more like a sister to me, the sister I never had."

Sarah gave Emily a hug. "Funny, I thought the same thing. I have two sisters. I miss them terribly, but here I never really had anyone my age nearby."

Sarah's eyes teared, which made Emily's eyes tear, too.

As they brushed them away, Sarah said, "Let's go

check on the men and make sure the soup isn't burning. I'll mix up the biscuits and when they're ready, we'll eat."

By midday, the men had cut the hole in the wall and set the framed window carefully in place. All that remained was to fill around the window with sod and stuff old newspapers in the cracks to help keep the air out. The boards nailed in place both inside and outside would also help keep out any air that could slip through.

After enjoying steaming bowls of soup with biscuits and blackberry muffins Emily brought, the men returned to work, finished the window installation, and started on a project in the barn.

When the men came in for supper, Sarah said with a smile, "Thank you, gentlemen. What a difference the window makes. The room is so much brighter, and now I can look out the new window and have a clear view of the garden and the creek as I do my kitchen work."

The sunlight illuminated the dining room as the two families sat down for the evening meal. "Now we'll save on lamp oil in both the morning and the evening." Sarah set the last dish of vegetables on the table, and Emily shared a jar of canned pickles and apple chutney as they sat down to enjoy friendship and fellowship.

"Now all the window needs is a curtain," Lydia said.

Jack added, "And shutters on the outside."

****

Sarah tended to Johanna while Emily helped Lydia with the breakfast dishes. The skies threatened rain. To avoid the worst of the storm, Emily hurried to pack the wagon while the boys carried several pumpkins from the root cellar and loaded them in the back.

"These should hold you all winter. Maybe Mrs. Frazer will fix you some pies," Jack joked.

"Yeah, and don't forget to roast the seeds, but be sure to save some for planting," Billy added.

"Thanks for all your help with the window and the barn, Seth. Don't forget, if you ever need a hand with anything, we're glad to help." Mark put his arms around both boys' shoulders.

Billy shook Seth's hand. "I want to say thanks for trying to save the little dog for us. I know you both did your best. I'm not upset with you. I was sad when Mark read your note." Billy looked down at the ground. "Another death was hard to take." He looked up. "I had a name and everything. I thought we could name him Lucky if Jack and Lydia liked the name. But now I'll name my pinto Lucky because I'm lucky to have my own horse, and I figure he's lucky to have me, too. I guess deep down I knew the little dog might not live, but I sure hoped he would. Lydia and I talked about the dog's death. She helped me realize sometimes things happen and we can't explain why."

"Thanks, Billy. We're glad you understand." Mrs. Frazer kissed Billy's cheek and climbed up to sit on the wagon seat.

"Please try to come again before the snow flies, or weather permitting, I'll see you sometime in March to help take care of the baby for a few days." Sarah waved good-bye, and Seth and Emily rode away.

Chapter Twenty-Two

Mid-October, Sarah announced, "The rest of the garden vegetables need to be picked and preserved."

The boys had been covering the plants nightly to keep them from the light frosts. This would be the final picking. They would cut the cabbage and make sauerkraut, and dig the rest of the potatoes, beets, and carrots to store in the root cellar. Everyone pitched in to help.

The sound of the new voice in the family rang out long and often, taking Sarah away from tasks. Lydia helped with Johanna when she could. Chores lasted long into the evening, but the children turned the work into fun, using teamwork. They even made a game of times tables and easy arithmetic problems part of the day's events.

Sarah, exhausted and ready for bed, said, "We have canned, pickled, dried, and prepared all the garden vegetables and herbs we grew. The root cellar shelves and crocks are full. Pumpkins fill empty nooks and crannies. I hope there's enough to last until our garden produces again."

But will there be enough? The new barn is filled to the brim with hay and grain. Will the livestock survive until spring if this year's winter is like last year's? All Sarah could do now was pray.

****

The corn was the only thing left to harvest after the last hard frost. The waiting gave Mark and the boys time to fix a few things before the cold and snow hit the Kansas plains.

Since there would be a few weeks before the corn could be harvested, now was a good time for Billy to ask if he could travel to Kansas City and see what he used to call home. He would assure Mark that he'd be back in time to help pick corn and cut the stalks. He wanted to return before the snow started. Already more than a year and a half had passed since he and his father left town. He wasn't sure what he would find, but he recalled there was a special girl in his life back then. He wanted to see if he could find her. Their families spent many hours together. Surely his friend would understand why he so desperately wanted to find a portrait of his parents.

He needed to talk to Mark alone, so he could explain his plan. Mark would understand better than Sarah. He wouldn't stay long, only enough time to see old friends and gather some memories. And on his way to Kansas City, he'd stop and give Elizabeth his letters. He had a fistful this time. Besides, he wanted to ask her father an important question.

Billy waited for Mark to fetch a bucket of water and followed him out the door.

"Can I talk to you for a minute?" Billy asked.

"Sure, what about?" Mark said.

"I'd like to go back to my home in Kansas City and find some of my family's belongings. My father and I left so quick, he never told me what happened to our things. I'd like to find my parents' portrait that hung in our sitting room. My parent's faces are a blur in my mind. I need that portrait to remember how they looked and to keep them forever alive in my heart. Before you say no, please hear me out," Billy pleaded. "My father was well known in town. He had lots of friends that came to the house. If I could find them, maybe I could find our belongings. I'd only be gone about two weeks."

"This trip means a lot to you, doesn't it, son." Mark raked his fingers through his hair.

Billy looked at Mark, his eyes telling the real story as he picked up the bucket of water.

"I understand your need to return home, but I don't like the idea of you going alone. I should go with you, but I can't leave Sarah and the baby right now. I'll talk with her and have an answer for you tomorrow." Mark followed Billy back to the house.

****

Before they turned out the lamp to sleep, Mark said, "Billy has asked to return home to Kansas City for a visit. He wants to find his parents' portrait, reconnect with friends, and share some memories. He says he desperately needs to find that portrait."

"Why, he's just a boy. To travel on his own with all the political unrest in Kansas wouldn't be safe. Does he have to go right now?"

"The portrait is special, like our new photograph. He's old enough, but I agree the timing is not the best. He wants to go before the snow flies so he can get back to help with the corn. He'd be gone for about two weeks, most of the time spent on the road. There are enough little towns between here and there that he'll be safe, and I'll give him money so he can get word to us if anything happens."

"Get word to us? Waiting for a letter or a wire could be too late. If he has to go, you should go with him."

"I can't leave you alone with the baby that long. He'll be fine. He really wants to do this on his own."

"Well, I don't approve, but you make the final decision. He trusts and respects you for saving his life. If you think he'll be safe and can handle this himself, I'll trust you too." Sarah kissed Mark on the cheek before turning on her side.

Mark turned out the light but couldn't sleep. *Was letting Billy go alone the right decision?* He slept fitfully, trying to come to peace with a decision he could live with. *If I allow him to go, he'd have to promise to be careful. He could be careful and something could still happen. The boy is smart. I'm sure he's seen more than usual while living with Rusty. But what if something happens to him? I'd never forgive myself. This is the first time he's asked to do something like this. It means a lot to him to find that portrait. By spring, who knows if he could still locate it? It will be two years next spring since everything happened. If I say no, he could go anyway and possibly never come back. I don't want to lose him forever. He's part of our family now. He'd break everyone's heart if he up and left altogether.*

****

Mark made his decision and told Billy in the morning he could return home on his own. Feeling guilty for not going along, Mark gave him ten dollars for expenses in case something happened and he had to send word, and Lydia fixed him food for his journey.

Billy packed and left right away. Camping under

the stars and being responsible for himself reminded him of his time with Rusty, when there were nights he was so cold he thought he'd freeze before morning or starve to death watching Rusty eat while he got to pick the bones.

When he arrived in Dead Flats, he rode straight to Elizabeth's house, desperately wanting to meet her father. He had seen Mr. Parker once, when Elizabeth pointed him out. A tall, business-looking man, like Billy's own father. He knocked on the door, and Elizabeth answered.

When their eyes met, Billy said, "I'm so glad you're home. I've missed you. I can't stay long, but I wanted to drop these off for you." He offered a stack of letters.

"You *did* write." Elizabeth gave him a hug and took the papers. "Wait right here. I have some for you too," she called back over her shoulder as she scurried up the steps, and she returned shortly with her letters tied with a ribbon. She handed them to Billy.

"Is your father home?" Billy asked, standing straight and tall.

"Why, no, he's still at work. Why do you ask?"

"I want to ask his permission to court you if you'll have me. I'm on my way to Kansas City right now to look for some of my family's old belongings, and I'm going by myself. Ma and Pa are letting me go alone, so surely they'll let me come to town more often to see you. You're not seeing someone else, are you?"

Elizabeth took a step back and cleared her throat.

"No. A boy asked me to a birthday party, but I went with my girlfriends." She took a breath. "I'm not seeing anyone."

Billy's heart skipped a beat. He put her letters in his pocket and took her hands. "Would you like to see me more often?"

"Yes, of course I would."

"Then tell your father that on my way back I'd like to talk."

"You mean it?"

"Yes, I want to court you proper, Elizabeth."

"I'll tell him."

The words were barely spoken before Billy kissed her, a kiss like the last one they shared. One he hoped she'd remember until he returned. "I have to leave. I'll read what you've written on my journey to Kansas City. They will give me something to look forward to each night." He kissed her check, stuffed the letters in his saddlebag, jumped on Lucky, and took off.

On the road, Billy spent one night in a small town when rain threatened the sky. The town didn't have a bank, only a few stores, a hotel with a saloon, and a stable. Billy was thankful the stable owner offered him a dry place to sleep, and he bought oats for Lucky.

Saddle sore and tired, he was able to arrive in Kansas City the afternoon of his sixth day of travel. Once in town, he and Lucky headed straight for the house he used to call home. The outside looked as he remembered, but the flowerbeds his mother once nurtured with pride were now a shamble. He continued down the street to find his friend's house. He and this girl were friends growing up, and her parents would certainly remember him. Their families were close before his mother died. They could share some memories. He found the house, but things looked different. When the door finally opened, he didn't recognize the person, so he asked, "Is this the Ross's house?"

"Yes, this is the Ross's residence," said the woman.

"Is Lillian home?" he asked.

"And who are you?" the woman at the door inquired.

"My name is William Paul Henry." Billy took off his hat. "My family used to live in this town, right down the street. My father was a lawyer. My mother died, and my father and I left heading west. It's very important that I see Lillian today. Is she here?" Billy asked again.

"Oh, yes, I remember your family now," said the woman. "You've grown into a man, Mr. William. Come in, please. Miss Lillian is somewhere. You wait. I'll fetch her."

After waiting for what seemed an eternity, Lillian finally stepped through the door.

"Billy Henry! It's been over a year since I've seen you." Lillian invited him into the parlor and offered him a chair.

When Billy laid eyes on her, he swallowed hard and did a double take. Lillian was breathtakingly beautiful. This was the same girl whose braids he used to pull and tease about her red hair.

"L...Lillian, it...it's good to see you again," he managed to finally say.

"Billy, I thought you headed west with your father."

"We left, but I didn't get far. I returned because I need to talk you. Will you help me? Really, I want to talk about when I lived here with my family."

"Of course. Would you like a glass of milk and something to eat?"

"Sure," Billy said without hesitation as they walked to the kitchen. "I've been on the trail for days so I could find an oil painting, the one of my parents that hung in our sitting room. Do you remember? I don't know what my father did with everything we left behind, but I am hoping your parents can help me. Are they home?"

"I remember the portrait; your mother's eyes were captivating." Lillian set out a plate of food and poured a glass of milk. "My mother's here, but father is still at work. I'll go get Mother. She might know something."

"Wait a minute, Lillian." Billy took her hand. "Tell me about yourself. What have you been doing the past year? Do you still play the piano and sing? I remember you singing in our living room the year before my mother died."

"Yes, I still play," said Lillian, "and I am seeing George Weber now. You remember him? We've been courting for about a year now and hope to wed when I come of age."

"Oh, that's right." Billy let go of her hand. "Your birthday's in April, on the twenty-eighth, and mine's the eighteenth. I always teased you about being ten days older."

Just then, Lillian's mother walked into the kitchen. "Lillian, who is this young man, and what is he doing in our kitchen?"

Lillian straightened. "This is Billy Henry, Mother. You remember him and his family? He would like to talk with you."

"What do you mean? Billy, where's your father?

Isn't Jacob with you?" Mrs. Ross looked at the boy's clothes.

"No, Mrs. Ross, he died over a year ago. We never even made Marysville before two men attempted to rob the stagecoach for the payroll and one of the first shots killed Poppa. This past year was hard." Billy looked away for a moment. "But I'm doing better now."

"You poor boy. I'm so sorry, Billy. Why, your mother Adeline and I were best friends. I knew your family well. I remember like it happened yesterday. Your mother died giving birth to a little boy. Her death hit your father hard. Jacob couldn't forgive her for sacrificing her life to save the baby. She loved that baby and knew he was a healthy boy before she took her last breath. The Fillmore family took in the baby when Jacob left town to relocate. He said he had to get away, start over. What a dreadful time that was for everyone."

"You mean I have a brother?" Billy could hardly breathe. He stood frozen in place. "Why didn't Father tell me?"

"Mr. Weston, at the bank, could tell you more," said Mrs. Ross, placing a hand over her mouth. "Jacob Henry and he were good friends. I'm not surprised your father didn't tell you about your brother. He couldn't stand to look at the baby, and the doctor removed him from the house the day he was born. Your father loved Adeline with all his heart. He would have done anything to protect her, but when she insisted on having your brother at the cost of her own life, I think her decision broke your father's heart."

"You speak the truth, Mrs. Ross. Father was never the same after Momma's death," Billy admitted. "That's why we left so quickly. I guess he couldn't deal with Ma being gone and the baby alive. Now everything makes sense. Who are the Fillmores, and where do they live?" asked Billy. "I have to see my brother."

"They live on the other side of town, on Pike Street," Mrs. Ross explained. "The house is on the left, with a big elm tree in the front yard. Why Mrs. Fillmore would take in another child when she already had two young girls of her own is beyond me."

Anxious to see his little brother, Billy sprang to his feet and asked, "Do you mind if I come back tomorrow and visit again, Mrs. Ross?"

"I'm free midmorning, but I have a busy afternoon planned," Lillian said.

"Thanks for everything, Mrs. Ross. I'll see you tomorrow, Lillian." Billy headed out the door.

"I have a baby brother," he said aloud over and over again as he rode Lucky to Pike Street. When he knocked, a woman opened the door. Billy blurted out, "Hello, my name is William Henry. Where's my brother?"

A puzzled look crossed her face. "Who are you again?"

"I'm William Henry. I was told you took in my brother when Father and I left town."

"Oh, my heavens! Well, can you prove you are who you say?" said Mrs. Fillmore.

"Ask Mrs. Ross and her daughter Lillian. They live near the West End Church. I was just there. They know who I am. Now can I see my little brother? What did you name him?" Billy asked. "Where is he?"

"Wait a minute, young man," Mrs. Fillmore said. "You need to talk to Mr. Weston, at the bank. He'll explain everything. He was a good friend of your father. Go see him. He can answer all your questions." She pointed toward town. "Yes, go see Mr. Weston. He can explain." Mrs. Fillmore closed the door.

Billy didn't have much choice. He had so many questions. He walked to the bank to find Mr. Weston. Luckily, the bank was still open, and Mr. Weston was there. Billy introduced himself, and remembered Mr. Weston as a friend of his father's who visited the house often. He'd always been pleasant, and Billy hoped he would have the answers he needed.

"Hello, Mr. Weston. I'm William Henry, Jacob Henry's son, and I need to talk to you."

Mr. Weston looked surprised to see him and immediately asked, "Where's your father, son?"

"Father is dead. Shot and killed during a stagecoach robbery." Billy recounted the story again. "The sheriff in Marysville said the two men were wanted outlaws. My father's buried there. The sheriff will tell you. He turned me over to an old peddler who sold his wares out of his wagon from town to town and treated me like his slave. He tied me to the wagon so I wouldn't run away." Billy rubbed his wrists remembering the pain. "Lord knows I wanted away from him, and I finally got away. Now I live with a nice family on a farm about thirty-five miles west of Dead Flats. I just found out I have a little brother that Father never told me about."

"I'm sorry you lost your father and for the last year you had to endure. I tried several times to find your father. I wired different cities along the trail west where I thought he might settle, but my wires were, of course, never answered. Your father had me sell your house and his business. The money was to be wired when you settled. Most of the money is still in an account."

"What do you mean 'most'?"

"Well," Mr. Weston said, and then paused. "Your father wrote up legal documents I'm holding for him."

"What else do you have of my father's?" Billy asked. He was desperate for answers and sincere about wanting to understand what happened a year and a half ago.

"Do you have a place to stay tonight?" asked Mr. Weston. Before Billy could answer, he said, "Come stay with me, and we can figure out this situation together. The bank will close soon, but I must finish up some paperwork." Mr. Weston gave Billy directions to his house, shook his hand, and told him to meet him there at six-thirty for supper.

Chapter Twenty-Three

A cold spell blew in chilly winds that reminded Mark he'd need to set a trap line again this winter. The pelts would fetch some extra money. He'd like to take both boys along this year. Jack went with him last December. Mark would remember that trip as long as he lived, and the secret he and Jack shared about a wet, cold, life-changing night that brought their relationship closer, ending with Jack finally calling him Father.

He was sure Billy had never been trapping and would enjoy learning. But Mark wasn't sure about leaving Sarah alone with the new baby for any length of time this winter. *Well, maybe a week at a time would be all right?*

As Mark sat propped up in bed writing a list of the things he wanted to finish before the snow started, he said, "I'd like to take Jack and Billy with me trapping this December. Just for a couple of weeks. We'd be back before Christmas. Selling the pelts would give the boys a chance to earn some money of their own."

"Are you sure they'll want to go?" Sarah asked.

"Oh, I'm sure, but we can wait until Billy gets back and ask them." Mark kissed Sarah goodnight, turned down the lamp, and rolled over to sleep.

****

After breakfast, when the children were outside doing their chores, Sarah, still sitting at the kitchen table said, "Well, I agree. You're right. Both boys will want to go trapping. I'll be fine. Lydia is very helpful. I can take care of Johanna and Lydia can get her Christmas presents finished. We'll have plenty of things to do together. You won't be gone that long, and the boys will need a break by then."

Mark ran his fingers through his hair. "They'll both want to go along, I'm sure, but we'll ask them. I'll take good care of them and keep them safe."

"I'm sure if they're with you, they'll be safe. You love them both as if they're your own." Sarah kissed his cheek.

****

Only six days had passed since Billy left for Kansas City, but already everyone missed him. *He should be there by now and getting ready to return.* Mark heard pebbles bounce off the wooden target when Jack released his slingshot. Soon the sound ended and Jack walked into the house.

Sarah looked up. "Why aren't you outside doing something? You're never in the house during the day."

"Nothing's fun without Billy here. I'm going to read a while." He grabbed a book from the bookshelf and slumped down in a kitchen chair.

Lydia sat at the table, sewing the lace she bought on the sleeves of a blouse. After all, she would be twelve soon, and she had to dress appropriately like a young lady. She took a few more stitches, looked at Mark, and asked, "When will Billy be back?"

"He should be home in a week or so. He's probably in Kansas City already. He needs a few days to find his parents' portrait, and then he'll head home."

Sarah looked up from her quilting, long faced and

eyes tearing.

"I can tell you're worried about him, Sarah, but Billy will be fine. I gave him a little extra money in case he needed to send a wire. We made arrangements that if he wasn't back in two weeks, I'd ride to town and check for news." Mark assured her, but Sarah's expression didn't change.

"I'm not sure we made the right decision letting him go by himself. Maybe you should have gone with him," Sarah said.

"He'll be fine," Mark replied. *But what if something did go wrong?*

To change the mood, Mark brought in a pumpkin from the root cellar and set it on the table. "Lydia, would you make a pumpkin pie for tonight? You're real good at making the crust."

"Sure, I'll make a pie today," Lydia said.

"And Jack, are you up for a ride to check on the corn?" Mark wanted to get out of the house, and a ride would do them both good.

"All right," Jack agreed.

"Grab the gun in case we see something fit for supper." Mark stood. "You can finish your book later."

Mark winked at Sarah. Keeping the children busy wasn't easy.

As Mark and Jack approached the fields, Mark said, "As soon as Billy gets back, we'll pick the corn and cut the stalks. We can use the stalks as bedding to help stretch the straw this year."

"I wish he was back already." Jack stared across the field.

"I know you miss Billy, Jack, and I'm sure he's missing us too," Mark said. "I'm sure there'll be enough feed for the herd this winter. At least we won't have to worry about losing any cattle."

"If only Father could have seen this year's crops. He'd be so proud. He always worried about the crops." Jack gazed out over the land he helped clear.

"Not only will the corn be ready to cut, but it's also time to round up the herd, make sure they're healthy, and see how many calves to expect next spring. The new bull was a good investment, and you know what that means—clearing more land and planting even more crops next spring." Mark yanked back the husk on an ear of corn. "Nope. Not ready yet.

"Let's take the long way home since we didn't see any critters on the way out. Maybe a rabbit or two, or a couple of ringnecks will give us a shot for dinner. We haven't had fresh meat for a while."

Mounting Button, Jack slid Mark's old gun into the scabbard. "Hey, maybe you'll win the rifle again next year, Mark. I doubt anyone ever won a gun twice in a row."

"I think I'll let someone else have a chance next time."

"I have two more years before I can try for the rifle. That's plenty of time to practice. Then maybe I'll win and finally have my own gun."

Rounding the corner of the harvested oats field, sure enough, two rabbits were not quick enough when Jack's sharp eyes caught them off guard. "Dinner tonight—rabbit." Jack jumped from Button and collected his prizes, holding their hind legs.

"Good shooting," Mark said. "I'm proud of you, Jack. I'm not sure I could have gotten both of them. We haven't had much time together lately. How about we take a whole day next week and go hunting, before Billy returns?"

"You mean it? A day of hunting, just the two of us? I'm sure Ma would like fresh meat for the pot."

"Yes, just the two of us." Mark grinned.

****

Back at the house, Jack showed the rabbits to Lydia and Sarah. "Are the hides good for tanning yet?" Jack asked.

Mark tugged on the fur and some came off in his hand. "No. The fur isn't ready yet. The weather has to get colder and stay cold for a spell. When the fur won't pull away from the hide, it's prime. Don't worry, Jack. There'll be more opportunities."

The pumpkin still sat on the table, and Lydia still sat sewing.

Mark was very proud of Lydia. She took on the household responsibilities since the baby arrived. She gladly took care of the cooking and the cleaning, but the laundry was never her favorite. At least that chore was only once a week, and Jack or Billy took turns helping if they were around.

"Did you forget about making pie?" Mark pointed to the pumpkin.

"Oh, that's right—pie." Lydia put away her sewing and rushed to the kitchen. "I'll have a pie in the oven in no time."

Just then, Johanna woke up from her nap and let out a cry everyone heard. Sarah picked her up, Jack prepared the rabbits for supper, Lydia started mixing the piecrust, and Mark took off his coat and hat and ran his fingers through his hair, still thinking of Billy. He prayed he'd return safely and be home on time.

Come mealtime, the rabbits tasted delicious, pan fried, and Lydia cut the pumpkin pie in eight pieces.

Chapter Twenty-Four

Billy's stomach growled after his long day. He hadn't eaten since before he heard the news of his brother at Lillian's house. He still couldn't believe the baby lived and his father never told him. He imagined what it'd be like, being a big brother. *I could teach him how to hunt and fish, ride a horse, and run a farm. What would Jack and Lydia think about having a brother? Sarah and Lydia already have their hands full with Johanna. I'll take care of him myself. He won't be a bother. Surely a one-and-a-half-year-old boy can't be that much trouble.*

With time to kill, he wandered in and out of a few stores he used to frequent and nodded to people on the street he recognized but couldn't recall their names. Passing his father's old law office, he remembered spending many hours after school waiting for his father to finish paperwork before they walked home. His mother always had supper waiting for them, and they would discuss the events of the day at the table. The shingle over the door no longer read, *Henry—Law Office*. Now the office was a shoe repair shop. He almost walked in, then kept walking.

He thought briefly about staying in Kansas City, but his life had changed. There wasn't any reason to stay. He liked his life with his new family on the farm and missed them.

At the stables, Billy paid Lucky's daily boarding fee and cleaned up a little. He walked to the Westons' house, and just as the town clock chimed the half hour, he knocked on the door. An older woman welcomed him, then escorted him to the parlor.

"Please join us," said Mrs. Weston. "I knew your mother well. She was a dear friend, and I miss her."

Before Billy could ask, Mrs. Weston said, "We know you have many questions. Let me start with your mother's death and your little brother." Mrs. Weston took a deep breath and exhaled slowly. "Billy, please try to understand your father's decision. Your mother took ill the last months before your brother was born. You may remember her in bed frequently, and the doctor visited almost every day. She became weak and had a difficult time. She held on long enough to give birth, hold her child, and learn the baby was healthy. She so wanted to give your father one last child, and she did, right before her heart gave out."

"I remember the doctor coming, but I thought he came on account of the baby, not because of Momma's heart." Billy asked, "Would she have lived if there was no baby?"

"No, Billy," said Mrs. Weston. "She would still have died. Her heart was too weak to support her. Your father held her hand up to the end. They loved each other so, and they both loved you very much. When your mother died, your father was so grief-struck he told the doctor to take the baby away. He couldn't bear to hold the child that your mother gave her life for. He said every time he looked at the baby the boy would remind him of the loss of his only true love. His heart broke when she took her last breath." Mrs. Weston's eyes teared.

"He had you to focus on. He wanted to give you a good education and hoped you'd follow in his footsteps as a lawyer. He knew he wouldn't be able to take care of the baby. Fortunately, the doctor found a good home for the boy with the Fillmore family. They had two girls and wanted a boy to carry on their name, because Mrs. Fillmore couldn't have more children. They seemed like a perfect match. They took the little boy in and now love him as one of their family. They even kept the name your mother gave him, Steven."

"Yes, I remember Momma said a boy would be named Steven, and if a girl, Victoria." Billy sat straighter in his chair. "But why did Poppa lie to me?"

"Maybe he didn't have a chance to tell you, or he might have told you after he had time to deal with his own emotions. Please don't say your poppa lied. We'll never know. He might have told you the truth eventually." Mrs. Weston took a hanky from her pocket.

"The day after your mother's burial, your father packed, and you both left town. Before he left," said Mr. Weston, "he spoke to me and asked if I'd oversee the selling of the house and his business. He told me he was moving west to start over. He would open his practice in another town where he wouldn't have to talk to people who knew his situation. He said he couldn't bear being in the house without your mother. He left with you on the stage without saying good-bye to anyone. He promised to wire or write for the money when he was settled."

"So you have the money from the sale of the house and Poppa's business? At the bank you said you had most of the money. What happened to the rest?" asked Billy.

"Well, you see, son…" Mr. Weston tamped tobacco into his pipe, lit it, and took a puff. "When your father never sent a wire, and I couldn't find him, I gave some of the money to Mr. and Mrs. Fillmore to help them raise Steven. They fell on hard times last year. Your father's money helped get them back on their feet. I didn't think he'd mind, since they were raising his son in a good home."

"I want to see him. I want to see my little brother," said Billy. "Mrs. Fillmore wouldn't let me."

"In the morning, I'll go to the Fillmores and explain who you are and that you want to meet your brother," said Mrs. Weston.

"I want more than just to meet him." Billy stood abruptly. "He's my brother. I want him to come home with me. I'm sure the Fillmores have been good to Steven and love him, but I'm his big brother. I'm his true family, and I'm not leaving unless Steven comes with me. You know Momma would want her sons together, even if Poppa didn't. Please make them understand we need each other like their girls need each other."

"Now, Billy, sit back down. You do have a point. I believe Adeline would want you together, but are you sure your new family will want another child to raise, another mouth to feed?" asked Mr. Weston.

"We won't be a hardship if you wire the money to the bank in Dead Flats in Riley County. Steven and I will be able to help with supplies and save until we can settle a piece of land of our own. I'll wed soon, and we'll raise Steven. How much of my father's money is left?" Billy asked.

"I knew you'd ask, so I looked up the amount before I left work. The account has grown to more than ten thousand dollars. That surely will get you started." Mr. Weston leaned forward. "I'll wire the money to Ogden, Kansas. The bank president there is an old friend of mine. He'll make sure your money gets to your bank in Dead Flats safely. With the money, you could follow in your father's footsteps like I know he wanted. You should at least consider college."

"No, I've already decided I'd rather be a farmer or a cattle rancher. I told father I didn't want to go to college. With that much money, Steven and I can have a good life. Now all I need is to find my parents' oil portrait. Poppa commissioned the painting for Momma for their tenth wedding anniversary. She cherished that painting. As long as I remember, the portrait hung in the sitting room. Do you have any idea where the portrait is?" Billy asked.

"The people who bought the house placed many of your family's things in the attic, waiting on word from your father where to send them, once he settled." Mr. Weston looked down. "It might still be there. Or, after a year and a half with no word, they may have gotten rid of everything. I hope for your sake they haven't. I'm sorry your life turned out this way, Billy. I know this wasn't your father's intent. I'll take you to the house and introduce you to Mrs. Myers in the morning. We'll see if she still has some of the items. Now let's eat, son. I'm sure you're hungry from your long journey and all the excitement."

Billy cleaned his plate, his mind spinning from all the information the day brought.

"You get a good night's rest, Billy, and in the morning we'll make our rounds," Mr. Weston told him.

Mrs. Weston took him upstairs to show him his room. Billy washed up before crawling into the big bed with clean sheets and soft blankets, a welcomed comfort after sleeping on the ground. The next thing he heard was a rap on the door and Mr. Weston calling him to come for breakfast. He dressed quickly, laced up his shoes, and finger-combed his hair before running down to the wonderful smell of bacon, eggs, and muffins coming from the dining room.

"Have a seat, young man." Mrs. Weston motioned to the seat across from her. "And how did you sleep?"

"I slept so good I forgot where I was when I woke up this morning," Billy replied.

"Help yourself. There's plenty of food, so eat as much as you like." Mr. Weston passed the muffins. "And then we'll be off. First stop will be your old house, to see if we can find the portrait you want so much."

Billy remembered he told Lillian he would see her this morning. She truly was a good friend.

After breakfast, Billy and Mr. Weston rode to his old house. Billy stepped onto the porch and instinctively placed his hand on the door handle to walk in as he had so many times before, then caught himself at the last minute and knocked. An older woman greeted them. Mr. Weston made the introductions, and Mrs. Myers invited them into the house.

"I've come back looking for an oil portrait of my parents, Mrs. Myers. I'm hoping you might still have or know where I can find some of the furniture, paintings, and the rest of the belongings that were left when you bought our house."

"Why, most of the furniture and the valuables we stored in the attic." Mrs. Myers motioned upward with her hand. "You're welcome to look."

"Is everything in the attic still mine?" Billy directed his question to Mr. Weston.

Mr. Weston said, "Well, yes, I guess everything is still yours."

"I had no use for the items and forgot they were even there." Mrs. Myers added, "Of course they're yours, Billy."

"Could I look now and see if there's anything I want to take home with me?" Billy thought of the stories he heard Mrs. Hewitt tell about the wagon train and how the things they brought from the east helped them get started on the farm. When he wed, the furniture and belongings would help him set up house. Everything legitimately belonged to him and his brother.

"I'd like to look for the portrait of my parents first, that hung in the sitting room. Do you recall moving the picture to the attic?" Billy inquired.

"Yes, I believe I do," said Mrs. Myers. "Let's go see."

Billy turned to Mr. Weston. "I might need to buy a covered wagon. Do you know where I can get one? I can use the money at the bank to purchase one, right?"

Mr. Weston answered, "Of course, the money is yours, Billy. If you want to take things home, you'll need a wagon. I'll check at the livery and the harness shop on my way to the bank."

"Good, I'll check with you later this morning. Once I have the wagon, I can start loading. I'd like to leave tomorrow."

"What's the hurry?" Mr. Weston straightened. "We need to talk with the Fillmores about Steven first. You can't expect them to just give him to you. This situation is complicated, and things won't be that easy. They've had him over a year now. They may not be willing to let him leave."

"Yes, they must. Steven's my brother." Billy wondered if they'd look alike.

"But Billy, you must be reasonable."

"I am being reasonable. He's my brother and he's going home with me."

The new owner, Mrs. Myers, spoke up as she led Billy to the attic. "If he's your brother, I believe he belongs with you. Now that's my opinion, but my opinion has carried a little weight in this town for some years now. I'm not acquainted with the Fillmores, but if they're reasonable people, they should come around."

Billy passed his old room with the door closed. "This used to be my room," he said, pointing. "Would it be okay if I look inside?"

"Why, sure." Mrs. Myers opened the door.

Billy looked in his old room. The furniture wasn't his, of course, and everything was arranged differently, another reminder that things were not as they once were.

"Come, let's see if we can find your parents' portrait." She put her hand on his shoulder and led him to the attic.

The first item in view when his head peeked above the top step was his father's desk. Memories flooded back to a better time, and he envisioned his father working late into the evenings, doing his paperwork while sitting at this desk. On top was the trunk from his parents' bedroom. His mother's father made the trunk when she was a little girl. His momma must have told him that story several times. So many of his family belongings he thought he'd never see again were now his. His mind swirled as he looked from one item to the next.

Then he heard Mrs. Myers call out, "I think I found it. Is this what you are looking for?" Billy turned around to see the woman holding up the portrait. Tears welled in his eyes. The blurred faces of his parents sprang to life again.

"Oh, yes, thank you." Billy walked over and embraced the portrait. Seeing his parents' faces made the journey worth the trip. Memories of the past year and a half flooded his mind, making him stop and reflect: his momma's funeral, his father shot by outlaws, having to serve as Rusty's slave until Mark rescued him. "My parents are with me again. Now I can see them whenever I want, and Steven will get to know them too."

Gaining his composure, Billy asked, "What time is it, please? I'm to meet Lillian Ross this morning."

"You best be on your way, then, young man. You don't want to keep a lady waiting." Mrs. Myers stepped back to let him by.

"Thank you for opening your home to me and storing my family's belongings. I'll be back later this afternoon with a wagon, if that is all right with you?"

"Yes, come back anytime," Mrs. Myers said. "I'll be home all day."

Arriving at Lillian's, he waited patiently until she arrived to greet him. Her beauty and fancy clothing surprised him.

"I'm sorry, Billy, I haven't much time. Did you find your little brother?" she asked.

"Yes, I found him, and I found the oil painting of my parents, too." Billy grinned. "Mr. and Mrs. Weston, friends of my parents, have been helpful. Oh, and thank your mother for me. I might never have learned of my little brother if she hadn't told me. We'll be going home tomorrow, Lillian. I wish you and George the best. I won't keep you. I know you have plans."

Just then a carriage arrived, and George jumped out. "Billy Henry," George shouted. "How have you been? Good to see you."

"Good to see you too, George. Do you still work on the family farm?" Billy inquired.

"I do, and we had our best year ever," George explained.

"I live on a farm now too. There's always something to fix on a farm, isn't there?"

George agreed and the boys reminisced for a while until Billy asked, "George, if you're not doing anything this afternoon, I could use a hand at my old house. There's furniture to pack into a wagon, and I sure could use some help."

George patted him on the back. "Sure, I can help. I'll meet you there. I remember where you lived."

Billy headed for the bank. *Oh, how different my life would be if Momma lived. Father wouldn't be dead, we would still be in our house, and Steven would have a real family and know our parents.*

At the bank, he connected with Mr. Weston and withdrew enough money to buy a covered wagon and a team of two good workhorses.

Mr. Weston said, "Come for supper tonight, Billy. Afterward we'll go to the Fillmores' and talk more about Steven. Mrs. Weston is there now trying to explain the situation and the fact that you want to take your brother home. But don't get your hopes up."

Billy made a good deal on the wagon and the horses at the stables and then stopped for a bite to eat at the hotel before taking the wagon to meet George. Billy carried everything he could handle himself to the front lawn. George arrived and helped with the heavy furniture like his father's desk, the dining room table, parlor furniture, a trunk, a filing cabinet, and some other odds and ends, and crates.

While carrying his father's desk down the attic stairs, a drawer slid out and almost pinned George to the wall. "You all right, George? I can't return you to Lillian all bruised and banged up or she'll never talk to me again."

"I didn't realize you were such good friends to begin with," George said.

"Now, don't go getting your nose in the air. Our parents were friends, and we often had to attend the same parties. I used to tease her, but that's all."

"Yeah, she told me the same thing. I just wanted you to say it. I plan to marry her."

"I know. That was the first thing she told me."

They smiled at each other. Once everything was on the lawn, they loaded items into the wagon like a puzzle, taking especially good care of the prized portrait.

"Thanks, George, for all your help. If you ever come to Riley County, look me up." Billy shook his hand.

"I might do that." George slapped Billy on the back and headed down the street to Lillian's house.

Planning ahead, Billy left enough space behind the seat for Steven and himself to sleep. He also figured he'd pack in that space the food and supplies that would get them home. He needed to show the Fillmores that he and his brother were meant to be together. Just because his poppa couldn't deal with the child was no excuse. Now that he learned the truth about his momma, Billy was determined he and his brother would never separate again. He sure hoped Mrs. Weston was making the Fillmores understand his love for his brother and the urgency that they leave right away. He promised Mark he wouldn't stay any longer than necessary. If he left tomorrow, he figured, he'd be a little late, but only a few days.

Billy drove the wagon to the stables, checked on Lucky, and left everything in the proprietor's care. Then he walked to the Westons' house for supper.

During the meal Billy asked, "Do you recall if I have any relatives? I don't remember anyone coming to the house."

"Come to think of it, your mother had a brother named Peter, Peter Hager. Your father didn't like him much. Called him a troublemaker and didn't want him around his family, given he was a lawyer with a reputation to uphold. As I recall, Peter was a bit of an outlaw and never settled in one place for long. Actually, this behavior started right around the time you were born."

"Was Peter older or younger than my momma?" Billy asked.

"About four years younger, as I recall," said Mrs.

Weston, "if he's still alive."

"How about Poppa's family? Anybody?" asked Billy.

"Your father was an only child, and his parents died young, leaving him everything they owned. That's how he got his start." Mr. Weston walked over and lit the fireplace.

"Now my parents are gone and left me a new start. I'm anxious to return home to the farm, but what about Steven? Did you talk to the Fillmores and tell them I would arrive in the morning to take him with me?" Billy took a drink of milk.

"I know you wanted to start back tomorrow, Billy, but to be fair to the Fillmores, I told them we'd come in the morning so they can meet you. They aren't sure you can handle the trip with a youngster. None of this is easy for them. They have to come to terms with the fact that they're losing a member of their family. Mrs. Fillmore wants time to pack Steven's belongings. She's not sure yet if she can let him go. She nurtured Steven as her own for over a year now. She needs a day or two to say good-bye. We'll visit tomorrow, and you can spend the day. You can't just walk in and take Steven. You aren't even sure he'll like you. Let's see how he reacts to you first."

"All right. But only one more day and then we must start back or I'm sure Mr. and Mrs. Hewitt will begin to worry." Billy cleaned his plate. "I guess it's best if I spend some time with Steven before we travel six or seven days together. I'm sure he can be a handful, and the trip home may take even longer if we have to stop to stretch and play every couple of hours. I better send a wire to the Hewitts tomorrow and let them know I'll be later than expected."

"I'll have the cook, bake, and prepare food for your journey home," said Mrs. Weston.

"Thank you, Mrs. Weston, that's thoughtful of you. I can't wait to meet Steven. I love him already and I haven't even met him. I'm sure Momma would want us to be together. You've both been very helpful. How can I ever repay you?" Billy gave them each a hug.

"Your father was a good man and a good friend," said Mr. Weston. "I'm glad to help get you on your feet. I'll wire the money to a bank in Ogden that I trust. You can stop there on your way home. You'll have to sign some paperwork once you arrive, and I'll give you a letter to show the bank president in order to release the money to your account. I've also been thinking about the route you should travel. It'll take a few extra days but will be safer with Steven along. You should stay to the towns and off the back roads less traveled. I've mapped out the route for you. We'll look it over in the morning and again before you leave."

"You're right, Mr. Weston, staying in towns along the way is a good idea. I'm going to buy a gun tomorrow to take with me. I'm a good shot. I'll feel safer having a weapon in the wagon."

"Your mother would be pleased to see how you've grown up a fine young man and so responsible," Mrs. Weston said with a smile on her face.

"I am proud of you, Billy. Your mother and father would be proud of you too, son," said Mr. Weston. "You've had to grow up quickly, finding out all this news at once. Maybe I should hire someone to escort you home?"

"No. I can handle a team of horses, I'm good with

a gun, and if anything happens, I can handle everything on my own. We'll be fine."

Chapter Twenty-Five

Billy awoke bright and early and was dressed before Mr. Weston called him for breakfast. Today marked one week since he started his journey and left his family. He admitted more than a twinge of nervousness to himself. Would Steven like him or cry and run off after they were introduced? Billy never dealt with any children before. He said a prayer asking for strength and courage, love and understanding. Today would be difficult for everyone involved.

After breakfast, Mrs. Weston and Billy walked to the Fillmores' house. Mrs. Weston properly introduced Billy to Mr. and Mrs. Fillmore, who greeted him politely and invited him in, taking him immediately to his brother Steven, who was sitting on the floor playing with a carved horse, cow, pig, and chicken; blocks were stacked in the corner.

When Steven looked up, Billy saw the resemblance right off. Steven had his mother's eyes and his father's square jaw, the same as he had. It wasn't difficult to tell they were definitely brothers.

Billy got down on the floor to play so Steven wouldn't be afraid of him and said, "Hello, Steven, I'm Billy, your brother. Our mother would be very happy to see us sitting here together because we belong together."

Steven was a good-natured little boy, bubbling

with laughter and excitement. Billy gathered a pile of wooden blocks and stacked a pyramid. Steven knocked them down and giggled. They did this several times as the Fillmores looked on.

"Okay, Steven." Billy scooted closer to sit beside his brother. "How about I tell you a story and show you the layout of the farm you'll come to love as I do?" Billy placed a block on the floor. "Here is the farm house. This house has only one level, with a loft where we'll sleep. Here is the barn where we keep the animals." Two blocks marked the spot for the barn. "The corncrib is here next to the barn. This is the corral, and here is the storage shed. A little stream runs right here." He motioned with his fingers. "In the barn we have horses, a mule, two cats, and Daisy, our milk cow." Billy placed the horse and cow beside the blocks. We also have lots of chickens in the chicken coop."

When Billy said the word chicken, Steven picked up the carved chicken and held it in his hands.

"I have a horse named Lucky. I named him Lucky because I'm lucky to have him. Mark gave him to me. My own horse. I always wanted one. He's waiting at the stables. I'll make sure you get a horse of your own someday, Steven." Billy smiled at the thought of them one day riding horses together.

A laugh escaped Mr. Fillmore when Steven whinnied like a horse and sat on Billy's lap awaiting the rest of the story as they played with the blocks and animals.

Mr. and Mrs. Fillmore in silence slipped out of the room to give the brothers time alone.

"When we arrive at the farm, you'll meet your other brother, Jack, who is thirteen. You also have a sister named Lydia, who is eleven, and a new baby sister. Her name is Johanna. You'll like your new family, Steven. You'll get to learn new animals. And I'm sure Lydia will let you play with the cats. You'll get to explore the farm, and you'll come to love it there the same as me."

The door opened, and the two Fillmore girls ran in to play with Steven. Time had flown by. The girls sat on the floor and played with their brother while Billy talked to the Fillmores in the kitchen.

"Based on what I witnessed today," Mr. Fillmore said, "you shouldn't have any problems with Steven. He took right to you. The girls are young. They'll miss their little brother, as will we." He gestured to his wife. "We took him in and treated him like our own. He's a part of our family, and I'd be lying if I said he won't be missed. But we understand you wanting your brother with you. He's your flesh and blood. He belongs with you now, but letting him go isn't easy."

Mrs. Fillmore dabbed her tear-streaked cheeks.

"I could write and let you know how we're doing. Would that be all right?" Billy asked.

"Yes," Mrs. Fillmore immediately replied. "We'd appreciate a letter from time to time."

"Well, we only get to town a few times a year, but I'll send one every chance I can," Billy said. "I promise to keep your memory alive for Steven. Do you have a family photo I could take to remember you by? A portrait of my parents was the real reason I returned home. I couldn't remember their faces and needed to find the portrait."

"Why, yes, we do have a photograph I can give you." Mrs. Fillmore retrieved one and handed the photo to Billy. "We had two taken this summer. I'll make sure to include one in Steven's belongings."

"Thank you, for everything. Is there anything else I should know?" Billy asked.

"Well, he usually takes a nap in the morning and afternoon. If he doesn't, he gets a little cranky." Mrs. Fillmore cracked a smile. "He really likes fruits and vegetables and loves carrots. In fact, I'll fill a sack with some for your trip home. Other than a cold, sore throat, or cough from time to time, he's very healthy. He is a good boy," Mrs. Fillmore said. "We'll all miss him, but I realize now you will take good care of him. He should be with you. You're his brother. I've been thinking about what I would want if my girls were ever separated. I'd want them to find their way back together."

"I understand," Billy said.

Billy stayed and played with Steven and the girls until time for the little boy's nap. Before Mrs. Fillmore took him upstairs, Billy took Mrs. Fillmore's hand. "Thank you again for everything you've done for Steven. Your love for him is obvious, and you've raised him well. Please understand why I must take him with me. I love him now, too, and will give him the best life I can." Billy gave her a kiss on the cheek. "I'll get the wagon now and pack everything, so we'll be ready to leave early in the morning."

Mr. Fillmore helped load Steven's things for the long journey home. Handing Billy clothes and toys made giving him away final. They shook hands.

Billy wanted to leave before sun-up to get a jump on the day. That way, Steven would sleep for a few hours. The girls would say their good-byes tonight, and hopefully leaving this way would make the separation easier on everyone.

Billy returned the wagon to the stables, checked on Lucky, and walked to the telegraph office.

"I've never sent a telegraph before," Billy admitted to the man behind the counter.

"Well, you want to keep the message short. Every letter counts," the man said. "The note will have the date and time stamped when it arrives, and if the person is expecting the telegraph, you don't have to include your name."

He thought for a minute and sent the following:

In KC/STOP

Leave tomorrow/STOP

With time on his hands before going back to the Westons', he took a walk to his old school, then through town, noticing all the changes that took place in a year and a half. He found himself on the front steps of Lillian's house, knocking on the door. The woman who answered told him to come in.

Lillian hurried down the steps and smiled when Billy looked her way. "I thought you left yesterday, after you loaded the wagon."

They stepped outside.

"No. I had to wait an extra day for the Fillmores to pack my brother's things. I stopped to say good-bye. We'll head back tomorrow. Hard telling when I'll be this way again. I wanted to thank you for being a friend I could count on. You have a good man in George Weber. Thank him again for helping me load the wagon yesterday. Living on a farm, you don't have friends around much, but you have lots of family support."

"Your life sure has changed, hasn't it?" Lillian

gazed into his eyes. "I remember coming to your house at Christmas. You would always tease me, but I really didn't mind. You take care of yourself, Billy, and if you ever come back this way, please look us up. I'm glad you located what you were looking for, and I am glad you came to our house first when you arrived. Do you have a girlfriend back home?"

"I do. Her name is Elizabeth Parker, and I hope to start courting her soon. Any advice for me? You know things girls like."

Lillian took Billy's hand and led him to the porch swing. "Girls like to be treated special. When you're together, she likes others to know you're together. She'll have her own opinions. Let her be right sometimes and make her own decisions. Always look your best, as she will for you. This is the best advice I have. If she's smart at all, she won't let you get away."

"Gee, thanks." Billy stood. "I'll remember everything you told me and do my best. George is lucky to have you as his girl. I better get going now. I don't want to take up too much of your time. If I do come back this way again, I'll look you up for sure."

Lillian leaned over and gave Billy a kiss on the cheek. "Good luck on your journey home." She turned and slowly closed the door.

****

Walking back to the Westons' house, Billy stopped at the hardware store and picked up a rifle and ammunition. He now had a family who loved and wanted him, a little brother to protect who would look up to and depend on him, and a wagon full of his family's belongings that held precious memories. This was his chance to start a new life. His thoughts turned to Elizabeth. They'd marry, build a home, and raise a family. He couldn't wait to see her and share his good news. He had already been gone too long. He knew the Hewitt family would worry when he didn't return home as planned. He hoped they'd understand when he showed up with his little brother. Once they heard his story, they would understand he didn't have a choice. After finding Steven, he couldn't leave him behind.

At the supper table, Mrs. Weston said, "Your parents would be proud of you, Billy, for wanting your brother with you. I know your mother would want her boys to grow up together, knowing each other, and being involved in each other's lives. You are making this possible."

After supper, the men discussed the route Mr. Weston laid out for Billy's journey. Billy avoided some towns on his way to Kansas City since he hadn't wanted to draw attention. Now, with a wagon and a young boy, traveling from one town to the next in case the wagon needed repair or Steven became ill would be best. Billy could buy grain to feed the horses and food would be easier to come by. This new route would take longer but would be roads a wagon could easily maneuver.

Mr. Weston stood and shook Billy's hand. "Here's a little extra money for the trip, and I promise to wire the rest to Ogden before you arrive. I trust that bank." He gave Billy a letter. "Make sure you give this to the bank president. Good luck on the trip home."

Mrs. Weston gave him canned fruits and some vegetables to help with meals on the road. The Westons' cook sent along jelly, breads, sweet muffins, and biscuits for the journey. Billy thanked the Westons one last time and climbed the stairs.

Crawling into bed, he prayed he wouldn't have any problems on the journey and turned in early.

****

Billy double-checked the wagon, assuring everything was packed, and tied his horse Lucky to the back. Just as promised, Mrs. Fillmore prepared Steven for traveling. "Here are extra vegetables from the garden. They're washed and ready to eat for your long ride home. And here is one last crate of things I found around the house after you loaded the wagon yesterday."

"Thanks, Mrs. Fillmore. I appreciate everything you and Mr. Fillmore have done for us." Billy nestled Steven in the special space he arranged right behind the wagon seat. Before pulling out, Billy waved. "Thanks again, and I promise to write and let you know we arrived safely."

Finally, the brothers' united journey home began. Billy had his parents' portrait that he so longed to find and a wagon full of his family belongings he thought he would never see again. He could start a new life, possibly with Elizabeth. He now had new responsibilities on his shoulders he never imagined, and getting Steven home safely was his first priority.

Billy followed the map he and Mr. Weston drew and knew the fabricated story he would tell if someone asked why a sixteen-year-old was traveling with a toddler across country by themselves.

Billy was familiar with many of the little towns he passed through, from when he traveled with Rusty peddling elixir. Some of the towns brought back harsh memories of days he would rather forget. He kept to

224

well-traveled, dusty, and often rutted roads so he wouldn't be far from help if needed. He figured the trip in the wagon would take a week or more, depending on the weather.

Billy dug through Steven's belongings until he located the photo Mrs. Fillmore packed, and showed it to the little boy when he cried. After a few days, the crying stopped. Billy found ways to entertain Steven in the wagon. He made up stories about Lydia's cats. When Steven refused to play behind the seat or sit on his lap while he drove the wagon, they'd stop, stretch their legs, and have a snack. While the toddler napped in the morning and afternoon, Billy took time, as they bumped along, to read Elizabeth's letters. When he wasn't reading, he thought about what he'd tell the Hewitts when he got home.

Every day the boys got better acquainted with each other and bonded. They did look an awful lot alike. Steven liked the songs Billy sang to help pass the time. They looked for animals and birds along the road. The food Mrs. Weston and Mrs. Fillmore packed saved Billy time, and he didn't have to worry about hunting for meals. Each day was a new experience. This trip changed his life forever, and he couldn't wait to get back to the farm to share his surprising news with the rest of his family.

The town of Ogden was the next stop on the journey home. Afraid they wouldn't arrive before the bank closed, Billy took shorter breaks and ate while riding in the wagon. If they didn't arrive in time, they'd have to wait until the next morning, which would put them further behind.

As he recalled the number of evening campsites

since he left Kansas City, and all the extra stops and time spent with Steven taking breaks and playing games to keep him occupied, the trip now extended several days past his originally planned arrival date. His family was sure to worry, and Mark would be riding to town to check for a wire. If he got to the bank today and sent another telegram, he'd get home in three or four more days.

Chapter Twenty-Six

Sarah worried something happened when Billy didn't return in two weeks. "Surely Billy should have been home by now," she said to Mark when the children were out doing their evening chores. "I know something's happened. Don't you think you should ride out and track him down? Aren't you even a little concerned?"

"Let's give him one more day. If he's not back tomorrow morning, I'll ride toward town and see if I can find him or find word if anyone's seen him. Maybe he stopped off in town to see Elizabeth, the girl he's sweet on, and he'll be home tomorrow."

"Well, if that's the case, be firm with him and explain he disappointed us, making us worry unnecessarily."

Mark smiled, and Sarah relaxed a little. "I'll ride to town tomorrow, sweetheart."

During supper Mark said, "I told your mother if Billy wasn't home tomorrow morning, I'd go to town and see if I could learn anything. He may have sent a telegram."

"Can I go along, Father? I'm worried about him too." Jack sat up straight in his chair.

"Sure you can, son, but let's pray he returns tomorrow and everything is all right."

****

Sarah busied herself to make the time pass faster, but she couldn't shake the feeling of concern. One day late she could understand, but she couldn't think of another reason why Billy shouldn't have returned unless he was hurt. *What if he's in trouble? He's alone, and has nobody to help him. Oh, why did I let Mark talk me into this plan in the first place? Never again. Never again will I willingly let one of my children go someplace alone and so far away.*

A somber mood surrounded the Hewitt family breakfast table the following morning with Billy missing from his usual chair. After breakfast, Mark packed his horse for the worst-case scenario of needing to travel to Kansas City, while Jack packed his own saddlebag for a three-day round trip to Dead Flats. Sarah fixed them both a cloth sack of biscuits and some vegetables from the garden to take along.

"If I have to go beyond town to find him, Jack will return and I'll head toward Kansas City. Either way, I'll find Billy and return him home safe," Mark promised.

As Mark and Jack rode off, they looked back to see Lydia and Sarah waving good-bye.

****

Mark and Jack rode all day, arriving at the old oak tree campsite with no signs of a recent fire. They filled their canteens and kept riding, putting them closer to Dead Flats every hour.

Jack sighed. "I hope we find him tomorrow. Then we can all go home together."

"I hope you're right, son. Your momma has worried enough."

They stopped for the night, built a fire to heat water for coffee, and ate some of the food Sarah packed for them.

"Let's get to sleep, so we can get up early," Mark said as they washed up in the creek. He let the fire burn out, and they crawled into their bedrolls, staring up at the millions of stars in the dark night sky before falling asleep.

****

At sunrise, Mark and Jack drew their jackets tighter and wrapped scarfs around their necks before heading east. As they approached the town's outermost boundary, they heard the Dead Flats clock chime nine times.

"The first place we'll look is Elizabeth's house. I'm hoping she has seen him. But if she hasn't, I'm going to have you ride back to the farm and tell your mother I'm heading for Kansas City to track him down." Mark rode close to Jack and tipped his hat. "It will be your job, Jack, to keep her reassured until Billy and I return."

"Elizabeth lives on this street. Billy described the house as a two-story, with a front stoop, shutters on the windows, and a painted brown door. Do you think it's too early to call on Miss Elizabeth?" Jack asked.

"I don't think so," Mark said. "I'll explain what the situation is, and I'm sure they'll understand."

Mark and Jack rode to the house, dismounted, and Jack stayed with the horses while Mark knocked on the front door. He took off his hat, ran his fingers through his hair, and waited for the door to open. Mrs. Parker, Elizabeth's mother, answered the knock.

"Hello, can I help you?" Mrs. Parker asked.

"Hello, Mrs. Parker. I'm Mark Hewitt, the father of Billy Henry. He and your daughter Elizabeth know each other from the Harvest Festival. Have you seen him in the last few days?"

Mrs. Parker said, "Yes, my daughter talks about Billy fondly, but it's been over a week since he dropped by."

"Well, Billy rode to Kansas City alone and hasn't returned yet," Mark said. "He's a few days past due."

"I can assure you I have not seen the boy, but let me call Elizabeth, and we can ask her together." Mrs. Parker called out, "Elizabeth, can you come here, please?"

Elizabeth recalled meeting Mark. "I know you. Your family adopted Billy. Is he here?" she asked, trying to look around Mark to see if Billy was standing outside.

"No, Billy took off for Kansas City on a trip. I just stopped to ask if you've seen him since he dropped by a couple weeks ago." Mark shifted his stance.

"I haven't seen Billy since he dropped off letters for me and told me he was leaving. He said he'd stop on his way back. He asked to speak to Father, but he wasn't home. I can't wait to see him again." Elizabeth tucked a strand of hair behind her ear. "So Billy isn't with you today?"

"No, not today. But I'm sure he'll be back soon."

"Good, I miss him."

Mark said, "I'll tell him when I see him." He didn't want to upset Elizabeth and waited until she left before saying, "Thank you for letting me talk to your daughter, Mrs. Parker. I must keep searching for Billy. He's a good boy. I pray he's all right. If he should stop by, please send him home. His mother is concerned. She doesn't need this stress now. Her hands are full taking care of our new baby."

"I sure will, Mr. Hewitt. And I'll tell Elizabeth if she sees Billy, she should do the same." Mrs. Parker turned and placed her hand on the door handle.

"Thanks again," Mark said and walked to where Jack stood. "No luck, Jack. I'm going to check for a wire and stop at the postal office before we head to the hotel for a bite to eat. I'll meet you there. If you want to stop at the hardware, you'll have time."

Jack took off for the store.

Mark tied Ruby to the hitching post. *I was a fool to let him go all that ways alone. I pray there's a wire. I don't know which route he'd take to come home, so I could easily miss him. I should have gone with him or had him wait until next spring. If anything happened...*

He arrived at the telegraph office. "Hello," Mark said to the tall, slim man behind the counter. "I'm Mark Hewitt. By chance, has a message from a Billy Henry arrived from Kansas City for me?"

"Why, yes, indeed, I received a message from Kansas City last week. I have it right here, but the message was only two lines. Nobody else has claimed it. This could be it," the man behind the counter said.

"I was taking a chance one arrived with news about my boy."

"Here. Does this make sense to you?" The man said, handing Mark the telegram.

Mark read:

In KC/STOP

Leaving tomorrow/STOP

"This date stamp shows the telegram arrived days ago." Mark showed the man.

"Yes, I remember I was just about to go get

supper," the clerk said.

"This message is from my son." Mark thanked the clerk and headed to the postal office.

A grin covered his face when the postmaster handed him a letter addressed to Sarah. She always loved hearing from her mother and learning of news from back east. After all the worrying over Billy, Mark was sure she'd enjoy the letter.

Mark met Jack in high spirits at the hotel. "Good news. We received a wire from Billy. He was still in Kansas City, but he's on his way home. He could still be a day or two away, so I'm sure I'll catch up with him."

After a quick bite to eat, Mark said, "I'm going to head east and should meet up with him tomorrow or the next day. You'll be all right to ride home alone, won't you?"

"Of course. I rode home alone after Momma had the baby. I'm not afraid."

"Good. You take the telegraph and this letter from your grandmother to your momma so she doesn't worry anymore. Billy and I should be home in three days, four at the latest."

"Here, Mark, take this. I'll be home late tonight or tomorrow morning and can fill up on Ma's leftovers. I'm sure she'll hold a plate. You'll need the food Ma packed more than I will."

"Thanks, son. This food will make my journey a little easier."

"I wish I could go along." Jack untied Button from the rail.

"I know, but its best I travel alone and you head back to protect our family."

"Be careful, Mark." Jack mounted his horse. "But Mark, what if you can't find Billy? Or what if your paths don't cross and he gets home before you? What should I do?"

Mark let out a sigh and smiled. "I'll find him one way or another. We'll come home together. But if he gets home before me, don't worry and don't come after me. I know my way. You and Billy stay home and take care of the family."

****

Mark rode east out of town. Riding all day, he stopped that evening beside a creek and watered his horse, filled his canteen, washed off dust from the road, and ate some bread with blackberry jelly that Sarah packed and an apple from along the trail. Once refreshed, he again rode until darkness made travel difficult. He hobbled his horse and lay on his bedroll for a few hours of sleep.

At first light the next morning, he traveled on. *I should catch up with Billy sometime today.*

Chapter Twenty-Seven

Billy drove the wagon into Ogden late afternoon in time to get to the bank before closing. He knew this town. He knew where the bank was located. He also recalled a roadhouse where they could eat supper. He entered the bank with Steven holding his hand; he approached a teller. Lifting Steven up and resting him on his hip, he asked, "Is Mr. Benson here? I must speak with him today."

A man stepped forward. "I'm Mr. Benson, and who, may I ask, are you?"

Billy took out the letter and handed the envelope to Mr. Benson. "This should explain everything."

Mr. Benson read the letter. "Dead Flats, you say. Is this where you'd like me to wire your money when I receive word you have opened an account there?"

"Yes," Billy said. "But a few weeks may pass before I can get there to open the account."

"No problem, Mr. Henry," Mr. Benson said. "Your money is safe in this bank. Have your banker wire me your account number, and I'll take care of everything."

"Thank you, Mr. Benson." Billy shook his hand before setting Steven down. "Oh, can you tell me where to locate the nearest telegraph office? Is there one in town?"

"Across the street and two blocks down." Mr. Benson pointed to his left.

"Thanks for everything." Billy and Steven walked to the telegraph station and sent word to Mark in Dead Flats that read:

In Ogden/STOP

Arrive two-three days/STOP

While in town, they would eat at the Main Street Roadhouse, down from the Ogden Bank. When he and Rusty peddled in this town, they set up their show near the alley next to the roadhouse, but Billy never ate there, of course. He still had money Mr. Weston gave him for the trip, so they'd enjoy a hot meal while they could.

Later, after traveling another five or six miles out of town, Billy reined the horses and wagon off the road. He unhitched the team, tied them and Lucky securely to some trees, and prepared to spend the night. Steven fell asleep, giving Billy time to think.

Finally, things were going his way. He would have money to buy a parcel of land, and he and Elizabeth could start their own farm. He mused about a beef ranch and clearing land for a big vegetable garden. Maybe he'd raise vegetables to sell in town. He didn't mind getting his hands dirty and enjoyed watching the plants in Sarah's garden and the fields grow. He could sell them out of his wagon like Rusty sold his wares. His family would have enough food in the pantry so they would never go hungry. Billy wanted his dream to come true. He wanted Elizabeth a part of his life and hoped to marry her when she turned eighteen.

Whatever he did, he wanted Steven with him. He would take full responsibility for his care. He knew his mother would want him to raise Steven, and he wanted that too, although he worried about what Elizabeth might say.

Thoughts were tumbling through his mind. He needed to sort everything out before he could start courting Elizabeth. He considered stopping in Dead Flats to see her, but he couldn't let his family worry about him any longer than necessary. He'd go straight home and see her in a few weeks, when he set up the bank account. He could talk to her father then.

He closed his eyes, thoughts a jumble, and he dozed off. He awoke with Steven standing over him patting his chest. Rain fell lightly. Billy lifted Steven into the wagon and hustled to gather their blankets and gear so they wouldn't get soaked. He heard the rumble of distant thunder. Getting home and not getting rained on at least once would have been too easy, he mused. Of course, the thunder appeared to be in the west, the direction they had to travel.

Steven fussed a little when he heard the thunder, but Billy assured him everything would be all right. The toddler played behind the seat until the horses were fed and watered. Billy filled his canteen from the water barrel and made peach jelly bread for the two of them, which would be breakfast. About to climb up onto the wagon seat to leave, he spotted a rider approaching.

He fetched his gun from the wagon and got out as the rider stopped in front of his horses.

"I mean you no harm," said the man. "I'm heading to Dead Flats. Am I on the right road?"

Billy recognized the man from the roadhouse last night. He lifted the gun and rested it tight to his chest and said, "You're on the right road. It's a good day's ride by horseback, if you ride straight through."

The man wore a long coat, had a heavy beard, and

looked tired. He said, "Thanks for the information." After he tipped his hat, the stranger rode off.

Billy thought himself fortunate coming this far without any problems, and he prayed this man wasn't lying in wait to ambush him up the road. The man seemed nice enough, just wanted directions, didn't even ask for food. Billy didn't want any trouble, so he'd be more cautious the rest of his journey.

A few miles down the road, the rain became heavier. Billy worried about possible holes in the wagon's canopy. Not wanting his valuable family possessions to get ruined, he stopped and checked quickly to make sure his prize possession, the portrait, was safe. Everything appeared dry for the time being.

Over a week passed since they left Kansas City. He was thankful the Fillmores packed all of Steven's toys to keep him busy on the long ride. Steven still asked for his momma and about his family from time to time, but he hadn't cried once today.

The rain let up midmorning. Both brothers were ready for a break. Billy rested the horses on the side of the road. Now only mist filled the air. He gave Steven a snack and took note that the food was running low. He'd build a fire tonight, if weather permitted. A hot meal would taste good after a damp, dreary day.

In three or four nights, if the rain didn't slow their pace, they'd be home. The road turned into muddy ruts, and Billy feared they might not make it as far today as originally planned. His family's worry troubled him, but the telegram should ease their concerns. He wouldn't be surprised if Mark was already in Dead Flats awaiting his arrival.

Chapter Twenty-Eight

Evening drew near and still no Billy. Mark rode hard and long every day, stopping at towns along the way. He'd check with the sheriff and leave Billy's description and information and then ride on to the next town and do the same. No one remembered seeing the boy on a pinto.

With little rest and less food, Mark rode into Kansas City on the fourth day. He'd eat and rest soon, but first he needed to find someone Billy talked to while in town.

Mark knew Billy's father was a lawyer. Someone would have to remember him. He'd start at the bank. A lawyer would've known a banker, for sure.

Walking up to the counter, Mark asked the teller, "Can I talk to the bank president?"

"Do you want to open an account, sir? If so I can help you."

"No, I need to talk about a mutual friend."

"That would be Mr. Weston. Wait one minute, and I'll see if he can talk to you."

"Tell him it's important."

Mark worried about Billy and what may have happened, traveling that distance by himself. Sarah would be worrying too. The entire family loved Billy.

"I'm Mr. Weston. How can I help you?"

"My name is Mark Hewitt."

"Yes, Mr. Hewitt. I heard all about you and your family from Billy Henry. He stayed with my wife and me while he was in town. His father and I were good friends. Come with me, Mr. Hewitt." The banker led him to his office and closed the door. "Have a chair. I assume Billy arrived home all right. Why are you here?"

"No, I haven't seen Billy in over three weeks. When did he leave?"

"He left over a week ago. He found more than he expected when he arrived. He learned he has a brother, and all of his family belongings were still in his old house. His father left them all behind when his mother died. Billy packed everything in a wagon and took his brother with him. Don't worry. I sent a man to follow him to make sure he got home safely. But he sent a telegram to let you know he'd be late. Your paths must have crossed and you missed each other."

"I did receive a telegram, but a short one that only told me where he was and when he left. He didn't mention his brother or that his trip home might take longer. Did he locate the portrait he so desperately wanted to find?"

"The portrait and much more. His wagon was full when he left. I assure you, he had food and money enough to get home, and as I said, I sent a man to keep an eye on him from a distance, even though he wanted to make the journey on his own. He's a brave young man."

"Yes, a man. Sounds like he took on a lot of responsibility. You say Billy has a brother?"

"You see, his mother died giving birth, but Billy's father never told him the child lived."

"It must have been quite a shock." Mark ran his fingers through his hair and sat back in his chair.

"To say the least. I'm sure the brother is a surprise for you as well. Let me pour you a drink." Mr. Weston handed Mark a shot of whiskey.

Mark downed the shot. "Well, I guess I best be on my way. I'm sure Sarah will be surprised when he arrives with a wagon and a brother. Relieved, but surprised. I'm glad to know he's all right. I still have corn to harvest and a good five days' ride to get home. Thank you, Mr. Weston. You're sure your man looked after him the whole way?"

"Yes. I paid him well, and I trust the man. Billy will arrive safely. Please don't tell him I had him followed. He so wanted to make the journey on his own." Mr. Weston stood and shook Mark's hand.

"No need to tell him. Thanks again, for everything you've done." Mark put on his hat, let out a sigh of relief, and headed for the door.

"One more thing," Mr. Weston said. "As a banker I probably shouldn't say this, but as you know, with all the civil unrest in this county right now, not every bank is safe. I'm afraid, with the talk of war, your money may not be safe at your bank in Dead Flats. You may want to keep some on hand in a safe place. When times are tough, banks get robbed, and I'd hate to see you lose everything Billy told me you've worked so hard to build."

"Not a bad suggestion. I'll have Billy do the same." He walked to the hotel across the street for a hot meal and thought about what he just heard. What surprised him the most was Billy had a little brother. He could only imagine Sarah's shock when Billy arrived with a wagon and a brother. *Heck, he could be home already.*

After finishing the last hot meal he'd eat for a while, he headed west, relieved to know someone followed Billy to make sure he arrived home safely. Now he worried how much of his life story Billy would tell Sarah.

Chapter Twenty-Nine

Jack rode until dark, slept until dawn, and got home in time for the midday meal. "Here, Ma, see for yourself." Jack handed Sarah the telegram. "And this came for you, too." He handed her the letter from his grandmother.

Sarah read the telegram aloud. A smile appeared on her face and she sat down in relief. She tucked her mother's letter in her apron to read later.

"Billy hadn't arrived at Dead Flats yet, so Father rode east. He figured he'd catch up with him in a day or two and then they'd come home together."

****

On the fourth day, Billy drove the wagon into the yard as Sarah stood at the stove preparing the evening meal. Jack heard the horses and ran out to give a hand. Billy was opening the barn doors to pull the wagon in when Jack caught up with him.

"What's all this?" Jack eyed the wagon and then heard noise coming from inside.

Steven poked his head out and smiled at Jack.

"And who is this?" Jack quickly asked.

"It's a long story. I'll tell everyone when we're inside. Can you help me with the horses? We're starved. I hope Ma made enough food."

"She expected you and Father today, so she cooked plenty. Where is Father? I thought he'd be with you."

"Father? I haven't seen him."

"Father rode out of Dead Flats four days ago hoping to catch up with you. We got your telegram saying you were on your way. What took you so long?" Jack unhitched the horses, led them to a stall, and gave them oats.

"The wagon and my little brother slowed me down." Billy untied Lucky from the back of the wagon. "Grab water for the horses, would you, Jack, and I'll start brushing them down and drying them off. Hurry, I'm hungry."

Lydia yelled from the door, "Ma said you have ten minutes and we're eating."

"All right," Jack called back and ran the water to the barn.

"I heard her," Billy said, and set Steven on the barn floor with a toy to play with.

"What's his name?" Jack asked.

"Steven. My momma named him before she died."

The boys quickly finished with the horses and the three of them entered the farmhouse.

Jack said, "Look who's home!" He stepped aside to reveal Billy holding Steven.

Sarah gasped and ran to give him a hug. "You're all right. We were so worried. And who do we have here?"

"His name is Steven, and he's my brother." Billy stood straight and tall. He set Steven down, who immediately walked to Lydia, raised his arms, and said, "Up."

Lydia couldn't refuse Steven's smile, and picked him up.

Billy said, "Steven, can you say 'Lydia'?"

Steven repeated a child's version of the name that sounded like "Lidy."

Billy pointed to Jack and said, "This is Jack."

Steven said, "Jk."

Billy stood beside Sarah and said, "And this is your new Momma."

Steven said, "Ma."

Sarah hugged Billy and kissed his check. "Where's your father? I thought he would be with you."

"I haven't seen Father. We must have missed each other on the road, but I'm sure he'll be home soon."

"Sit down and tell us all about your travels and your little brother." Sarah retrieved a pillow from the bed so Steven would be closer to the table.

****

Billy recounted his journey in its entirety. He spoke of arriving in Kansas City and learning about his brother and the Fillmores raising Steven after his mother's death. He recounted staying with the Westons and how they helped him find the portrait and his family belongings, and then the trip home.

By the time Billy finished, Steven was tired and ready for bed. Billy got a clean nightshirt from the wagon and took him up the ladder to put him to bed. The little boy fussed a little, until Jack and Lydia climbed in bed too.

Billy asked Sarah, "If you're not tired, could we stay up and talk a while?"

"Of course, Billy." Sarah carried the lamp to the table beside her chair. "Is there something on your mind?"

"Well, my little brother being here will change everything and mean more work for everyone. I want you to know, I'll be responsible. I mean, I'll take care of him, and he won't be a burden to you. Johanna takes a lot of your time, so I'll help out more. I can help wash clothes, keep Steven out of trouble, and pick up after him, and still help with all my other chores, too.

"Along with Steven, my parents left me the money from the sale of our house and my father's business. I have to go to Dead Flats and set up a bank account, and then the banker in Ogden will wire the money to my account so I can buy extra food or whatever you need." Billy paused and took a deep breath.

"You aren't upset with me, are you? I couldn't leave Steven in Kansas City. He's my brother. My momma would have wanted us together. I know she would. My father gave Steven away, but only because he loved my momma so much he couldn't bear to be reminded about the day she died, and he couldn't forgive Steven for living and her losing her life. But Mrs. Weston told me my momma would have died anyways. Her heart gave out. Birthing Steven didn't kill her." He brushed a tear away.

Sarah knelt beside his chair. "No, sweetheart, I'm not at all upset with you. We are your family, and Steven is now part of our family too. We'll manage; don't worry. You're right. Having a little one running around is different than Johanna, who is still carried everywhere. Steven will keep us all busy and on our toes to make sure he's safe and doesn't hurt himself. It'll take him time to adjust to all of us as well, but we're family. I'm glad you trusted your heart and believed we would welcome Steven into our home. Mark will be pleased, too.

"Why don't you go get some sleep? Tomorrow will

be a big day for Steven, with so much to see and explore." Sarah kissed his forehead.

"You're right. And I have more to show you in the morning. I want you to see the portrait of my parents." Billy stood and walked to the loft's ladder, turned, and said, "Good night, Mother."

****

After all the news and excitement since Jack and now Billy returned home, Sarah finally sat down to read her mother's letter.

October 2, 1859

Tidioute, Warren County, Pennsylvania

Dearest Daughter,

I'm not sure when you will receive this letter, but I wanted to write and thank you for the photo of your family. I think I have shown the photograph to everyone in town, and your father and I want you to know we are proud of you. You have a very handsome family. My, how the children have grown, and how nice to see your new son, Billy. I visited with both Samuel and Mark's mothers in town, and they agree the photograph was a pleasant surprise. They appreciated you thinking of them with your precious gift. I'm sure they will be writing soon as well.

By now you have probably added another member to the family, and I can't wait to read if I have another granddaughter or grandson. From the way you are carrying, I say the baby's a girl, but your father is hoping it's a boy for Mark. The baby will be loved and that is what matters.

We're hoping for a letter soon to let us know the baby is healthy and what you named him or her. I so wish I could be there to help you. I remember the feedings and changings keeping me busy with all four of my children. Remember to take time for yourself. Your health is important now too.

I'm sure big sister Lydia will be a help with the new baby. Please write and give us all the details.

Your father and siblings are all in good health at the moment. Your father is anticipating the Christmas holiday, and we have already started purchasing a few extras to make this a festive year. My shelves are full. Emma informed us she would like her soon-to-be new in-laws to dine with us for a meal. I'll write and tell you all about the outcome.

Please know I'm praying you have a perfect delivery and a healthy baby.

All my love, sweet daughter,

Mother

****

The following day, the boys took Steven along to do the chores in the morning. Billy set him down on the floor with an armful of blocks, and the boys completed their work as usual. They looked in Steven's direction every once in a while when they heard him chattering or the blocks tumbled. And then, when Billy looked after feeding the horses, he was gone.

"Jack, is Steven with you?"

"No, I thought he was with you."

"I don't have him, and I don't see him anywhere." Billy called his name. Nothing. He ran outside and called his name again. Nothing.

"Find him?" Jack called from the barn after searching thoroughly.

"No."

"Well, he's not in here. I've looked everywhere."

Billy ran to the well and looked down. No Steven. He ran to the chicken coop, calling the little boy's name. There sat the toddler, legs crossed, with a chicken on his lap, letting him stroke its feathers from head to tail.

"I found him," Billy called.

Jack ran around the corner of the barn toward Billy's voice just as Steven let out a giggle.

Billy picked him up. "Well, you're not afraid of the chickens, are you? Lucky thing that chicken liked you, or you'd be crying right now. They peck at Lydia sometimes when she gathers the eggs, and they know her."

"Let's not tell Ma about this," Jack said.

"Yeah, I'll have to keep a closer eye on him from now on." Billy dusted off his little brother, carried him back to the barn, and kept one eye on him at all times.

After finishing their work, the boys gave Steven a tour of the farm. He already found the chicken coop. Billy carried him around the house and pointed out the root cellar, showed him the well and explained not to crawl on the rocks. They showed him the barn, told him the stalls with animals were off limits, and showed him where he could play near the wagons.

"Watching after Steven is a lot of work." Billy exhaled.

"Don't worry. I'll help you, and so will Lydia. He'll get to know the place, and every year gets easier," Jack offered.

"But he's only one and a half. He's got a long way to go until he can do for himself." Billy sighed.

"You're together, Billy. Isn't that what you wanted? I can't imagine not having Lydia around.

You're Steven's big brother. He'll look up to you."

"Yeah, I know. We're all family, and that's why I brought him home with me." Billy set Steven on the ground and took his hand to let him walk.

"You just said we're all family," Jack reminded him. "We'll all help take care of him."

****

While Steven and Johanna were napping, and Jack and Lydia were outside doing the wash, Sarah said to Billy, "You told me about your mother's death, but you never talk about your father. I realize you may be angry with him for not telling you about your little brother, but you've never told me anything about your father."

"My father was a good man. He was a lawyer back in Kansas City. He wanted me to become a lawyer too, but I never liked the idea. He wanted me to go to college and follow in his footsteps. That day, when we were on the stage, I told him I didn't want to be a lawyer. He was upset, said we'd talk later, but later never came. He died that day."

"I know your father was shot during an attempted stagecoach robbery. Mark told me about the sheriff giving you to a peddler." Sarah leaned forward.

"Yeah, he was shot by one of the outlaws. But the man who saved me was a farmer. At least that's what the driver called him. I don't know his name. Then the sheriff gave me to Rusty, who didn't treat me very good. I didn't like him. I sure was glad when Mark rescued me. I never met him before, but for some reason I trusted him after we talked a while. I almost didn't come here, but Mark told me about his family and the farm. He said you didn't own any slaves, that you worked the land yourself. By the time we arrived, I already knew all about you. Mark talked the whole way home about his family and the farm, so I thought I'd give farming a try, and here I am." Billy stood. "I should probably go help Jack chop some kindling wood."

"So Mark saved your life getting you away from Rusty?" Sarah awaited the answer.

"I wouldn't be here today if he hadn't gotten me away from him." Billy walked to the door.

"Well, I'm glad you're here with us, and I'm glad you found Steven and brought him home, too." Sarah leaned back in her chair, and Billy walked out to help Jack.

Sarah thought long and hard about what Billy said. *"I was glad when Mark rescued me. I never met him before, but for some reason I trusted him."* Did Billy misspeak? Didn't he remember Mark from the stage holdup the year before?

Chapter Thirty

Mark took the same roads back to Dead Flats, stopping only twice for hot meals and to feed and water Ruby. Darkness covered the street when he rode straight through town trying to get home to Sarah and his family so their worry and concern would end.

When he arrived at the old oak campsite his family always used, he stopped and took a short sleep. Awake and on the road before dawn, his thoughts turned to what he'd tell Sarah if Billy revealed the true story about the stagecoach robbery. No good answer came to mind. He rode all day and arrived home in time for supper.

Sarah ran out to greet him. If Mark hadn't heard about Billy's brother, she would tell him. And if Mark already knew, she would explain she was fine with them both staying.

Mark no more than got off Ruby before Sarah plunged into his arms. They embraced as if they hadn't seen each other for months instead of days.

Mark whispered, "I love you, Sarah," and gave her a warm kiss.

Sarah responded, "Where have you been? I've been worried. And there is something I must tell you before we go in the house."

"I've been to Kansas City, and I already know about Billy's little brother. I talked to a friend of the family, who told me the whole story." Mark hugged her again.

"They're both our family now." Sarah laid her head on his chest.

"I agree, and I'm glad you understand. I knew you'd accept them. They need us." Mark placed his hand on Sarah's back and drew her close. "Our family just keeps on growing." He chuckled.

"You must be hungry. Come in and meet the newest member of our family as soon as you're done in the barn." Sarah turned when the door opened. There stood Jack, standing beside Lydia holding Johanna's basket and Billy with his brother Steven in his arms.

"I'll give you a hand with Ruby, Father." Jack ran out to help.

****

The table was laden with food, and all six chairs were full for the first time as the Hewitt family enjoyed their first meal together, with little Johanna sleeping peacefully in her cradle, near the hearth.

Mark recounted his travels and welcomed Steven to the family. Thankfully, everything worked out for the best.

After supper and the dishes were done, Lydia served apple pie.

Mark yawned. "Everyone needs a good night's sleep, because tomorrow we start on the cornfield."

"Jack and I checked the field yesterday, and it's ready to pick," Billy said.

"We escaped the drought they predicted this year," Jack noted. "I'm sorry for the townspeople and farmers who left the area fearing they wouldn't survive the predicted drought. We had a good crop year. Even our pumpkins grew bigger than usual. We'll have to plant more to sell next year."

Billy put Steven to bed and showed Mark his parents' portrait and the photo of the Fillmores, then shared some details about his trip, including the money waiting at the Ogden bank.

****

As promised, the following day Mark and the boys started on the cornfield. After almost a week of picking the corn, and another week and a half cutting the stalks and hauling everything to the barn, the corn filled the corncrib and the task was completed. Thankfully, everything was out of the field before a heavy rain let loose and turned the field into mud.

The following week, Mark and Billy left for town to take care of Billy's bank account arrangements. Minding Mr. Weston's advice, they both took half of their money home, where they would find a good place to hide and keep the money safe.

Billy then headed to the Cattlemen's Association office to talk to Mr. Parker, Elizabeth's father. He introduced himself, shook hands, and asked for a moment of Mr. Parker's time.

"I know who you are," Mr. Parker said. "I'm glad to see you're back from Kansas City. Have you stopped to see my daughter yet?"

"No, sir. I wanted to talk to you first. I'd like your permission to court Elizabeth." Billy stood straight and tall.

"Well, it's good to finally meet you. Elizabeth tells me you live with the Hewitt family." Mr. Parker looked him up and down.

The stare Billy received penetrated his soul, but he

held his ground. "Yes, sir, that's right. We had a good year and just finished harvesting our corn."

"I appreciate a man who's not afraid of a little physical labor. Farmers and ranchers keep this county growing. How often do you intend on visiting?"

"As often as I can, sir. I mean, with winter coming, I won't get to town as often, and not much during the planting and harvest seasons, but other than that, as often as possible."

"Well, Billy, if courting you is what my daughter wants, I'll agree."

"I plan to go talk to her right now, sir. I have lots of news to share with her. Thank you, Mr. Parker. I'll never do anything to harm your daughter."

"If you do, son, you'll answer to me."

"Yes, sir. Thank you again. You have a good day."

Billy hightailed it out of there so fast he didn't remember closing the door. He walked to the hardware store to meet up with Mark.

"What'd he say?" Mark asked.

"He said yes, I can court Elizabeth. I'm going over there now. Don't worry, I'm not going to mention the money my folks left me, but I am going to tell her about my brother and finding my parents' portrait. I'll meet you at the hotel at twelve-thirty."

"All right, but not a minute later. We need to head home tonight." Mark shook Billy's hand. "This is a big step for you, son. I hope everything goes the way you want."

Billy shook Mark's hand and said, "Thanks, Father." Then he took off down the street to Elizabeth's house.

Chapter Thirty-One

Mrs. Parker answered the door.

"Hello, Mrs. Parker, is Elizabeth home?" Billy said politely.

When Elizabeth heard his voice from the top of the stairs she ran down into his arms. "You're back. I worried you might not return from Kansas City. Mr. Hewitt stopped here a few weeks ago and asked if I'd seen you. What took you so long?"

Billy held her tight, picked her up off her feet, and swung her around. "It's a long story, and I don't have a lot of time, but let me start by saying I talked to your father and asked his permission to court you, and he said yes." He kissed her tenderly and set her back on her feet.

Mrs. Parker gave them time alone.

"Billy, that's wonderful." Elizabeth squeezed his hands. "I figured he would. My momma really likes you, and I think she talked Poppa into saying yes."

"I told him I'd treat you real good, and I mean it. I may not be here for every party or event, and if you want to go with friends, I want you to go, as long as it's not with another man."

"Don't worry. You're the only man I want. Now tell me what happened in Kansas City." Elizabeth led him to the parlor, and they sat on the settee together.

"Well, I found what I went searching for. I found

my parents' portrait. The woman who bought our house put all the furniture and things in the attic. She was real nice. She even let me look in my old bedroom, but nothing looked the same. I can't wait to show you the oil painting. I also brought back a wagon full of furniture and some of my old belongings.

"I met up with old friends, and my friend George Weber helped me pack the wagon. The town looked a little different after a year and a half. Town life isn't for me anymore. Farm life is much better."

Elizabeth interjected, "I've never spent much time on a farm. In fact, I've only ridden past a few. Father talks about when he grew up on a farm, but when he and Momma got married, they bought this house and Pa got into the cattle buying and selling business," Elizabeth shared. "I'll have to talk to him about living on a farm."

"I'm sure he'll tell you farming is a lot of work, but you're working for yourself and your survival depends on everything you do. You'll see. You can come visit and stay with me on the Hewitt farm next summer for a few weeks. Then you'll see firsthand what I mean.

"Oh, and back to my trip. I also found something I didn't know I had. You won't believe this. I didn't at first either."

"Well, tell me!" Elizabeth's eyes opened wide.

"I have a little brother."

"A real live little brother, and you didn't know?"

"My momma had the baby and then she died. I always thought the baby died, too. Poppa was devastated when he lost Momma, and he took us out of town as soon as possible. We were on our way to Colorado when the stagecoach holdup I told you about happened. He never told me that the baby actually lived. Poppa couldn't bear to look at the child after Momma gave her life in order to have the baby. Wait until you meet him. We look a lot alike."

"Oh, my, that must have been a surprise." Elizabeth turned toward him and gave him a hug.

"I'd say more than a surprise. A shock, surprise, and delight, all wrapped in one. I didn't think the Fillmores, who were taking care of him, were going to let me have him, but they came around. I brought him home with me, too. His name is Steven."

"You mean you brought your little brother, Steven, back with you to the farm?"

"I didn't have a choice. I knew Momma would have wanted us to grow up together, even if Poppa couldn't bear to take the baby with us."

"How did the Hewitts feel about another small child? Didn't Mrs. Hewitt just have a baby?"

"Yes, she had a baby girl named Johanna. We all have our hands full. You can't turn your back for a second or Steven is into something. But he's learning. Mother says it'll take time for him to get to know us and to explore the farm. He really likes the chickens."

"My, you had quite an interesting trip to Kansas City. Just think if you'd never gone back."

"I know. And I realize this is a lot of information."

"When do you think you'll get to town again? I don't imagine you had time to write any letters or read any of mine."

"I read a few of yours on my ride home, when Steven napped, but I didn't have a chance to write one."

"I have some for you." She ran to retrieve them and Billy stuffed them in his coat pocket.

"I promise to write and tell you everything. I've been thinking about our future." Billy took her hands. Then he heard the clock chime the half-past mark. "I'm sorry. I have to hurry to meet Father. We're getting a head start on our trip home so Mother isn't alone. Well, she's not alone, but Father hates being away too long."

Billy took her in his arms and kissed her, leaving her almost breathless. This was the kiss she longed for. His kisses stirred her heart.

"You've given me lots to think about, Billy."

"I'll be back at least once before the snow flies. I'll find some excuse to get away for a day, but I don't know when." Billy took her hands in his and looked into her eyes. "I'll see you soon." He kissed her forehead and dashed out the door.

Chapter Thirty-Two

Billy and Mark arrived at the farm the next morning. As Billy dismounted, he heard the house door slam and saw Steven run toward him.

Billy picked up his brother, twirled him around, and carried him while he led Lucky into the barn. He then said to Mark, "It's a good feeling being missed by someone you love, isn't it, Father? Maybe this means Steven is accepting me as his brother." Billy put Steven in an empty stall to play while the men unsaddled their horses.

"Yes, the best feeling ever. You and your brother share a special bond that can never be broken. You may have your disagreements throughout life, but you'll always be brothers and you'll both always be a part of the Hewitt family." While brushing down Ruby, Mark said, "I'm glad you brought Steven home. It's a man's commitment.

"Asking Mr. Parker to court Elizabeth is also a commitment you mustn't take lightly. If you think she's the helpmate for your life, your relationship will take time to grow into certainty." Mark fed the horses while Billy hung up the bridles and saddles. "With Steven and your responsibilities on the farm, you may not always get to town when you want. But you'll work things out somehow. I'm proud of you, son." Mark patted his shoulder.

"Thanks. That means a lot, Father."

Finished with their chores, the two men and little boy headed to the house. Mark carried a package of fabric and yarn he picked up in town in case anyone in the family, especially the two newest members, needed new clothes between now and next spring.

Inside, Jack was busy cutting vegetables, Lydia kneaded bread, and Sarah sat near the hearth feeding Johanna. Billy chuckled at the sight of Jack wearing one of his mother's aprons.

"Wait until you have to do the vegetables." Jack snickered. "Momma says everyone has to help pitch in with additional chores."

"Boy, are we glad you're back." Lydia looked at Billy. "Steven really missed you. Did everything go all right in town?"

"Everything went great." Billy set his brother down to play, but the toddler immediately stretched out his hands and said, "Up."

"Mr. Parker agreed to let me court Elizabeth. I told her about finding the portrait. She's happy for me. Then I told her all about Steven. She sure was surprised. I know in time she'll come to love him too."

****

After supper, Lydia took Steven to the loft to read stories before bed. The boys headed to the barn to talk more about what happened in town. Mark fixed Sarah a cup of tea, and they sat at the kitchen table to talk.

"I took half of our savings out of the bank today, and Billy brought half of his home, too. The banker in Kansas City recommended we take precautions. He said with all the civil unrest, the bank may not be the best place for our money right now. We'll find a safe place tomorrow. What would you say if I carved a cross for Billy's parents and we bury the money up under the old elm tree? Then Billy would have a place to visit and to talk to his parents."

"I love the idea. You can talk to Billy tomorrow and see what he thinks. You know, I hate the thought," Sarah said, "but war could happen all too soon. The conflict will divide this country and make people take sides against one another. Fighting could reach our farm and we might be forced to leave. Mark, I worry for our children. I'm afraid for our lives."

"I don't think anything will happen until after the presidential election, but it's best to be prepared. And speaking about being prepared, when you have time, will you put together a supply list for our next trip to town? I'm sure we won't need much more, but Billy offered to buy extra staples because of Steven, and he's itching to see Elizabeth. Let's let him help with a few items, and he can fetch them while he sees his girl."

"Billy grew up on this trip. I see the change in him already. I'll make the list, and I'd like to write to our families back east and tell them about Johanna and Billy's brother. But right now I have a question for you."

Mark straightened. "What's on your mind, sweetheart?"

"I had some sleepless nights while you were away. Something Billy said got me thinking. I've a question on my mind, and there's a puzzle I need you to help me solve. Billy said the first time you two met was when you rescued him from Rusty. But you told me you first met Billy during the stagecoach holdup. I think perhaps I have the answer figured out. You tell me if I'm wrong." From across the table, Sarah took Mark's hands in hers.

Mark's heart beat rapidly, and a rush of heat enveloped him. *I knew this day might come. Sorry, Samuel, but I won't lie to our Sarah again.*

Sarah said, "Please be honest with me, Mark. I must know the truth. I think I've pieced together what happened, but only you can tell me if I'm right." Still holding Mark's hands, she continued, "I've concluded you didn't meet Billy at the stage robbery."

"Billy told you the truth, Sarah. I discovered him in town working for a peddler selling elixir and caught sight of the birthmark on his neck. In addition to Billy's name, his birthmark was one of the details I knew about him. Walking past the peddler's wagon, I took a chance and called out 'Billy.' He responded, and I knew he was the same boy. I gave the peddler details I found out from the sheriff to prove I knew the boy's parents. I said the boy had family and I'd make sure he got back to them.

"Everything I told you about Billy is true. The boy needed help, and I asked myself what Samuel would have done and followed my heart." Mark brushed a tear from Sarah's cheek.

"Let's go back to the stagecoach robbery," Sarah said shakily. "I believe Samuel was involved, not you. Billy said when the driver told the sheriff the story of how things happened, a farmer saved them. But the sheriff thought you were Samuel when you collected the reward money. And if I'm right, why weren't you with Samuel during the robbery?"

Mark leaned forward and took a deep breath. Sarah had released her hands of his and he reached to hold them again, but she resisted. "Are you sure you want to hear the answer to your question, Sarah?"

"The truth. Please tell me. Were you the one who shot the outlaws and foiled the robbery?"

"No, it wasn't me. I wasn't even there. I pray to God every day for forgiveness that I wasn't. Maybe things might have gone differently if I were. I accidently left my canteen behind when we stopped for a break. I returned to get it while Samuel rode ahead to hunt. That's when he spotted the stage; the wheel had come off. Everything happened so fast. He foiled the robbery but was shot during the shootout. Afterward, Samuel told the stage driver to tell the sheriff what happened so their stories would match when he collected the reward, but he never gave the driver his name.

"I heard the shooting, and when I reached Samuel as he was riding back to find me, he had lost a lot of blood, too much blood. When the bleeding wouldn't stop, we both knew he couldn't survive. He told me what happened and deliberately gave me the details I'd need to convince the sheriff I was him. He asked me to collect the money and pay off his debts." Mark's eyes welled with tears. Telling the true story suddenly made everything too real. *Please God, let Sarah understand and forgive me.*

Mark knelt beside her. "Sarah, you must believe me. I would have traded places with Samuel. He had everything to live for. He was thinking about you and the children always. He made me promise to never tell you the truth and swear to take care of his family. I gave him my promise. His last words were what I told you before, 'Tell Sarah I love her.'"

Tears streamed down Sarah's cheeks.

"Please, Sarah, I stayed on to help you and keep my word to my best friend. I would have kept his secret and taken my promise to my grave."

Sarah wiped her tears with her apron. "He didn't want me to know he killed two men, did he?"

"No, he knew how you felt about taking another's life and didn't want you to think of him as a killer. He didn't want his death to be for nothing. He said you'd call it blood money and not want any part of it, but he knew his debts could be paid off and you wouldn't lose the farm if you had the reward, so I claimed the money and paid off the debts. We did this all for you and the children.

"Before you and I were married, I almost told you the truth about Samuel. He died a hero in my eyes. Then I told myself, in the end, all a man has is his word. And if I couldn't keep a promise to my best friend, what kind of man was I?" Mark took Sarah's hands in his and gave them a light squeeze. She replied in kind. Mark took her in his arms and said, "Our love for each other grew out of mutual respect." Mark held her shoulders and gazed into her tearful eyes. "Please tell me you learning the truth doesn't change your love for me."

"Oh, Mark…" Sarah's hands framed his face. "I know you were only looking out for me and keeping your promise to your dear friend. You are a man of your word, and I understand now why you lied about the money. You lied to keep your promise to Samuel."

Sarah wept and clung to Mark as he embraced her. When her tears finally subsided, she said, "Thank you for being honest. Telling those lies must have been difficult for you.

"We must keep Samuel's secret. There's no need to tell Jack and Lydia the truth. Let's let them remember their father as the honorable man he was. And let's pray Billy never realizes that the farmer was really Samuel. Now I know Samuel died a hero. If he hadn't been there to stop those two men, more people may have died, and Billy might not be with us today. Samuel shot in self-defense, just as you did saving Lydia and me from those two thieves who were ready to commit dire acts to get the rifle. They would have killed all of us to get what they wanted. I could never think of you or Samuel as a killer."

Mark cradled her on his lap. His lips brushed hers. "I love you, Sarah. Little Johanna is proof of our love."

Gazing at this man she loved so fiercely, Sarah said, "And I love you, Mark. Now more than ever." She caressed his face and kissed away his tears.

"Sarah, fate ruled when I made my promise to Samuel. That promise brought us together in love, manifested itself in the joy of our daughter Johanna, and brought Billy and Steven to us to make a complete family with Jack and Lydia. We are all here, safe, and under one roof, as Samuel would have wanted. Together we'll watch our children grow and have families of their own. We'll survive whatever comes next, war included. We're strong because we've learned the true meaning of unconditional love."

A word about the author...

Authoring a historical romance novel has always been a dream of Judy's, and now writing has become her second career. She devotes a portion of each day to improving her craft at her home in the northwestern mountains of Pennsylvania.

Second Chance Life is the second book in her series A Plains Life. Book One, *Settler's Life*, was released in September 2018.

Living a simple life, Judy enjoys the wildlife and nature surrounding her, a cup of coffee in the morning, and curling up in the evening with her husband and their cat, Miss Kitty.

Judy also loves to hear from her readers. You can contact her through her website and sign up for her newsletter at:

https://judysharer.com

CPSIA information can be obtained
at www.ICGtesting.com
Printed in the USA
LVHW081711230121
677302LV00044B/457